Andersonville Violets

ANDERSONVILLE VIOLETS

A Story of Northern and Southern Life

HERBERT W. COLLINGWOOD

Introduction by
David Rachels and Robert Baird

THE UNIVERSITY OF ALABAMA PRESS
Tuscaloosa and London

*Published in Cooperation with the
United States Civil War Center*

First paperback edition
Copyright © 2000
The University of Alabama Press
Tuscaloosa, Alabama 35487-0380
All rights reserved
Manufactured in the United States of America

Originally published in 1889 by Lee and Shepard Publishers

1 2 3 4 5 6 7 8 9 . 08 07 06 05 04 03 02 01 00

Cover design by Michele Myatt Quinn

∞
The paper on which this book is printed meets the minimum requirements of American National Standard for Information Science–Permanence of Paper for Printed Library Materials, ANSI Z39.48-1984.

Library of Congress Cataloging-in-Publication Data

Collingwood, Herbert W. (Herbert Winslow), 1857–1927.
    Andersonville violets : a story of Northern and Southern life /
  Herbert W. Collingwood ; introduction by David Rachels and Robert Baird.—1st. pbk. ed.
      p. cm.—(Classics of Civil War fiction)
  Originally published in 1889 by Lee and Shepard Publishers.
  "Published in cooperation with the United States Civil War Center."
  Includes bibliographical references. ISBN 0-8173-1061-4 (alk. paper)
  1. United States—History—Civil War, 1861–1865—Fiction. 2. Andersonville Prison—Fiction. 3. Andersonville (Ga.)—Fiction. 4. Prisoners of war—Fiction. 5. Mississippi—Fiction. I. Title. II. Series.
  PS1359.C53 A53 2000
  813'.4—dc21   00-055199

British Library Cataloguing-in-Publication Data available

INTRODUCTION

David Rachels and Robert Baird

I.

Herbert Collingwood never knew why he went deaf, though he speculated that the gradual failure of his hearing began with a babyhood bout of scarlet fever. In his meditation on deafness, *Adventures in Silence* (1923), he wrote that he "wandered slowly and gently along the road [to the Silent Land], each year coming a little nearer to silence, yet working on so easily and unobtrusively that the way [did] not [seem] hard and rough." But in his dreams, sound never faded. While asleep, Collingwood could hear music as well as ever. Unfortunately, this music was frozen in time. He heard not a note of jazz or ragtime or any other contemporary music. Rather, he heard only "grand operas and songs of the Civil War and the following decade; these last are plaintive melodies for the most part, for New England, when I was a young man, was full of 'war orphans,' who largely dictated the music of the period."[1] Among these orphans was Collingwood himself, for he and his four siblings lost their father to the war.

Thus, it seems fitting that Collingwood took the Civil War and its aftermath as the subject of his only novel. The passionate *Andersonville Violets* (1889) reflects his hope that his father did not die in vain. Collingwood felt that his father had died for a worthy cause—the reunion of the United States—and this cause had, of course, triumphed. But the younger Collingwood's brief migration to the South made clear to him that the two regions were joined only as a body. Their spirits remained worlds apart. If, indeed, the death of his father was not to be in vain, then there was work left to be done. *Andersonville Violets* was his contribution.

Herbert Winslow Collingwood was born in Plymouth, Massachusetts, on April 21, 1857. He was the son of Rebecca Richardson Collingwood, a teacher, and Joseph W. Collingwood, a fish dealer. Joseph supported without question the policies of Abraham Lincoln, and he felt that in the Civil War the Confederacy would reap what it had sown. He mustered with the 18th Massachusetts Infantry on August 24, 1861. He would be the captain of Company H. Like many, Joseph Collingwood felt confident that the war would be brief.[2]

His middle son, Herbert, who was four at the time, would retain only one memory of his father. Herbey, as his family called him, and his older brother, George, had angered their mother and were sent to bed to await the return of their father. Shortly after six o'clock, Joseph arrived home. Rebecca greeted him with an order, which she intended the boys to hear as well: "Now, Joseph, you go right up and whip those boys! They would not mind me, and *you must do it.*" Joseph and Rebecca argued briefly before he finally began climbing the stairs to the boys' attic bedroom. Joseph went to the bed and beat on a pillow while "growling" at the boys: "*Now,* will you mind your mother when she speaks to you?" The boys played their parts by screaming in pain. The charade worked so well that Rebecca hurried upstairs to defend George and Herbey and to chastise Joseph for being too hard on them. In less than a week, Joseph would leave for the war. "If I were starting on his long journey," Herbert later wrote, "I should be likely to treat my children in the same way." It was "a beautiful memory."[3]

On December 13, 1862, at the Battle of Fredericksburg, the 18th Massachusetts advanced closer to the Confederate lines than any other Union regiment, and as a result they suffered 126 casualties. Among these was Joseph Collingwood. Rebecca learned from the newspaper of her husband's wounds. On December 19, Colonel Joseph Hayes wrote to her with good news: Joseph, who had been shot in the leg, had walked off the battlefield, and he was expected to recover. On December 24, however, Hayes had a more difficult letter to write: Joseph had died shortly after an operation to remove a ball that had lodged near his spine.[4]

Many years later, Herbert located a veteran from the 18th Massachusetts who had known his father well. They had even shared a tent together. Collingwood was eager to learn more about his father, but an old and famous senator—Collingwood does not give his name—talked him out of it. He warned Herbert that the old veteran knew his father "as just a plain, common man, probably with most of the faults of humanity. Let him alone! If at your age God has permitted you to retain an ideal of any human being, keep it pure. Take no chances of having it blackened!" Herbert took the senator's advice.[5]

Collingwood bristled at the notion that the Civil War

was "a mere skirmish" compared to the Great War. "Perhaps so," he wrote, "if we count only money and men, yet our part in this recent conflict was but a plaything in intense living, in sentiment, and breaking up of family life, as compared with the war of the sixties."[6] Collingwood, of course, wrote from experience. And while he clung to his single memory of his father, he doubtless learned a great deal about the war from his mother. He dedicated *Andersonville Violets* to her memory.

Though Joseph Collingwood did not live to raise Herbert, the boy became a farmer, as his father had wanted. He graduated from the Michigan Agricultural College in 1883, composing the commencement poem for his class and calling it "On the Threshold." Collingwood was determined to be not just a farmer but a writer as well. His aspirations may have been fired as a youth when he worked at a publishing house where he ran errands for Henry Wadsworth Longfellow, Ralph Waldo Emerson, John Greenleaf Whittier, and Oliver Wendell Holmes. Forty years later, Collingwood bragged of being the only man alive who had eaten peanuts with this illustrious group.[7]

After crossing the threshold, the Massachusetts native decided to move south. In Starkville, Mississippi, as the editor of *The Southern Livestock Journal,* Collingwood began his lifelong career as a farm journalist. He had come to Mississippi to "reform and uplift the South." His bosses were known locally as Colonel O'Brien and Sergeant Hill. Both were veterans of the Civil War; Hill had been with Nathan Bedford Forrest at Fort Pillow. Collingwood did most everything for the *Journal:* he edited the paper, set the type, ran the press, mailed the papers, and swept the office. His raisons d'être, however, were his editorials. He was especially proud of one that broke a local strike, but he thought that his masterpiece would be an editorial on "The South's Future."[8]

This editorial fell predictably flat. With the ignorant pride of youth, Collingwood read his piece to Colonel O'Brien and Sergeant Hill. Only years later did Collingwood recognize "the humor of it": two veterans who "must walk softly all their remaining days amid the ruins and the melancholy of defeat" were forced to listen to a boy "without the least conception of what life must have meant to the Southern people . . . pouring out dreams of a future which seemed even beyond the vision of an Isaiah." Said Sergeant Hill: "Fine. Splendid. I reckon you'll have us all in Heaven 40 years hence?" And for Colonel O'Brien it was hardly worth responding: "Fine. Fine. I hope I'll be here to see it; but today I saw that paper collector from New Orleans in town. We can't pay his bill. He'll have to leave on the night train. Better shut up the office."[9]

Collingwood left the South aware that he had not changed it but still hoping that he might. In 1885 he began work as an editor at *The Rural New-Yorker,* a weekly paper for business farmers. He became editor-in-chief in 1900, a job he held until his death on October 21, 1927. During more than forty years as a farm writer, Collingwood lost neither his love for literature nor his faith in the power of art:

> The future of this land, and all it means to us, lies in the hands of little children. . . . And this future will be safer with poetry and imagination than with the multiplication table alone.

I know about this from my own start in life. I was expected to be satisfied with work until I was 21, and then have a suit of clothes and a yoke of oxen. One trouble with the farmers of New England was that they thought this a sufficient outfit for their boys. I think I might have fallen in with that plan and contented my life with it had it not been for a crude picture which hung in the shop where we pegged shoes. It was a poor color scheme, a perfect daub of art, in which some amateur artist had tried to express a thought which was too large for his soul. A bare oak tree, with most of its branches gone, was framed against the Winter sky. It was evening; a few stars had appeared, and the sky was full of color. The artist had tried to arrange the stars and the sky colors so that they represented a crude American flag, with the oak tree serving as the staff. His great unexpressed thought was that at the close of the Civil War God had painted His promise of freedom on the sky in the coloring of that flag. As a child, that crude picture became a part of my life. I have never been able to forget the glory of it, as I have forgotten the meanness, the poverty, the narrow blindness of our daily lives, so that all through the long and stormy years, wherever I have walked, I have seen that flag upon the sky. . . .

Collingwood was a farmer, but he was a writer as well, and he noted with pride that his reading included not only *Rural Credits* and *Manufacture of Chemical Manure* but also Dante, Whittier's poetry, and Lowell's essay on Abraham Lincoln. And though most of his published books

INTRODUCTION

bore titles such as *Chemicals and Clover; Or, Farming with Concentrated Dung: A Record of Successful Farm Operations in New Jersey, Where High-Grade Complete Manures and Sod Supply a Cheaper Manure Than That Obtained from Keeping Live Stock,* he also wrote personal essays and fiction.[10]

Andersonville Violets was born of the same youthful optimism that had taken Collingwood to Mississippi. Given that the book was copyrighted in 1888 and published in 1889, he probably began it soon after leaving the South in 1885. He still hoped, in some measure, to change the course of history, but now he stated his goal modestly: his novel of both North and South "would present food for sound and healthful thought."[11]

The book begins inside the infamous Confederate prisoner-of-war camp. Perhaps in an effort to show that the similarities of his protagonists transcend their differences, Collingwood names them both John: John ("Jack") Foster is an Andersonville guard, and John Rockwell is an Andersonville prisoner. When Collingwood introduces Foster, the Confederate guard is thinking of Lucy Moore, the girl he left at home. When Collingwood introduces Rockwell, the Yankee POW's thoughts are at home, too. He pines for Nellie Sinclair, who did not return his declaration of love when he left for the war. Thus, *Andersonville Violets* is not without romance, but these potential marriages of Southerner to Southerner and Northerner to Northerner are secondary elements of the plot. Of central concern is the relationship between Rebel guard and Yankee prisoner.

In prison John nurses Archie Sinclair, Nellie's brother. As John yearns for Nellie, Archie becomes her surrogate, and the relationship between the two men, who are known among the prison guards as the "babes," becomes increasingly homoerotic: "Archie was a little, delicate fellow, with golden hair, and a face like a girl's. . . . A strange intimacy sprang up by degrees between the two men. . . . John almost worshipped his little companion. Archie grew to look more and more like Nellie. He had the same gentleness. . . . [John] carried him tenderly about, thinking and talking of the little girl at home" (9, 13, 16). The novel's plot is set in motion when John spots a bunch of violets within the prison, and Archie, delusional and dying, asks for them. There is only one place where flowers can grow in Andersonville, only one place where the prisoners have not trampled all life into the ground: inside the dead line. Any prisoner who crosses this miniature fence of stakes and scantling is liable to be shot. Thus, when Archie asks John to retrieve the flowers, he is asking him to risk death.

John considers Archie's request not because John is suicidal but because Archie does not want the flowers for himself: he wants them for his sister. John enlisted after seeing Nellie sewing a flag for their hometown company. She is, therefore, more than the girl whom John loves: John has no family, so he fights for Nellie, both literally and figuratively. "You said you loved her once," Archie reminds John, "and now you are not ready to pick her a few flowers" (19). In this way Archie questions John's loyalty not only to Nellie but also to the Union.

The Rebel who guards the violets is, of course, Jack Foster, and he has been watching the interaction between John and Archie. Jack is not the sort of incompetent guard commonly associated with Andersonville; he has fought at both Gettysburg and Chancellorsville. Having clashed

INTRODUCTION   xiii

with the Yankees himself, he respects them, and he feels as well a kinship with the two "babes": pressed in a letter from Lucy, Jack carries his own violets. When John risks his life by speaking to him, Jack can bring himself only to raise his gun. When John tells Jack that he must retrieve the flowers, the guard lowers his gun.

After John scrambles across the dead line, another guard shoots at him. Jack's failure to do the same results in a charge of treason. There is, however, little suspense in this episode, for Collingwood titles his fifth chapter "Dishonorably Discharged." Jack would prefer execution to a life of disgrace, so he begs his comrades to kill him. Significantly, the men of his former company march away "sullenly," without shooting him and without saying a word (40).

After Appomattox, the lives of Jack and John take predictably divergent paths in which Jack is defeated and downtrodden and John is happy and prosperous. Here Collingwood's experiences in Mississippi are crucial, for he notes in his preface that his "pictures of Southern life are taken from personal experience" (v). When John moves south to Mississippi—like Collingwood, he is trained in agriculture—he finds a sorry lot of farmers. Many spend their time lounging about; they stand only to go in search of more comfortable seats. Others may work, but they raise too much cotton and not enough food. At best, the Southerners "[seem] to understand that a change must be made, yet they [have] neither the patience nor the energy to go through the slow process of development" (241).

But Collingwood makes clear that the problem facing Southern agriculture is not mere laziness but the system that makes it possible: sharecropping. A perplexed John seeks out Colonel Fair, who explains: "They [the white land owners] live on the niggers. . . . They rent out their land to niggers, and make the poor black fellers do all the work, while *they* hold down them chairs and take the money. . . . It's mighty easy, I reckon, to make money outer niggers if a man only has a tough conscience. I reckon a heap of the men here have got consciences like sole leather" (245). The Colonel goes on to illustrate—on a piece of scrap board with a pencil—how the creative accounting practiced by land owners leaves the sharecroppers in debt, with the cost of mules, harnesses, rations, and interest always greater than the monies made for that season's cotton crop.

Thus, *Andersonville Violets,* despite its title, moves well beyond Andersonville and the war years. Collingwood, a thoughtful observer of social conditions, farming practices, and local attitudes, hoped to shed light on problems that still plagued the South—and by extension still plagued the United States. His insightful short list of problems includes antiquated farming practices; the injustice of sharecropping; the "Negro Question"; and the crippling, stubborn pride and anger of the defeated South.

Such issues alone, however, may not keep readers turning pages. The true power of *Andersonville Violets* lies in its characters and their struggles toward reconciliation and redemption. These, in turn, gain their force from Collingwood's personal experiences with Southern farming conditions, with the defeated South, with physically and psychologically injured veterans, and with men and women of stoic integrity. But at the symbolic center of the novel's hope for the future lies a nightmare from the past: Andersonville.

II.

Andersonville Violets is a fascinating document in the cultural history of Andersonville prison. This history begins with a seemingly simple question: Where should the Confederacy have kept its prisoners of war?

At first the Confederacy had held its prisoners mostly in Richmond. As the war progressed, however, the capital became an increasingly poor place to hold POWs. The city was no longer able to supply the needs of its swelling POW population, and the Southern government was forced to import goods to the area, which drove up local prices. To make matters worse, as the need for fighting men thinned the corps of competent prison guards, the citizens of Richmond increasingly feared prison breaks, and Robert E. Lee himself noted that the prisoners would prove a serious problem if the Union attacked Richmond. Thus, in November 1863, the Confederate government began scouting sites for a new POW camp.[12]

General John Henry Winder commanded the Department of Henrico, which in practice meant that he ran the city of Richmond. He sent Captain William Sidney Winder, his son, to select the new prison site. Sidney Winder chose a plot of land near Andersonville, Georgia, that seemed perfect: although the site was near the railroad, it was isolated and thus safe from attack; the surrounding woods would provide lumber; and a branch of Sweetwater Creek would provide water. With the site chosen, General Winder sent Captain Richard Winder, his second cousin, to oversee the construction of the prison, Camp Sumter—not to be confused with Fort Sumter—which would soon become known as Andersonville.[13]

Andersonville's first prisoners arrived on February 24, 1864. By May 1, the stockade's population had exceeded 10,000, the intended capacity of its sixteen and a half acres, so it was expanded to enclose more than twenty-six acres. But the prison was soon overcrowded again: on August 12, its population peaked at nearly 33,000. This overcrowding problem was exacerbated by the Northern government's suspension of all prisoner exchanges. The sticking point was escaped slaves held as POWs: whereas the North insisted that these black soldiers simply be exchanged, the South insisted that they be returned to their owners. On August 24, 1864, the *New York Times* urged the Federal government to "exchange the white prisoners, man for man at least; if no better can be done for the negro troops now, their time will come anon." By this time, however, Union General Ulysses S. Grant stood firmly against exchanging any soldiers at all. Grant knew that Federal POWs were suffering, but he also felt that Confederate POWs would quickly return to battle. Grant concluded that exchanging POWs would mean a higher mortality rate for his soldiers in the field, and this was not acceptable.[14]

Andersonville was nothing more than an open-air pen—a field surrounded by a pair of oversized walls. Captain Henry Wirz faced the difficult task of managing this overcrowded stockade. He did what he could for the POWs, but his efforts had little effect. His plan to build latrines was abandoned when he could find no shovels in that remote region of southwest Georgia. As a result, the prison, along with its water supply, became a cesspool. There was lumber for barracks, but it proved impossible to get nails. Once the population of the stockade passed 10,000, it became nearly as difficult to find adequate rations. Because there were never enough fruits and vegetables, scurvy and intestinal diseases ran rampant. Prison doctors, who sometimes ran out of medicines entirely, could do little. Nearly 13,000 prisoners died.[15]

After the war, the victorious North hung Andersonville like an albatross from the neck of the defeated South. When John Winder, now commissary general of all Confederate prisons east of the Mississippi River, died before the end of the war, Henry Wirz inherited the role of scapegoat. During Wirz's trial for war crimes, the *New York Times* editorialized that "the trial now going on in Washington has a marked national importance. It is not so much the wretched creature, WIRZ, who is on trial, as it is the temper and spirit of the authorities of the late rebel government. They are charged with having starved and tortured thousands upon thousands of Union prisoners who had fallen into their hands,—[of] having, intentionally and systematically, deprived them of shelter and of food,—of having withheld from them all care during sickness,—of hunting them like wild beasts, of killing and maiming them for the most trifling offences,—in a word, of conduct toward them which should brand them forever with the scorn and contempt of the civilized world."[16]

Even before the trial had started, newspapers such as the *Times* were prosecuting the Andersonville commandant with any evidence that came to hand. As Wirz's day in court approached, the New York paper published a letter purportedly written by a Southerner intimately acquainted with the horrors of Andersonville. The letter, which was signed only with "S.," was introduced by a series of front-page headlines that included, "AN INCARNATE FIEND" and "Infamy Never Before Equaled in the History of Man." The letter was part fact and part fiction. One of its more remarkable fictions concerned the distribution of rations. S. claimed that when the population of Andersonville peaked, the systematic distribution of rations stopped. Instead, the prison gates would be "slightly opened" and the food would be "thrown" inside, where prisoners would fight for it. Thus, the strongest prisoners and those nearest the gate captured all the food, and the rest starved. And if it were not bad enough to starve the weak, the Andersonville jailers, according to S., found flimsy excuses to execute the strong. During the winter, he reported, groups of thirty prisoners were allowed to leave the prison under guard to gather wood. They were allowed one hour to do this. If they stayed out longer, they were charged with "violating their parole," tried, and executed.[17]

Immediately below this letter from S., the *Times* published a short letter from Wirz's counsel, who wrote, "We protest against trying the Southern Confederacy in the person of Capt. WERTZ [sic], and we ask for him a suspension of public judgment until the proper evidence upon which to form it is furnished in a reliable shape." In a subsequent letter to the newspaper, S. stated the obvious: if Wirz's counsel "[sought] to prevent a judgment being passed upon the conduct of their client, they [had] begun their efforts too late."[18]

It would have been difficult enough for Wirz to defend the reality of Andersonville, but the military tribunal that oversaw his court martial might as well have been run by the editors of the *Times*. The tribunal's president, General Lew Wallace (later of *Ben-Hur* fame), acted as a de facto prosecutor. As a matter of course, he allowed all evidence, hearsay and otherwise, that damned Wirz, and he disallowed all evidence that might have helped Wirz's defense. The prosecution argued that the Confederate government conspired to ruin the health of POWs in an attempt to weaken the Federal war effort. In addition to Wirz's role in this larger conspiracy, Judge Advocate Norton P. Chipman claimed that the Confederate jailer personally beat and executed Yankee prisoners. Chipman had no problem "proving" his case, for his witnesses outdid each other in inventing tales of Wirz's villainy.

On November 10, 1865, Wirz was hanged. It was the first and the only execution for crimes committed during the Civil War. On the next day, the *Times* expressed its hope that "the long strain of excitement over the awful disclosures of the trial is among the events that all good men will hasten to forget."[19] If "all good men" had honored this request, then the memory of Andersonville would not have ripened for Herbert Collingwood's purposes. In the years after the Wirz trial, the nightmare of Andersonville burrowed deeper into the American consciousness, largely through the words of Andersonville diarists. Like the protagonists of *Andersonville Violets,* the best-known diarists were both named John: John McElroy and John Ransom. McElroy and Ransom each had an agenda, and neither agenda included dispelling myths of Andersonville. This would be left for Collingwood.

Andersonville diaries fall into two general categories: those written while their authors were actually in prison and those written, expanded, or fabricated after the war. The former, while of more value to historians, are typically brief, elliptical, and repetitive. They are filled with entries such as Asbery C. Stephen's notation for February 27, 1865, which said only that it was "cloudy and dull all day."[20] Not surprisingly, the poetic and reflective accounts of McElroy and Ransom were composed after the war.

At the age of ten, John McElroy left his recently remarried mother in Kentucky and went to St. Louis to work as a devil in a printer's shop. Through his own efforts he learned Shakespeare and a number of languages. After moving to Chicago, he enlisted in Company L of the 16th Illinois Cavalry. On January 4, 1864, Sergeant-Major McElroy was in camp in Jonesville, Virginia, when he was captured in a surprise attack. At seventeen, he found himself touring Confederate POW camps.

His *Andersonville* (1879) was originally serialized in the newspaper he edited, the *Toledo Blade*. When published as a book, it ran over 650 crowded pages and sold more than 600,000 copies.[21] The origins of this memoir, as well as its great length, point to what historians distrust about McElroy: his apparent attempt to become, in the words of historian William Marvel, the "poet laureate" of Andersonville.[22] McElroy's *Andersonville* indulges every newspaper trick and literary tool of the era, including poems, tables, maps, letters, military orders, popular ballads, religious hymns, slave work songs, courtroom testimony, copious line drawings, and for good measure, allusions to, paraphrases of, and quotations from Greek and Roman mythology; Homer; the Books of Job, First Samuel, Exodus, and Matthew; Shakespeare; Coleridge; Byron; Darwin; and the epitaph of the Spartans who fell at Thermopylae.

Like McElroy, John Ransom was trained as a printer. On November 6, 1863, the twenty-year-old Ransom, a quartermaster of the 9th Michigan Cavalry, was captured by Confederate cavalry after a day of heavy fighting in eastern Tennessee. To the casual reader, the details of his *Andersonville Diary* (1881) ring true. It seems a genuine, if loquacious, prison journal. As we might expect of a quartermaster, Ransom returns again and again to the daily condition of the men's rations. His first meal at Andersonville of corn meal, beef, and salt is "splendid," but soon he is complaining that the corn meal has been "ground, seemingly, cob and all, and it scourges the men fearfully."[23] The details of his involvement in Andersonville's makeshift economy and the narrative of his declining health seem trustworthy.

The surprisingly objective tone of Ransom's diary also inspires confidence. At first he discounts the rumors of Wirz's cruelty in punishing disobedient prisoners, though eventually he vents that the Andersonville commandant possesses "not an atom of humanity." Even then, however, he gives Wirz credit for helping to put down the Raiders, who terrorized their fellow prisoners, and for allowing POWs to travel to Washington to plead for the renewal of prisoner exchanges. Here Ransom's bitterness is directed not at his captors but at his own government: "Rough that it should be necessary for us to *beg* to be protected by our government."[24]

This bitterness makes perfect sense given the circumstances behind the actual composition of his book. Ransom represents his "diary" as having been written while he was a prisoner. However, in "Johnny Ransom's Imagination," Marvel demonstrates that Ransom's narrative is dominated by "anachronism" and "wholesale exaggerations and misrepresentations." Among the grossest misrepresentations is simple plagiarism: for an account of the overthrow of the Raiders, Ransom steals from McElroy. An authentic Ransom diary may never have existed, as Ransom claimed that the original was lost in a fire. In any case, the work that he published was cobbled together while he searched for a government pension.[25]

Thus, though both men suffered at Andersonville, neither McElroy nor Ransom was concerned with historical accuracy. McElroy, driven by literary ambition, and Ransom, driven by financial gain, delivered the Andersonvilles that suited their purposes, and in so doing they helped to buttress many myths. Most important for readers of *Andersonville Violets* are the diarists' depictions of the Andersonville guards. This ragtag lot, most of whom were unfit for other service, were stationed in sentinel boxes perched around the top of the perimeter of the stockade's inner wall. These men did kill prisoners, though not as frequently as McElroy and Ransom indicate. In his entry for May 6, 1864, Ransom writes that "nearly every day, some one is killed for some trifling offense, by the guards." McElroy concurs: "I think I hazard nothing in saying that for weeks at least one man a day was killed at this place. The murders became monotonous; there was a dreadful sameness to them. A gun would crack; looking up we would see, still smoking, the muzzle of the musket of one of the guards on either side of the creek." Both McElroy and Ransom report the rumor that any guard who killed a Yankee received a thirty-day furlough.[26]

In actuality, there were no furloughs for trigger-happy guards, and in all, they killed only eleven prisoners.[27] But in the wake of the Andersonville trial and the diaries of McElroy and Ransom, the public—especially the Northern public—thought that it knew the truth about what went on at Andersonville. In the decade after McElroy and

Ransom, Collingwood offered a contrary view. Of course, *Andersonville Violets* does not apologize for the Confederacy itself—Collingwood notes that the Confederates fought for "the mistaken idea of Southern independence" (6)—but Andersonville is another matter. Collingwood hits near the mark when he argues that the horrible living conditions at the prison were not the fault of the Confederates but a sad fluke of history: "The Southern leaders probably desired to locate their prison in some healthy spot where the prisoners would be safe from attack. The rude chances of war crowded so many into the stockade that it became a perfect den of disease" (15).

From the beginning of *Andersonville Violets,* Collingwood plays with readers' conceptions of the prison. When he introduces Jack Foster, Collingwood evokes the homicidal guards of Andersonville mythology: Looking out over the stockade, Jack is "smiling as only men smile who are greatly pleased" (2). He is, however, no sadist; Collingwood explains that the Rebel guard's thoughts are far from Andersonville. Then, when Jack refuses to fire his weapon at a prisoner who crosses the dead line, reader expectations are undercut further still. Yet Collingwood's portrayal of the guards does not avoid myth. We are told that Jack and his fellow guards have orders to shoot not only those prisoners who cross the dead line but even those prisoners who dare to speak to them. In truth, many guards and prisoners had lively relationships, not only talking together but also conducting business. Collingwood apparently shared the common belief that Andersonville guards required little provocation before killing their charges, a belief that is crucial to the opening chapters of *Andersonville Violets.*

In the popular imagination, these villainous guards were mere servants to Andersonville's great villain, Henry Wirz. Thus, Collingwood worked to subvert readers' conceptions of the prison commandant as well. Wisely, Collingwood portrays Wirz with restraint. The Andersonville commandant enters the novel without fanfare. Indeed, Collingwood does not even identify him by name, for his readers would not have needed a formal introduction. Wirz, who utters only seven words in the novel, appears "glum and savage" with "no possible hope for mercy in [his] savage face" (37). He and Jack meet in a room that is "dismal and bare, in keeping with the war's justice" (36). Wirz is eager to make an example of Jack, lest the prisoners should feel emboldened by such signs of weakness to storm the stockade walls. After a perfunctory trial that foreshadows the "dismal and bare" justice that Wirz himself would later face, Jack is sentenced to execution by firing squad.

But Jack, as we have seen, is not executed. At the last moment, an order comes repreiving him by virtue of "his previous good conduct" in the war. Who is responsible for this order? Collingwood does not say. If we limit our list of possibilities to characters who appear in the novel, then it could have been written by no one but Wirz. Perhaps this is the reading that Collingwood intended. He may have reasoned that his audience would reject any portrayal of Wirz that was explicitly sympathetic. Thus, he could redeem the Andersonville commandant only by implication.

Though only the first seven of the novel's twenty-three chapters are set at Andersonville, the awful specter of the Confederate POW camp stands at the thematic center of *Andersonville Violets*. Much of the remainder of the novel explores the question posed by the seeming oxymoron of its title: Can something so terrible give rise to something beautiful? How will Jack Foster put the shame of his dishonorable discharge behind him? What will John Rockwell make of his life when the nightmare of Andersonville is over? And what will happen should the two men meet again, after Appomattox? If *they* can put the war behind them, might the rest of us do the same?

When young Herbert Collingwood hoped to "set the world on fire," he imagined a place "as dry as a stack of hay in a drought—only needing [his] little flare of flame to start it going." Instead, he found in Starkville, Mississippi, that the world more closely resembled "a soggy swamp."[28] Collingwood returned to the North more humble and more realistic, but with his ambition intact. With *Andersonville Violets*, he hoped to do his part to help heal his nation's wounds. He hoped to help finish the job that his father had started.

NOTES

1. Herbert W. Collingwood, *Adventures in Silence* (New York: The Rural New Yorker, 1923), 20–21, 48, 95.

2. Donald Thompson, "Biographical Sketch of Joseph W. Collingwood," unpublished manuscript. Thompson's research on the Collingwoods is based largely on the letters of Rebecca and Joseph, which are held at the Huntington Library, San Marino, California. No history of the 18th Massachusetts has yet been written. The regiment is currently being researched by Thompson, Tom Churchill, and Steve McManus.

3. Collingwood, *Adventures in Silence*, 89–94.

4. Thompson, "Biographical Sketch of Joseph W. Collingwood."

5. Collingwood, *Adventures in Silence*, 92–93.

6. Ibid., 91.

7. Herbert W. Collingwood, *On the Threshold: Commencement Poem, Class of 1883, Michigan Agricultural College* (Boston: C. W. Calkins, Printers, [1883?]); Collingwood, *Adventures in Silence*, 73.

8. Herbert W. Collingwood, *Hope Farm Notes* (New York: Harcourt, Brace, 1921), 191–93.

9. Ibid., 194.

10. Ibid., 18–19, 63; Herbert W. Collingwood, *Chemicals and Clover; Or, Farming with Concentrated Dung: A Record of Successful Farm Operations in New Jersey, Where High-Grade Complete Manures and Sod Supply a Cheaper Manure Than That Obtained from Keeping Live Stock* (New York: Rural Publishing, 1892).

11. Herbert W. Collingwood, *Andersonville Violets: A Story of Northern and Southern Life* (Boston: Lee and Shepard Publishers, 1889), v. Hereafter page numbers are cited parenthetically in the text.

12. Ovid L. Futch, *History of Andersonville Prison* ([Gainesville]: University of Florida Press, 1968), 2–3.

13. William Marvel, *Andersonville: The Last Depot* (Chapel Hill: University of North Carolina Press, 1994), 14–16.

14. Futch, *History of Andersonville Prison*, 5, 31; Marvel, *Andersonville: The Last Depot*, 27, 41–44, 53, 180, 191–92; "The Union Prisoners at Andersonville," *New York Times*, August 24, 1864, 4. Futch objects that "it is illogical to argue that since exchange would have saved lives, refusal to exchange *caused* deaths" (118–19), but this looks

like a semantic quibble. Even if we agree that the Northern refusal did not cause the deaths, the fact remains that if the Southern pleas to exchange prisoners had not been ignored, the POWs would not have died, and this was a foreseeable consequence of the refusal.

15. Marvel, *Andersonville: The Last Depot,* 45, 52–53, 86, 154, 206–7.
16. "The Trial of Wirz," *New York Times,* September 9, 1865, 4.
17. "An Incarnate Fiend," *New York Times,* August 4, 1865, 1.
18. "Letter from the Counsel of Capt. Wertz [sic]," *New York Times,* August 4, 1865, 1; "The Andersonville Torturers," *New York Times,* August 8, 1865, 2.
19. "The Execution of Wirz," *New York Times,* November 11, 1865, 4. For the details of the Wirz trial, see U.S. Congress, House, *Trial of Henry Wirz,* 40th Cong., 2nd Sess., 1868, H. Doc. 23, serial 1331.
20. *The Diary of Pvt. Asbery Stephen in Andersonville,* ed. Oscar F. Curtis (Bloomington, Ind.: Monroe County Historical Society, 1973), 33.
21. *Who's Who in America,* vol. 6, ed. Albert Nelson Marquis (Chicago: A. N. Marquis, 1910–1911), 1223.
22. Marvel, *Andersonville: The Last Depot,* 172.
23. John L. Ransom, *John Ransom's Andersonville Diary* (1881; reprint, New York: Berkley Books, 1994), 53, 67–68, 81, 87, 118.
24. Ibid., 64, 92, 107, 126.
25. William Marvel, "Johnny Ransom's Imagination," *Civil War History* 41 (1995): 181, 183, 184, 188.
26. Ransom, *John Ransom's Andersonville Diary,* 75, 109; John McElroy, *Andersonville: A Story of Rebel Military Pris-*

ons (Toledo: D. R. Locke, 1879), 190.
   27. Marvel, *Andersonville: The Last Depot,* 172–73.
   28. Collingwood, *Hope Farm Notes,* 189.

Andersonville Violets

TO THE MEMORY OF

𝔐𝔶 𝔐𝔬𝔱𝔥𝔢𝔯

THIS LITTLE VOLUME IS AFFECTIONATELY DEDICATED.

PREFACE.

THE writer has long felt that a story of Northern and Southern life might be written that would present food for sound and healthful thought, unblinded by partisan feeling or sectional hatred. The war is over forever. It can never be fought again. We have but one flag. It is the duty of all patriotic citizens to lend their best efforts to the task of looking at the causes of the war and its results, fairly and intelligently. A story of Andersonville prison, told by a soldier in the Confederate army, suggested this volume. The Northern scenes are taken from life. The pictures of Southern life are taken from personal experience. An effort has been made to give an exact report of the state of affairs found by one Northern immigrant.

HERBERT W. COLLINGWOOD.

RIVER EDGE, New Jersey.

CONTENTS.

CHAPTER		PAGE
I.	JACK FOSTER'S LETTER	1
II.	THE BABES IN THE WOODS	9
III.	THE ANDERSONVILLE VIOLETS	18
IV.	A PLAN FOR ESCAPE	25
V.	DISHONORABLY DISCHARGED	35
VI.	THE ESCAPE	42
VII.	SOL'S VICTORY	53
VIII.	THE NEGRO CABIN	68
IX.	JACK FOSTER'S WELCOME	76
X.	BROTHER HILL, THE PREACHER	88
XI.	BREEZETOWN'S WELCOME	103
XII.	AFTER THE WAR	122
XIII.	A SOUTHERN TOWN	139
XIV.	COLONEL FAIR	153
XV.	THE MAN AT THE DOOR	164
XVI.	RUN TO RUINS	179
XVII.	THE GERMS OF A NEW MANHOOD	199
XVIII.	THE ANDERSONVILLE SENTINEL	209
XIX.	BOB GLENN WANTS HIS PAY	227
XX.	JACK FOSTER'S TROUBLE	239
XXI.	THE NEGRO QUESTION	248
XXII.	AUNT JINNY'S FAVORITE STORY	254
XXIII.	FADED FLOWERS OF ANDERSONVILLE	260

ANDERSONVILLE VIOLETS

CHAPTER I.

JACK FOSTER'S LETTER

THE sun came sullenly climbing up the high Georgia hills. The sky had heralded a pleasant morning, but the angry face that pushed up over the hills gave the lie direct to its joyful proclamation. The sun came slowly. First one hand reached up among the stars and drew a long streak of crimson over the tops of the hills. Then the arm slowly pushed the black curtain of night back to make a place for the scowling face that followed.

There was nothing attractive in the face of the country upon which this angry gaze was bent. Dry, rolling sand hills, covered with thin pine forests, stretched away on every hand — wide stretches of dry sand and old fields with great gashes cut in them. Off to the left a high pine stockade ran around the ridge of a small valley. The logs seemed to push sturdily against each other — like soldiers who wait an oncoming charge. This stockade lay directly in the path of the sun and that gloomy individual was obliged to pass over it.

The sun hung back with all its might, but there was no help for it. At last it made an angry start and darted a long stream of light over the dry sand-hills and thin pines, and up to the hateful stockade. Jack Foster turned on his beat just as the light splintered against the logs. Even when pushed thus far to the wall, the sun seemed to rebel a little. Slowly it followed its advance guard up past the regular mounds in the hideous graveyards, past the ugly barracks and huts, up to the stockade itself. There it paused as if to cover its eyes before climbing the rough barrier that hid so much of horror. It seemed to wait for extra strength, and then, of a sudden, it sprang to the top as if to flash with all its speed over the dreaded space and up the convenient hills beyond. It flashed full in the face of Jack Foster as he walked back along his beat.

Jack's face held such a pleasant expression that the sun stopped in utter surprise to examine him. Jack was smiling as only men smile who are greatly pleased. The sun seemed to drop its ill temper for the moment. It was so lost in wonder to think of such an unheard-of thing that it halted in its tracks as if to assure itself that the smile was genuine. Jack's face bore the examination well. The smile brightened perceptibly in the sunshine. The sun even smiled back and so far forgot itself as to take one look over Jack's shoulder. The sight was enough to call up all desire to escape, and it flashed over the yard and hurried on the wings of horror up the opposite hills. The sky before, noticing its eager face, blushed with pleasure at its approach. It glanced back only once, to throw a bright gleam on the barrel of Jack's musket. More from force of habit than because he was harder than the sun, Jack glanced down into the yard. He looked down into — *Andersonville!*

Andersonville! What a dreadful thrill runs through the veins at the word! Who has not formed some horrible picture of the place? What nameless agony the four walls held! What death in life was locked behind the heavy gate! What noble lives oozed away in that pen of despair! Jack saw it all as he glanced from his place. Gaunt, hungry, desperate men, with all the better feelings driven from them by suffering and disease — all but one, patriotism. There was not a man in that frightful pen who would not have raised his feeble hand to cheer at a sight of the old flag. The poor wretches came crawling out of their dens, and ranged themselves on the little hill alongside the ravine. How wistfully they watched the sun slide away to the western hills! They watched all in vain. Not for them that path leading up to the crimson sky. They could only sit and dream that the same sun looked down upon the friends at home.

Jack Foster did not smile because he was a rebel and these dreadful creatures were the hated Yankees. Far from it. He had learned to respect these Yankees after Gettysburg and Chancellorsville. They were brave men, he knew; and at Gettysburg a Yankee soldier had spared Jack's life when he might easily have taken it. When he first entered the army, he might have rejoiced at this dreadful picture, but three years of fighting had taught him a certain respect for his foes. He had been pained at first at the sight of so much wretchedness, but he had grown accustomed to it at last. He could not feel a very earnest sympathy for hungry men when his own rations were shortened and ofttimes dropped entirely.

There was nothing about the dreadful scene that made Jack Foster smile. That facial change was caused by something entirely foreign to the surroundings. The cause had come over the hills, far ahead of the sullen sun, from the world outside, where there were brightness and tenderness and kindly sympathy. It had touched the springs of Jack's heart, and set the whole machinery of his face in motion to manufacture a smile.

Jack held this wonderful stimulant in his hand, between himself and the prison, as he walked with the sun gleaming on his musket. It is easily described. It was nothing but a letter from Lucy Moore. He had others in his pocket. Jack carried these valuable documents about with him wherever he went. He had stitched a great pocket on the inside of his coat, and in this receptacle the whole correspondence was crowded. There were two of the letters — the best of them all, too — one written just after Fredericksburg, and the other at the time when McClellan was driven back from his position before Richmond — that were so badly worn that handling them was a somewhat serious business. But their very use had saved them. Jack had read them so many times that he now knew them by heart. He had made it a habit to say them over to himself time after time when he felt that he needed some great inspiration to nerve him on.

On that fearful third day at Gettysburg, when the lines moved out from under the trees, some of the boys noticed Jack reading his letters. There were some that smiled at him, but yet there were many that felt, at the sight, for a little package under the breast of the coat. Jack came sullenly back out of the fight, but many of the soldiers who smiled at him lay cold and still out in the valley, with letters that never could be answered.

Jack had selected for his morning's reading a letter written by Lucy just as the army stopped to draw itself together after the dreary retreat from Pennsylvania. That was the time when men needed all the brave words and tender consolation that women could give them. The soldiers knew well enough when Lee reeled back for the last time that the life of the Confederacy was doomed. There was no thought of giving up the fight, however. They called Gettysburg a "drawn battle," and every man set his teeth hard and made a vow that the cause should go down in glory.

This obstinate feeling had been intensified all through the dismal retreat. The men who toiled back to Maryland, through the mud and wet, listening to the groans of the wounded, and thinking of the dead men lying on the battle-fields behind them, of the women waiting with white faces in the lonely Southern towns, reformed themselves, when next they reached Southern soil, into a desperate band, armed with the courage of despair. The women watching at home, in the lonely towns, held their friends at the front with letters of grim determination. Lucy had written Jack a letter that well expressed the feeling among Southern women at that day. They begged their friends to fight on. The letter had done Jack good at a time when he needed help. It had nerved him on to the bitter death struggle. There was one sentence that he was never tired of reading over.

"No matter what may happen — if you are only *true*, I will love you forever."

The word "true" was underscored, and Jack made his own estimate as to its meaning. It was the one great idea for which men were dying, and women were suffering, that he must hold true — the mistaken idea of Southern independence.

Jack's thoughts went back over the hills, as he marched slowly along with the letter in his hand. He did not look at the letter; he did not need to do so. He thought it over, as his eyes swept back over the bleak hills, still gilded with the radiance the sun could not help leaving. His musket fell loosely at his shoulder and he forgot the scene of misery so close at his side.

Over the hills, far away in that quiet Mississippi town, his dear little girl was thinking of him at this very moment. He could see her as she stood under the trees, looking sadly down the long street where *he* had marched so bravely away. Jack had often pictured her as she stood that morning when he marched down that beautiful street. He could tell just what she wore that day, even to the color of the ribbon in her hair. A mist had gathered before the honest fellow's eyes as he turned for a last look, and an ugly lump had risen in his throat. Jack could not understand why it was that he remembered everything so well. It is strange how the image of those we love, when viewed through the magnifying dew of tears, can never be put from sight, but will grow in distinctness as the years go by.

Who could help being true when such a dear little girl smiled through her tears? Who would not walk into death's door with a smile at the wish of such a woman? So at least honest Jack asked, and he grasped his musket more firmly as he thought of the danger he would gladly go through to add one ray of pleasure to the light in Lucy's eye.

It is a fact that such letters and such thoughts do not mean business after all. They add to the enthusiasm of a campaign somewhat, but when allowed their own way, they interfere with military discipline considerably.

It is a good plan to allow soldiers to read over their letters just before the bugle sounds a charge. The army will be doubled then, for with every soldier that rushes into the fight, the inspiration of a wife, a mother, or a sweetheart will go. A woman's smile — so tender in love, so terrible in hate — will add a brighter gleam to each flashing bayonet. When any intricate evolutions or any sober, earnest work are needed it may be well to keep the letters in the pocket.

Jack knew that he never could carry that letter in his hand, and, at the same time, hold his gun in exact position and keep the military step, so with a final reading he thrust the precious document into his pocket and straightened himself into a better position. He walked along slowly repeating, "no matter what may happen, if you will only be *true* I will love you forever." There was so much consolation in this thought — the fact of his failing to be "true" being so far out of the question, that Jack smiled again and glanced once more into the yard. He did not take his eyes away at once, for there was something there to interest him.

The "Babes in the Woods" had come out of their place into the sun. They were almost within a stone's throw of Jack's beat. The little one was lying on the ground with the big one sitting beside him. Jack had seen them in this position many times before.

CHAPTER II.

THE BABES IN THE WOODS

BABES IN THE WOODS! It was the only name Jack and the rest had for them. John Rockwell and Archie Sinclair, —th Maine Regiment, was the entry on the books, but the guards had never taken the trouble to find out their real names. When men once entered that pen of misery it needed some striking characteristic to single them out from the rest.

The name was somewhat appropriate in Archie's case, but great, raw-boned John Rockwell was anything but an infant. Archie was a little, delicate fellow, with golden hair, and a face like a girl's. Poor little man! He marched bravely away from the quiet Maine town, bravely and willingly, little thinking of the dreadful heat and agony of Andersonville. Life was full of promise, full of hope, when he kissed his mother and sister good-by. That was the time when the " On to Richmond " order seemed easy of execution. The army did, at last, go " on to Richmond," but it was over a weary and bloody road, covered with the dead bodies of those who failed at first. The little man had gone through many a hard fight without flinching, but the disgrace of captivity had weighed heavily upon him, and when at last he marched with the rest through the prison gate it was in the arms of stout John Rockwell. The slender form had drooped, and clung for support to the strong, rough, tender-hearted man who had seemed so like a brother to him.

Archie had not noticed, when the company went out under the great elms of old Breezetown, how wistfully John had glanced at sister Nellie. He did not know till long after that sad morning what a load John carried under his bright, new uniform. Nellie's "No" had crushed all the sunshine out of John's heart. Poor, awkward, blundering John. There was no one in the village to weep over him, or give him the strong hand-clasp or the smile that reaches to the heart. He had gone to the war almost alone.

Who can tell what the poor fellow thought as he went mechanically through his round of duty? The boys called him odd, and made him the butt of the whole company. Every old trick was played off on honest John, yet he never once complained so long as Archie was amused. The boys would all laugh at John when the mail came in, and the whole army sat down to read the home letters.

"She don't seem to write to ye, John! Who's run off with yer girl, John? Better go back an' see how things is."

Such remarks would always drive John away from the happy group, for he never got a letter. He alone, of all the army, seemed to have no friends at home. John liked to sit at one side — out in the shadow — and watch Archie as he read the home letters. He knew they always contained a line from Nellie, and he often saw a letter in her own handwriting. He could sit there and imagine what she wrote to her brother.

Archie was just like her — so John thought as he watched from the shadow. Small and slender, with blue eyes and hair like gold. John had worshipped her for years. He was only the " Widder Rockwell's boy," yet he had the heart of a nobleman. Many a day he had paused in his work to see her trip by like a little sunbeam. His love had been his one great secret and his religion. The thoughts she had inspired kept his mind pure, and brought him safely through a life filled with such temptations that thousands would have fallen.

When his mother died, John was left alone with nothing but his strength, his love for Nellie, and the well earned title of " Honest John." The war broke out, and all over the country thousands of young men rushed to arms. The great enthusiasm put souls into men who had seemed dull and stupid before. The whole village was ablaze with patriotism; all business was neglected. John saw Nellie at the "sewing circle," making a flag for the company to carry away. He put his name on the list of volunteers without a moment's thought. Then, the mighty spirit of patriotism giving him a wild courage, he spoke the words that the long years of waiting had told him were true.

Nellie laughed at first — how could she help it? This great blundering fellow who had always seemed so awkward. And yet in a moment she pitied him

— this strong man who was to face death at her brother's side. She knew he was sincere — he offered her all he had. She told him at last, very gently, that she could not love him. He went away from her with a love stronger than ever. He knew that it was a hopeless love, and yet he could not help it.

He would sit and think this all over, as he watched Archie read the letters. Archie seemed to John to care very little about these precious documents. Every now and then the old letters would be torn up and thrown away. John found, one day, a piece of an old letter from Nellie, with the words "I love you" written on it. It was only part of a long sentence; he could not tell how the words were used, but he sewed the little scrap on the inside of his vest. There it remained for many a day, and his heart grew very tender whenever he thought of it.

One day Archie met John alone.

"John," he said, "I've got a message for you. Nell sends her regards."

John blushed with pleasure, and stammered out his thanks. It was the first message he had ever received from a young lady. It seemed to him after this that Archie had been left in his special care. He watched over the slender boy as carefully as a mother would have done. Perhaps Nellie would write and thank him for it. There were many things that he could do to help the little man. He was tireless while there was a chance to win a word of thanks from the woman he loved. One message such as she sent before would have well repaid him for all his extra work.

A strange intimacy sprang up by degrees between the two men; strange because they had hitherto lived such widely different lives. Archie learned to lean upon his strong companion, to trust him with all his troubles, and to go to him for advice. He came to hold a great respect for John's great strong blocks of advice, rough-hewn and honest as himself, — chipped from a tough and bitter experience.

John almost worshipped his little companion. Archie grew to look more and more like Nellie. He had the same gentleness. He made a poor soldier, for he pitied his enemies.

Just before Chancellorsville, where they were captured, John had told Archie the great secret. He never would have spoken of it had not his little companion drawn it from him. The great companionship of danger had taught Archie to respect and love "Honest John." He wrote Nellie a long letter, painting with boyish enthusiasm John's good qualities, and asking her, for her brother's sake, to give one word of encouragement. John never knew till the hideous mouth of Andersonville yawned upon them that this letter had ever been sent. Archie and he were swept out of the army at Chancellorsville, and left behind when the gray wave went rolling forward into Pennsylvania.

It was a sad and bitter journey the prisoners made, with heads hung in shame, and idle, weaponless hands, toward the South. A dreadful, heartbreaking journey. Defeat behind them and hopeless captivity before, with the dreadful stories of cruelty magnified a thousand times, and the sickening thought that those at home were mourning their fate. The only news they could hear was the joyfully repeated cry that Lee was marching on through Pennsylvania, sure to pass the winter in Philadelphia, and thus cut the land of the Yankees in two.

The Southern people really believed that the turning-point of the war had come. So it had, in fact, but it turned as they little expected. Chancellorsville seemed to them like Waterloo, and Lee was like Wellington marching on Paris. People turned out at all the little villages to see the Yankee prisoners. How they hated the blue uniform. It was but natural that they should hate it. The Northern men had come among them as rough soldiers, with all the better feelings in them blunted by years of rude life and cruel warfare. How were the women to know that these stern, dusty men, who fought so savagely and burned the pleasant homes so cruelly, had wives and children of their own at home? The prisoners seemed to the great mass of Southern people like so many captured tigers. They were glad the creatures had been caught. They were glad to see them hurried on through the dust and the heat to the horrible prisons.

Many of the women, with sons of their own at the front, pitied Archie. He had been hurt in the battle, and he grew weak as the rough journey went on. The people did not taunt him as they did the others. At one place a little girl ran out from the crowd and handed him a cup of water. A woman dressed in the deepest mourning had sent the little thing on this errand of mercy. Archie and John never knew who she was. She may have been a Union woman, or some Southern mother whose dead son seemed to look out of Archie's eyes.

The prisoners were kept for a time at a small place in South Carolina, but when Sherman began to threaten Georgia they were moved to Andersonville. The Southern leaders probably desired to locate their prison in some healthy spot where the prisoners would be safe from attack. The rude chances of war crowded so many into the stockade that it became a perfect den of disease.

Poor little Archie grew weaker and weaker. John helped him on, divided his rations, and talked about Nellie. Archie's strength gave out at last, and, when he staggered up the sand hills and looked down upon his terrible destination, it was nothing but John's strong arm that held him on his feet. They marched down the hill to the gate. Archie would have fallen as they entered had not John caught him in his arms from the ground. There was no halt for that forlorn column, and so, keeping step with the rest, they marched in through the gates of death together — Archie in John's arms. The guards noted them, and gave them the name at once, "Babes in the Woods!"

No man can tell what these two suffered through these awful days. Archie grew weaker and weaker. His strength passed away from him slowly, and he came to look like a golden-haired ghost. John grew gaunt and desperate as he realized Archie's condition. He divided his rations with his comrade, and even sold both allowances in order to secure some little dainty for his weak companion. The most inoffensive of men before, he grew surly and desperate when Archie was hungry. He fought many a fierce battle with other prisoners for the possession of the scanty food. He lost his former title, and was now known as "Fighting John." It was not the famine and the disease that changed him, but the desire to do something that should make him worthier in the eyes of Nellie.

Day after day they lived on — through the dreary, rainy season, when the dreadful fever leaped over the stockade and laid its hot hands upon them, through the broiling days when they could only gasp for breath. It was a close contest with death for Archie, but still he lived on. John knew too well that his friend was dying. He carried him tenderly about, thinking and talking of the little girl at home. There was hardly a moment that he left the sick man's side. On pleasant days he carried Archie out of their dug-out, and laid him tenderly on the sand. There they would sit for hours and talk. They could remember so many things about the home folks now that had been crushed from memory before. Poor Archie really expected to recover. He made plans for the people at home. John knew better. He knew that the prison gates would only open for Archie's dead body. Their talk was always sure to centre upon Nellie. They were like "babes" surely when they reached this subject.

They were speaking of her, in fact, when Jack

Foster turned on his beat and looked down into the yard. Archie lay on the ground, with John's coat for a pillow. John sat at his side, pointing with his hand in the direction of the place where Jack was walking. He spoke so earnestly that Archie raised himself slightly and looked in the same direction. The sight evidently pleased him greatly, for he smiled and said something that caused John to turn and look squarely at the sentinel.

Jack could not hear any of the conversation, but his eyes followed the motion of the "little babe's" hand. The cause of the dialogue surprised him at first, and yet he could not help appreciating it. Down in the ground, just below where he was walking, grew a great bunch of violets. They were beautiful — the only flowers he had seen in the yard. Perhaps some brave angel had brought them, with averted face, up to the stockade, and then turned back in horror at the wretched picture of despair. Jack had never noticed them before. They were just inside the dead line — far removed indeed from the two "babes," for to cross that line meant death.

Jack gave the flowers but a moment's thought. There were sterner and pleasanter duties for him. He marched slowly on, thinking of his letters. Down in the prison the two "babes" still sat discussing the violets.

CHAPTER III.

THE ANDERSONVILLE VIOLETS

Poor Archie talked queerly that morning, when John brought him out into the yard. Happily for him, his mind had wandered out of the prison. He talked about the Maine home, the woods, and all the old scenes, till John felt sick at heart. What a dreadful mockery it all was! The horrible place filled with these desperate men, and this weak boy babbling wildly of the old scenes they both knew so well.

"And there's Nell," whispered Archie at last. Poor fellow, his voice was almost gone. "She's going with us, John. Ain't you glad? I know you are, for I remember what you told me. Come on, Nell. We can eat our dinner down by the old rock, and we'll make John pick the flowers for your wedding.

"What flowers shall we bring her, John? Violets, I say. You go and pick them, John, while I stay here and talk to her. I'll tell her all about the war — all we have been through; then I'll tell how much you love her, and she can't help saying 'yes,' for we have been such chums, you know. It will be all right, I'm sure, John. You go and get the flowers and let me talk to her alone."

John tried to turn Archie's mind away from the

flowers. He had pointed them out some time before, little dreaming that Archie would insist upon his getting them. To the fevered mind of the little man they seemed to be growing in the meadow at home. Archie did not know when he urged John to get them of the fatal dead line that held the flowers further away than the old home could be.

"Never mind about it now, Archie," John said. "Let's talk about the old times a little first, and then I'll get 'em. There's no hurry, you know, for we have all day before us. Look at the sun over on the hills there."

Archie lay without speaking for a little while. He watched the sun, far away now over the hills. The hills were bright with splendor, and it seemed to Archie's fevered mind like the opening of the gates of Paradise. The great hills seemed changed to a stair of gold. The opening of the gate was nearer to Archie than he thought. He lay and watched the sun till a cloud passed over the golden hills and closed for the moment the glorious gate. Then he turned back to the flowers.

"Come, John, why don't you go?" he whispered fretfully. "Now is your time. You said you loved her once, and now you are not ready to pick her a few flowers. Run, John, or I will never tell her what you want me to. You said you loved her once, now why don't you go?"

John never faltered for an instant. He knew well that to cross that line meant death, yet he never thought once of holding back when Archie said — "you said you loved her once."

He did not mean that Archie should see him make the sacrifice. He bent down and raised the "little babe" gently from the ground. How light the burden was.

"Come," he said, "it's getting hot here. I'll carry you back into the shade, and then I'll get the flowers for Nellie."

"All right, John, but hurry up; for Nellie can't stay long, you know, and this will be the last chance for you to show how well you love her. I think she will understand it, John, when you bring the flowers."

John carried him back and laid him under the shade of the bank of earth they had raised.

"Don't be long, John," said Archie, as the "big babe," with a most babyish moisture about his eyes, shook the little fellow's hand and started back to go through the test. "I'll talk to her about it while you are gone, John — never fear for me — she will do anything for me. Good-by. I will be telling her all the time."

And perhaps he was "telling her" while John Rockwell walked deliberately back to the dead line.

Jack Foster had watched the whole proceeding from his place on the stockade. Men in possession of such an amount of imaginative literature as he carried are apt to put a sentimental rather than a business-like interpretation upon such actions. We judge men's actions by imagining what we would do under similar circumstances. The frame of mind in which we find ourselves regulates our judgment.

The "little babe" pointing to the violets made Jack somehow think of the times when Lucy and he had placed such a value upon just such little flowers. In fact, he carried, in one of his letters, two dried violets that seemed of more value to him than all the remaining vegetation of the country. Jack could not help imagining some of the feelings of the " little babe."

Here was a little fellow shut up in this dreadful place, dying, it may be, longing for the sweet breath of these simple little flowers so near him. Perhaps he had a sweetheart of his own somewhere far away in that cold Yankee country. No doubt he loved her in his queer Yankee fashion almost as well as *he* loved his little girl.

Jack ran it all over in his mind as he glanced at the two men in the yard. What would he do in such a case? It seemed to him from the way the "big babe" looked when he picked the little one from the ground that he was desperate enough to dash over the line. Somehow, Jack rather expected him to do it. He knew well that he would have gone himself. What could he do if the attempt was made? Could he shoot this man for proving himself a hero? Could he disobey orders and risk the penalty? He was in a place of trust. Let the prisoners once rush over that line, and the small guard could never keep them back. He must obey orders, and shoot the "big babe" if he should make a dash for the violets, as Jack seemed to know he would do.

John Rockwell left Archie in the shade, and then walked slowly and grimly back to the place where they had been sitting. He did not pause here, but walked savagely on to the line. He looked desperate indeed as Jack glanced down at him.

Thin and gaunt, with famine-eaten flesh, and thin, bony hands held out before him, he walked savagely on, looking directly at Jack. His face told, by the long, deep lines pinched into it, of the two lives he had supported so long. His eyes peered out from two deep caverns under the broken visor of his army cap, which hung down over his forehead. His long hair fell about his face in wild disorder, and an unkempt beard thrust itself fiercely out from about his mouth. It was a face that Jack Foster never could drive from his mind. The blue uniform was torn, and hung in tatters about the gaunt prisoner. One sleeve was gone, the wasted muscles of the arm showing through the rent. One bony knee was brought into view at every stride. A desperate man the Yankee stood before the rebel to show, by giving his life if necessary, that not even the fevered imagination of a dying man should question his love. The other prisoners in the yard watched him. They crowded behind, at a short distance, to see what he would do. No one seemed to know his mission. All waited in silence. Desperately, like a man who has fought too long with death to fear it, the "big babe" walked up to the line. Jack paced slowly on. He brought his musket into position as the man advanced. No one saw it but himself, but, as he raised his gun, across his vision came the figure of his little girl — Lucy standing before the desperate Yankee. She put up her hand as if to motion him back. Her lip was trembling just as it did when he bade her good-by, and her eyes were beaming on him as they never had done before. The sentence in the letter he had been reading flashed through his mind. "No matter what may happen, if you will only be true, I will love you forever."

This was what she meant then. He must be true to himself. He dropped the point of his musket, and stopped for a moment in his walk. He fully realized what he was doing, but that face and figure were too dear to him.

John Rockwell came to the dead line and stood looking at Jack. "Rebel," he said, in a thick, hoarse voice, "I must get them flowers."

No one but "Honest John" would ever have thought of speaking at all. The guards had orders to shoot down all prisoners that spoke to them. It was here that Jack raised his musket, while the guard below him stopped to watch.

"I want them flowers. There's a young boy here dyin'. Let me get 'em for him, rebel."

He saw the musket lower, and, with one wild spring, he dashed over the line and dropped on his knees beside the violets. Jack never raised his musket, but the guard below him brought up his gun as John sprang back over the line with the flowers in his hand. The guard fired, and John fell over the line with a bullet scratch on his leg. The prisoners, at the report, hurried for shelter into the holes or behind the banks. Some of them peered out through the openings to see what would be done. Jack brought his musket mechanically to his shoulder and started back along his beat. He well knew what would follow.

The "big babe" lay for a moment on the sand. He tried to rise to his feet, but his leg seemed numb, and gave way beneath him. After a little he crawled slowly and painfully back to the bank where Archie was waiting. He carried the flowers in his mouth. He crawled slowly up to Archie's side, and gently placed the flowers on the boy's breast. A shout, fierce and exulting, went up from the hiding-places as he passed into the shelter. The prisoners came creeping out of their holes to admire this brave man.

In a few moments the steady tramp of marching feet was heard outside the stockade. The company halted at Jack's beat, and a new sentinel appeared. A new sentinel who glanced savagely down upon the prisoners, and seemed to dare any of them to make another dash. Between the files of soldiers Jack was marched back to the guard-house in disgrace. The musket he had carried so well was taken from him. Terrible war that allows no sentiment, no love to soften one of its harsh features!

"It was treason!" they muttered as they marched him back to the guard-house. "Death!" they whispered sadly as the doors closed on him. But Jack smiled in spite of it all. It was Lucy that stood before the Yankee; it was her hand that bade him lower his musket, and he was satisfied. He had been true to himself.

CHAPTER IV.

A PLAN FOR ESCAPE

ARCHIE looked up with a feeble smile as John came crawling back with the flowers. The fever had left the "little babe" at last, and he knew now that he was in the prison. As John placed the flowers on Archie's breast, the little fellow took the gaunt hand in both his feeble ones and raised it to his lips. The men understood each other. There was no need of speaking. When men are placed in such situations, the womanly qualities which they take from the companionship of their mothers and sisters will always show. Under ordinary circumstances both men would have laughed at such a demonstration of affection, but here, where a horrible death was grinning in their very faces, the true manhood came to the surface. It is the truly brave man, he who can look without flinching into the eyes of death, that is the tenderest when the danger is over.

"I am very sorry I made you go, John," said Archie, feebly, still holding the gaunt hand. "Did they break your leg?"

"I guess not," answered John. "It's only a flesh wound, I guess. It bleeds a little, but I can stop that."

John tore away the hanging sleeve of his coat, and prepared a bandage, with which he bound up his leg. There was nothing dangerous about the wound, and John felt disposed to make light of it.

"They can't hit nothin'," he said, gleefully. "They can't hit a barn door. That reb there where I jumped might have shot me easy. I saw the gun drop, and then I jumped. What do you s'pose made him drop his gun?" John knew nothing of the little woman who stood in front of him and turned Jack's musket aside.

Archie smiled wearily as John told the story of the flower-hunting. A number of the prisoners came from their hiding-places and gathered in a group to listen to John's story. Short, "thick-set" Maine men they were; all "home folks," with all that term implies. Most of them had marched with John and Archie out of old Breezetown. They seemed like a great family as they gathered in the sand to offer congratulations and sympathy. Stout, hearty fellows they were when the old elms bent down as if to whisper "good-by." They were fresh from home then. Now they were sadly changed. Worn by suffering, with ragged clothing hanging about their wasted bodies, they crouched in the sand.

There were no "play-day" soldiers in this group. The old New England patriotism is too strongly planted in her sons for any cruel treatment to tear it away. It is planted as firmly in the hearts of her sons and daughters as her gray old mountains are fastened to her breast. There was not a man in the

A PLAN FOR ESCAPE

whole company who would have turned his back upon the loathsome prison to shoulder a musket in the guard outside. They had suffered as not one man in ten thousand ever suffers, or dreams of suffering. None but old soldiers can ever understand what these men endured under the glare of the burning Southern sun. How they longed for the cool woods and pure breezes of old Maine. How grimly they waited and watched the life oozing away from them — the life that meant so much for " the folks " at home. In spite of all the agony they never dreamed of changing their faith.

There was one great, gray-bearded man in the group who seemed to be a natural leader. He was Archie's Uncle Nathan — they are all uncles or cousins in the old Maine towns. They all turned to him for counsel. A gruff old fellow he was — sunburned and grizzled, with a hatred for his foes that triumphed over all his privations. The old fellow had reason for his hatred. Three strong sons had marched behind him out of old Breezetown. They could not stay at home when volunteers were called for. Three strong boys — they were now lying back on the battle-fields — and he alone was left to tell the story to their mother.

He had made a small Union flag out of cast-off garments that he had been able to pick up. The blue parts had been cut from an old army coat. The white came from a cast-off shirt, and the red was utilized from a pair of torn stockings. He had stitched and pinned this curious mixture of colors together, doing his work when the guards could not see him. It represented the dear old banner under which they had fought. Uncle Nathan was proud of his flag. It was his dearest treasure. Once, when some of the company, wild with hunger, had vaguely hinted at going over, he had pulled out his flag and waved it defiantly in their faces. Not another word had ever been heard of surrender. There was too much hatred sewed into that flag.

Uncle Nathan smiled grimly as he put his hand on John's leg and examined the slight wound. He had never before been quite able to forget that John was only "the Widder Rockwell's boy."

"Ye done well, boy! Ye done well!" he muttered as he satisfied himself that no serious damage had been done. "Them guards can't hit a barn door. But what made ye go after them posies? Ye don't wanter risk a shot like that 'thout ye can git a grip on some reb's throat."

"Archie wanted 'em," said John simply. He did not consider it necessary to give any other reason; but Archie looked at him and smiled, and they understood each other.

The group of men, old friends and neighbors, who had gathered in the sand, viewed the sick boy compassionately. The old home feeling came strongly to them as they watched him. It seemed so terrible for him, the baby of the company, to be dying here, and they unable to help him or soothe his sufferings. How different such a sickness would have been at home, where all "the folks" would hasten with words of the tenderest consolation to draw the sting from death. These rough men did their best to speak tenderly; but home was too far away, and the "wimmen folks" could not come.

"Done it fer him, did ye?" said Uncle Nathan as he brushed the hair away from Archie's forehead. "It takes grit, I tell ye, to do sech things. It takes men from the State o' Maine ter show them rebels what grit is. Them's the kind o' men we raise to our town. Old Breezetown don't never take no back seat." He addressed this boasting remark to the prison in general.

"But what made that fust rebel hold up his gun? — he might have shot clean through ye with half an eye."

"I don't know," answered John. "I see him drop the p'int of his gun an' I give a jump."

" An' ye done well, John, ye done well. Give me fifty sech men as you be, an' I'll be out of this yard in half an hour. I see 'em take that fust rebel down. They'll court-martial him, I s'pose. It beats all how they do business. When they git a decent man on guard, they shoot him jest to keep in practice. It beats all," and Uncle Nathan, with a growl at the imperfect military system of the Confederacy, started away.

He paused at the end of a few steps, and came slowly back. His face showed that something of great importance was coming. He pulled from beneath his coat the rude flag he had carried so sacredly. He pushed the little banner into John's hand as he said, — "I'll make ye a present of that. I'll warrant you'll keep it too. It takes men o' grit to do sech a thing as that is, I tell ye. I hadn't no idee the Widder Rockwell's boy hed ser much in him. I'm proud of ye — yes, I be " — and he marched away, with a smile for Archie, while John thrust the flag into his pocket.

Uncle Nathan went away, but the rest of the men made quite a visit. There was nothing to do, and they felt that they might just as well stop there and talk in the shade, as to wander about in the sun. They were all desperately hungry, and it was but natural that they should fall into a discussion of foods. They had held many a Barmecide's feast in the prison before — indeed their greatest pleasure lay in attempting to

"Cloy the hungry edge of appetite
By bare imagination of a feast."

"I tell ye," began Tom Gove, "when I git back to the State o' Maine, I'm gonter git me the squarest meal you ever see. I want me some fish chowder. I'm gonter git that down to Bill Waterside's. Bill can make the best fish chowder that ever was eet. He takes his big kittle and puts him in fust a layer o' fish, then a thin patch o' pork, then a layer o' pertaters, then a layer o' crackers, an' so on to the top. When it comes out o' that kittle, there ain't nothin' better nowhere, I tell ye."

The water stood in Tom's mouth as he gave this recipe. He involuntarily extended his hand as if to secure a plateful of the delicious mixture. Bill Brown had decided to patronize home talent as far as possible. He was determined to secure a dish of his mother's baked beans.

"They beats everything," he argued. "I've seen my mother cook 'em time and agin. She parbiles 'em over night, an' then puts 'em in a deep dish with a piece o' pork on top. She puts in a little merlasses an' bakes 'em kinder slow. There ain't nothin' comes nigh 'em for taste" — and Bill drew a long breath as if to catch a faint whiff from the fragrant bean-pot just coming out of his mother's oven.

Dave Jackson was a trifle more of an aristocrat. It must be stated in explanation that Dave's mother was not particularly noted as a cook.

"I'm gonter stop to Boston an' get me a real good ham an' eggs. I know a place where they cook eggs so they slide right down your throat without butter."

And so the men talked on, laying plans for a time that never could come.

The crowd at last dropped away, and left Archie and John alone. They were glad of the chance to talk.

"I'm sorry I made you go, John," said Archie, gently — "but *you* will never be sorry for it, I'm sure."

"That's all right," said John, sturdily; "I ain't a mite hurt, and you got your flowers."

"But it wasn't for *me* that you went, John. I know all about it, John, and I am sure it will be all right some day." He clasped John's hand with a pressure that both men understood.

"I shall never see her again, John. I am sure of that now, but I want you to take a message from me — and you must live through here to do it. I meant to do so much for them, John, but it's all passed now, and I can only leave them to you."

John listened without a word. How gladly he would take the charge. He would live to fulfil it, too.

"I have written her a letter," said Archie, after a little. "You must give it to her, and tell her just how I wrote and sent it. Give her my love, John, and tell her that I meant all I have written her. I think she will believe it, too. I'm so tired, John. I think I will try to sleep a little."

John arranged the coat under Archie's head. The little fellow closed his eyes, and slept like a tired child. John sat beside him and brushed the flies away from the thin face. He glanced at the letter that Archie had given him. It was written on a piece of rough paper that had been torn from some package. The words were traced with a dim lead pencil, and then retraced with a pale ink that Archie had borrowed from one of the prisoners. John did not mean to read the letter, but his eye glanced instinctively over the rough page, and he read it through almost at a glance. His heart gave a great throb as he read: —

"DEAR NELLIE: I am writing this in the prison. It is the last time I shall ever write to you, for I do not think I shall live through another week. I am not afraid to die, for I feel that I have tried to do my best. John has promised to carry this letter to you, and I know he will live to do it. He will carry my love to you, too. I do wish you could know John as well as I do. What I wrote just before we were captured was not half strong enough. If you love me you never will marry any one till you know just what John is. He loves you better than he loves his own life. I know it, for he would die to-day for me, because I am like you. Good-by, comfort mother the best you can. I did mean to do so much for you, but it's all past now. John will tell you all about it; and if you could only know him, you would love him just as well as I do.
"ARCHIE."

John read this letter, and then folded it carefully, tearing off a piece from his ragged coat to serve for a covering. He opened his vest, and disclosed the piece of the letter to Archie with " I love you " written upon it. He fastened both papers with the pin, and buttoned the vest tightly about his throat.

John sat by Archie's side till the sun came back over the bright hills. Slowly it circled up over the prison, gradually it destroyed the shade where Archie was lying. The sunlight fell directly in the face of the sleeper, and, turn as he would, John could not keep him in the shade. At last he shook Archie's shoulder to rouse him. The sleeping man was cold and stiff. John had been watching the sleep of death.

The soldiers of the old Maine town came and viewed the body in solemn procession. There was nothing they could do or say. They had passed through too many horrors already.

Uncle Nathan and John carried the body into the shade. They threw a coat over the face, and arranged the violets on the breast. This was all they could do now. John's leg troubled him somewhat, yet he did his work. As they came back to their old place, Uncle Nathan whispered to John : —

" Are ye ready to make a dash agin, and push outer here ? "

John nodded. The letter under his coat throbbed at the thought of freedom. He felt that he must deliver that note. It had put a wild courage into his heart. Uncle Nathan chuckled with great satisfaction.

"I knowed ye would. I like yer grit fust-rate. We can show them fellers what kind of folks we raise to home in the State o' Maine. We must leave the boys here, and make a break for the lines."

Uncle Nathan detailed his plan. A number of the prisoners were called for to go out on the hills after firewood. He had gone once, and noticed, as he thought, a chance for escape. He proposed to John to go out, separate the guards, beat them down, secure their arms and ammunition, and make for the mountains. It was a wild scheme. Many a prisoner had been killed attempting it, but John was still ready to try. Anything rather than endure another month of Andersonville life. The two men shook hands. They were willing to make the trial. They went back to take a last look at Archie. There was no "scene," no painful leave-taking. John bent over and cut away one of the curls that struggled over the dead man's forehead. They threw the old coat back over the face, and it was all over. John and Uncle Nathan secured a position in the squad of wood-carriers. They went out through the gates, determined never to reënter them alive. As they marched up over the hills, they saw a file of rebel soldiers, with a man marching in the midst with his hands bound behind him. They were not near enough to recognize Jack Foster.

CHAPTER V.

DISHONORABLY DISCHARGED

WHEN Jack Foster found himself alone in the guard-house, his first impulse was to read his letters. There was just light enough in the dim room to enable him to see the words of the letter that he selected at random from his pocket.

This selection was not, on the whole, a happy one. It had been written just after Grant defeated Pemberton and drove him back into Vicksburg. The Union soldiers had marched through the village. Lucy had but spoken the feelings of all Southern women when she wrote, "I hate them all. If you ever neglect your duty, or show any mercy for these robbers and murderers, I will never speak to you again. But I know *you* never will come to any disgrace, for you love me too well."

Somehow, Jack did not feel exactly comfortable after reading this letter. What would she think of him now? He had spared a Yankee's life, and brought disgrace upon himself. Would she believe him when he told her the reason?

The thought was so unpleasant that he crowded the letters back into his pocket. This was the first time they had failed to bring him consolation. He put his hands into his pockets, and began walking up and down the narrow room. There was nothing particularly dreadful about the trial which he knew would soon be called. He had faced death too many times to fear it now, but the thought of Lucy's displeasure nearly drove him wild. As he paced slowly up and down, he caught the sound of marching feet outside.

"Halt!" The stern order brought both the marching guard and himself to a standstill. The door was unlocked and thrown open. Peering out into the bright light, Jack found himself confronted by two lines of soldiers, who were drawn up in front of the door.

The officer in command ordered Jack to march out and take his place between the lines of soldiers. Then at the sharp order, "Forward — March!" the squad advanced in the direction of the commander's office. Jack glanced at the faces of the guards as they marched on. He knew them all. There was not a sign of hope in any countenance. A group of officers stood about the door of the office. At the approach of the guard they passed inside. Jack, at the order, followed them, while the guard fell in behind to cover the entrance. And Jack Foster found himself on trial for his life. It was treason then to refuse to shoot a man for doing what any man would have done. It was a crime to be merciful. The room was dismal and bare, in keeping with war's justice. A few rough chairs and a dirty table covered with papers stood at one end. A few maps were hung upon the walls. The floor and walls were stained and rough. Jack stood in the middle of the room, while the guard ranged about the sides. Every eye turned to the prison commander. This personage sat at the little table. He seemed glum and savage, and the others glanced anxiously at him. A rough, brutal-looking man, he glared angrily at Jack, and nodded his head impatiently at the group of officers gathered about him, as if anxious to have the case ended. An example must be made of this sentinel. A few such cases and the prisoners would break over the walls. There was no possible hope for mercy in that savage face. Jack knew that his story would be wasted on such a man. A grim, hard feeling came over him, and he shut his teeth just as he used to do when the company marched into battle. He was too proud to beg for his life, and he knew he had no defence that could ever satisfy such a man. So he waited proudly for the result.

The trial was a very short one. The case against Jack was too clear to admit of any argument. The guard who had shot John Rockwell told the story as an outsider might have seen it. This man stated that he had seen the big Yankee talking with Jack. He had distinctly seen Jack lower his musket, and he had noticed the Yankee jump over the line. At this point he had deemed it necessary to take an active part in the exercise himself. He had taken a hasty aim and fired. The Yankee was, in his opinion, very badly hurt — his only regret was that he had not killed him at once. This story was told in a most dramatic manner, with many gestures and explanatory remarks. What did this man know or care about the violets or the little woman who had stood in front of the Yankee?

The officers listened carefully to the story, asking an occasional question. When the fluent sentinel had finished his oration, all eyes turned to Jack.

"Well, what have *you* got to say?" growled the commander.

What *could* Jack say? How could he tell about the sick boy, and the violets, and Lucy?

His reason must remain tied to his heart, for this sneering man never would believe him.

He looked straight into the commander's eyes as he answered, slowly : —

"Nothing, I reckon."

That was the end of the trial. At an order from the officer, the prisoner, surrounded by the guards, marched out of the room. Just as Jack turned, he saw his old captain rise from his chair to address the commander. The first words fell upon Jack's ear : "I plead for mercy for this man. I have seen him in battle, and I know there is not a braver man in the army." But here the door closed, and the rest was never heard.

Who can tell what Jack felt as he marched back to the guard-house? Who can tell what he thought when the sentence came — "To be shot at noon"? There are few men who can tell, few men who ever live such lives. After all the years of hoping and devotion it had come to this. And yet down in his heart there was still a feeling of satisfaction. He was glad, after all, that he did not shoot the Yankee. At last the time came. He had written a long, disjointed letter to Lucy and his mother, trying to tell them just how he had done his duty. The letter was in his breast-pocket when the guards came to march him away. His hands were bound behind him. Twelve soldiers, members of his own company, had been detailed to do the horrible work of execution. They dared not look Jack in the face as they bound him. Six of the guns were loaded, and six were empty. No one could tell which one he held. A merciful provision when one's friend stood up as a target. The men were silent. There was no one there to offer consolation to poor Jack. He started in a sort of daze to the place of execution. He could hardly realize his position yet. The sad-faced squad had hardly taken a dozen steps when a messenger dashed up with a paper in his hand. The soldiers halted almost without the order, while the officer glanced over the paper. Jack waited in dull anxiety.

"Reprieved," the officer said at last, with a curious glance at Jack. The squad sent up a shout, which was echoed from the barracks. The men were happy to know that they would not be called upon to kill a brother soldier.

There was a look on the face of the officer that Jack did not like. The rest of the paper was read as the soldiers unbound Jack's arms and heartily shook hands with him. Jack almost wished for a moment that the paper had never been written. He was pardoned in consequence of his previous good conduct, but, that his grave offence might be a lesson to others, he was dishonorably discharged from the service — never to enter it again. It was worse than the death sentence to a proud man. Many a man would prefer death to a life of imprisonment, where all hope and ambition must be starved out of him. Many a man would rather die than live in the midst of former friends who could only point the finger of shame and use him as a terrible example for their children.

The soldiers — Jack's old comrades — looked at each other in horror. "Dishonorably discharged" from the service they would give their lives for so willingly — for which they had suffered so much. With all a Southern man's love of honor and chivalry they recoiled from such a bitter disgrace. Better death than such dishonor. What true Southern man or woman could ever look upon a man who had been "dishonorably discharged." Such a stain would cling through one's life.

Jack felt the disgrace keenly. He turned white as death and the tears came into his eyes.

"Kill me, boys," he begged. "I can stand that, I reckon, but don't send me back like that."

But the squad of men marched sullenly back to the barracks — glad, yet sorry that the execution had been prevented. Glad that Jack was to live, sorry that such a terrible stain was to be put upon his character. Jack followed them slowly back to the prison walls. The soldiers who knew of his sentence seemed to shun him. There was no excuse that he could offer. It seemed as if his proper place was inside the heavy gate with the other prisoners. All his life was clouded. There seemed no hope for him. What would Lucy say to her dishonored knight?

As Jack passed slowly by the stockade, the gate swung open and the guard passed out, followed by a squad of prisoners who carried the dead. Jack turned carelessly to look at them. Archie's long, yellow hair straggled out from beneath the blanket that had been loosely thrown over him. Jack recognized the head at once. He stepped to the side of the cart in which the bodies were placed, and looked long and earnestly at the boyish face for which he had lost so much.

The soldiers who had charge of the work did not know of Jack's dishonor. They supposed he had been pardoned without any condition. They spoke to him as of old.

"It's the little babe, I reckon, Jack," they said. "See them flowers. He'd throw hisself mighty straight ef he had them at home, I reckon."

Jack glanced at the violets fastened in Archie's shirt. A strange impulse tempted him to take them.

"I reckon I'll keep them," he said, and he reached over and pulled them from their fastening. It would be something after all to keep these little flowers even if they had brought him such dishonor. He turned back to the barracks and the cart jolted on to the rude graveyard.

CHAPTER VI.

THE ESCAPE

UNCLE NATHAN and John marched slowly over the hills toward the woods. The gang, shortly after leaving the prison, had divided up into small squads which marched out in different directions. Each squad consisted of six prisoners and two guards. The prisoners understood that a single suspicious gesture would be fatal to them. The guards realized that prompt action would be necessary. The prisoners marched in front, Uncle Nathan and John in advance, while the guards followed in the rear. The four prisoners who followed the leaders were members of a German regiment from Pennsylvania. One of them could speak a little English, but their favorite means of communication was the rude dialect so common in the German districts of their State. These men made wooden and machine-like prisoners, just as they made block-like soldiers. They marched heavily on, with their eyes bent on the ground, punching great holes in the sand at each heavy step. Uncle Nathan had the most profound contempt for his fellow-prisoners. He knew they would be of no help whatever in his proposed dash for liberty.

"Them Pennsylvany Dutch," he whispered to

John, "don't know nothin'. One of 'em keeps settin' his big hoof right onter my heel. We can't make no dependence on them."

It was a strange-looking company. John walked painfully. His leg hurt him somewhat, but he dragged it manfully on over the sand, trying not to limp at all. He would not go back now. He had seen Andersonville for the last time. He looked wilder than ever. The cap with its drooping visor, the sleeveless coat, ragged and tightly buttoned at the throat, the gaping shoes, and the thin brown legs all added to his strange appearance. Uncle Nathan marched grimly at John's side. The old man had lost his soldier's cap. A square piece of the lining of his coat, with a knot tied in each corner, served for a head covering. His gray hair straggled down about his neck and ears, and his grizzled beard stood out in the wildest disorder about his face. The lines on his forehead and under his eyes had deepened until his face had drawn into a grim scowl. His gray eyes glistening under the heavy eyebrows spoke of the rough desperation that filled his soul. He had no coat — he had used the last of it in making his flag, and his vest hung in tatters. An attempt had been made to patch this latter garment with the side of an old meal sack, but this attempt had added little to the beauty or usefulness of the vest. His shirt sleeves were ragged, and the thin brown arms were bare from the elbows.

The "Pennsylvany Dutch" looked like walking ragbags. Their tattered garments shook about them as they marched solidly up the hill. They had never taken the least care of their clothing, and now their only covering consisted of a series of rags that seemed in constant danger of falling from them. If anything was needed to complete the ridiculous picture, the element was certainly supplied by the two rebel soldiers who marched at the rear of the column. One was a short, heavy Alabamian with a large, exceedingly hairy head and neck, that seemed bent on imprisoning his face in a forest of hair. His body promised to assume true aldermanic proportions when he should once more secure a close proximity to rations that would enable him to do himself justice. The spectacle of a fat man who has been deprived, for any length of time, of the good living that made him greater than other men, is a sad one. We feel that the form and face have been driven back from the proud proportions they once held. We watch such a man's smile with sorrow, for we feel that it ought to be, at least, an inch in advance of its present ground. The short soldier walked with short waddling footsteps, with his musket thrown carelessly over his shoulder, yet keeping a sharp lookout on the prisoners. He was dressed in the prevailing slouch hat and dirty gray uniform of the Confederacy. His coat, evidently made at a happier time, when its owner had access to a better table, hung in loose folds about his body. His reduced legs struck against the sides of his voluminous pants with about the significance of a blow against the side of a hanging carpet. Uncle Nathan had singled out this man as the easier of the two to handle. The other soldier was the exact opposite of his companion. A tall, gaunt Mississippian, with the long, thin legs and arms, lank hair and melancholy face, peculiar to the "piney woods" regions. A student of character will notice that men can be known by the character of the soil upon which they have been raised. A dry, thin soil is almost sure to produce long, thin men, who seem eager to grow away as far as possible from the earth that has barely supported them. On rich soil will be found men, thick and heavy, who seem to desire to walk solidly upon the good ground. The tall guard towered high above his comrade. He kept his dull, heavy eyes carefully fixed upon space as he marched solemnly on. His long, thin features and cadaverous cheeks contrasted strongly with the good-natured face of the man at his side, whose short legs were taxed to their utmost to keep in step. Both men, in addition to their muskets, carried revolvers at their belts.

The strange procession moved on over the hills with some semblance of order till the first valley was reached. Once out of sight of the camp, the discipline of the guards and the legs of the short man gave out together. The portly soldier stopped the long stride, and fell back to his more comfortable short step. The long soldier, with the accommodating indolence of his race, shortened his own step. Uncle Nathan and John instinctively slackened their pace, but the "Pennsylvany Dutch" went on with the same stride. They ran into the leaders so heavily that John and Uncle Nathan stepped to the side and fell in behind the progressive Dutchmen.

There was reason and method in this new movement. Uncle Nathan wished to get near the two soldiers and throw them off their guard. He had great faith in his conversational powers. The useless energy displayed by the " Pennsylvany Dutch " did not meet with the approval of the stout soldier. To him all extra motion was useless. They were not, to his mind, engaged in any walking match or any other event in which useless energy was required.

"Halt!" he shouted, in his most commanding tone, holding his musket with one hand, while with the other he pulled his capacious vest down into something like position. This vest movement seems to be the favorite motion of authority employed by fat men of good nature and small intellect. The Germans halted so suddenly that they ploughed great holes in the sand with their feet. They never moved their heads, but stood with eyes held directly in front of them, waiting for the next order.

"I reckon ye'd better go to the front an' march 'em sorter slow like, Bill," said the portly commander of the expedition, as he pushed his hat to one side of his hairy head. The long soldier, thus advised, placed himself at the head of the column without a word of argument. He kept his eyes straight before him, looking neither to the right nor to the left, as if confident that his comrade was fully able to manage everything in the rear.

"For'ad march! Slow!" ordered the commander, pulling his hat down over his forehead.

At the word Bill started at his most indolent pace, while the poor "Pennsylvany Dutch" went tumbling over one another's feet in their efforts to keep pace with the slow motion. The fat man toddled at the rear, fully satisfied with the success of his new arrangements. He grew quite communicative as they marched slowly on.

"I expect you Yanks ain't gut nary piece of terbacker, have ye? I done used mine all up," he began.

At the word "terbacker" Bill's face displayed its first sign of intelligence. His chin dropped into something like a smile, and one dull eye glanced back to take notes on the answer. There are various ways of reaching the souls of different men.

The question may be considered, by some persons, a very foolish one. What reasonable man could expect prisoners, suffering for want of the simple necessaries of life, to be provided with an article which is usually looked upon as a luxury? However, the question served to open the conversation, and is no more useless than many used for a like purpose. Uncle Nathan appointed himself as spokesman for the party. John and the "Pennsylvany Dutch" never offered any objection.

"No, we ain't gut none. Don't s'pose we can git none of you, can we? I was kinder in hopes we could."

The tobacco question, though easily exhausted, paved the way for an extended conversation, and, by the time the first woodpile was reached, Uncle Nathan and the fat soldier were on as good terms as their circumstances would allow. A discussion or conversation between any prisoner and his keeper must always be a trifle one-sided, but it is better than a complete silence. On reaching the pile, the first act of the commander was to suggest a rest. There was no attempt at argument on this proposition, and the whole party at once sat down in the sand, near a tall pine to gather strength for the return trip. The two guards sat a little to one side. The " Pennsylvany Dutch " sat directly in the sun, and fell at once into the discussion of some evidently interesting point, in their disjointed German.

" Whar be them fellers frum, Yank? " asked the Alabamian, pointing to the group.

" Them's what we call Pennsylvany Dutch," answered Uncle Nathan ; " furreners," he added, fearful lest the rebel might think these men came from his beloved State of Maine.

" Wall, Yank," continued the leader, reflectively, " them furreners is what done it. I'm doggoned if that ain't so. They've hurt us right smart, I reckon. Ef you all hed gut shut of them furreners, we shud be 'way on top of ye now. Them furreners is what's doin' it, I reckon."

Uncle Nathan found it hard to answer this statement calmly. He had his own ideas on the subject, and it was hard to keep them back. He knew that Old Abe, with the aid of men like his own from the " State o' Maine," had done more than all the " furreners " that ever breathed. Still, it was his present policy to keep his captors good-natured, and so he muttered shortly, —

"Mebbe so."

"Yes, sah. It's them furreners an' that twenty-nigger law thet's gonter do it, ef anything does. You all kin see that. Drop them furreners out, an' we'll march — wall, right smartly into your country." The geography of the fat leader was evidently defective; he did not care to assume the responsibility of giving any exact point at the North where he could safely march. "We is a heap better fighters than you all is. We can march all round ye, I reckon. When we marched up to Gettysburg, our company went by a house whar they wuz a couple of ladies sot out in front. I heard 'em whisper like — 'they march better'n our'n, but ain't they dirty?' But fer thet twenty-nigger law an' them furreners, we'd 'a' whipped ye."

Uncle Nathan was about to give his ideas concerning constitutional law, when Bill surprised every one by rising to his feet as a gentle intimation that the time had come for an action against the woodpile. The fat man followed Bill, and routed the "Pennsylvany Dutch" from their position in the sand. He had, evidently, taken quite a fancy to Uncle Nathan, and desired to reserve the lightest work for him.

"Bill," he suggested, "jest load up them furreners, an' start 'em in slow like. I'll sorter take these yer Yanks an' git some light-wood." "Fall in, Yanks! March!" and he indicated with his hand the direction in which the light-wood lay.

The two men stepped off with a farewell glance at the patient "Pennsylvany Dutch;" they were resolved never to see their fellow-captives again, unless the meeting took place within the Union lines. Uncle Nathan shook his head with grim pleasure at the thought of singling out this fat gentleman, who held such a poor opinion of the fighting qualities of Maine men. He meant to change that opinion decidedly. The melancholy Bill carefully loaded his Germans with logs. "Forward!" he ordered, in a doleful whine, and the gallant "furreners" started back to the prison. Bill followed, never looking back to see how his companion fared.

A short march through the pines brought the lightwood party to a pile of small, well seasoned sticks. The guard produced two long strips of rawhide from his pocket, and directed John and Uncle Nathan to bind the sticks into faggots of convenient size for carrying. He sat on a log during this operation, keeping a close watch on the prisoners. He evidently appreciated their society, as far as it went, but he did not propose to fall a victim to any of the evils incident to a close companionship. When the faggots were bound, he invited the prisoners to take another rest before returning. Uncle Nathan and John sat on the piles of wood, and the three men watched each other carefully.

It was a strange group. The rebel, affable and pompous, yet with his hand on his revolver, ready to shoot, at the least suspicious movement; the two gaunt prisoners praying for a chance to spring upon their companion. The rebel was evidently curious as to the origin and purpose of the "furreners."

"We done keptured a heap of them fellers at Chancellorsville," he began. "Stuart was sent ahead to run some Yanks back, an' we supported him. We fit thar right smart, fer half an hour, I reckon, when thar kem a rush an' some of you all's cavalry jumped right inter us. Stuart he wheeled like an' tuck 'em on the flank, an' we closed up an' keptured a heap of 'em. They wuz all Dutchmen, an' I'm doggoned ef they warn't all tied to their hosses. They didn't know nothin' about reinin', an' them hosses hed run away with 'em. Thar we stud yer, an' Stuart he kem up yer." He had traced the plan of the battle out in the sand with the toe of his boot.

"You all never seen Stuart charge, did ye?" To John's surprise, Uncle Nathan seemed to be suddenly converted to the cause of the Confederacy — or rather Stuart.

"Wall, I should think I had," returned the old man. "I see him charge on our lines once, an' I call it the grandest sight I ever see anywhere. He come way out ahead of his men, waving his sword — jest like this" —

Uncle Nathan had started from his seat in his great excitement. He waved his arm above his head, and, to give a better illustration of the action, he caught up a long stick with a huge knot at the end. The rebel sat looking on admiringly, all unconscious of the fact that the height of Uncle Nathan's ambition was to bring his head and the knot in close contact.

"Jest like this," said Uncle Nathan as he stepped nearer and held the stick high over his head. There was something in the old man's face that showed the rebel that this was no idle feat of gymnastics.

"Stand back!" he shouted, reaching for his revolver.

But Uncle Nathan's blood was up. It was life or death for him.

"Jest like this!" he said coolly, and the stick sung a song of freedom through the air, and fell directly upon the rebel's head. The owner of the head dropped his gun and fell back like a dead man.

"What d'you s'pose he thinks about furreners now?" asked the imitator of Stuart, as he threw away his stick.

It is more than probable that the guard had a most profound respect for the fighting qualities of men from the "State o' Maine" ever after.

There was no time to be lost. The prisoners held a hasty consultation and assured themselves that the fight had not been observed. With the strings of rawhide they bound and gagged the stunned rebel. It was all done in a moment, and then, securing the gun and revolver and ammunition, they turned to the north and hurried into the woods. It was to be a desperate race. They would never be taken alive.

CHAPTER VII.

SOL'S VICTORY

THE two prisoners had hardly disappeared under the trees when the portly guard began to show signs of life. His head was evidently harder than the stick. He had been left in a most undignified position — flat on his face, with his hands tied behind him. First, he shook as much of his portly frame as could be shaken at one time and uttered some sound which lost itself in the sand. At last, with one supreme effort, he rolled himself over on to his back, where he could view a small portion of the world. His mouth and face were well plastered with sand and blood, and altogether he did not present a most agreeable appearance. He struggled desperately to free himself, but the tough strings held him fast. He did his best to call for help, but the gag, firmly fixed in his mouth, prevented any escape of sound. There was nothing for him to do but to lie on his back and wait for help.

We may very naturally expect that his ideas as to what constituted the heart of the Union army changed somewhat. His aching head must have convinced him that the "furreners" did not monopolize all the fighting qualities of the army after all. Whatever the opinion of the ladies at Gettysburg might be in regard to the marching of the two armies, it was painfully evident that men from the "State o' Maine" knew how to strike a good blow. Our fat friend might, perhaps, have consoled himself with the thought that he was not the first man to be convinced so roughly of the truth of a proposition. There are plenty of men whose heads must be broken before the truth can enter. Truth pounded in with a club, however, is remarkably sure to stick. Our friend had but little time to devote to this thought. He was mainly occupied in trying to clear his mouth of sand. He lay, as it seemed, a long time in his uncomfortable position. The sun started down behind the hills and the first afternoon shadows came creeping out from under the trees to mock him. It was not until the shadows had danced cruelly over his sandy face that he caught the sound of footsteps. A moment later the melancholy face of Bill came peering over the pile of wood. Bill had never been called a handsome man, even by his wife, but his face seemed like the face of an angel as viewed through the mask of sand and blood that covered the face of the portly victim of the Maine men.

Bill had marched his patient "Pennsylvany Dutch" back with their burden, and watched them pass safely inside the stockade. Well knowing the brilliant conversational powers of his comrade, he did not wonder at first when the detachment came not. When, at last, several hours went by without bringing his friend, Bill grew anxious and with a small squad came out, to find him as left by the prisoners. The bands were quickly severed, and the wounded guard raised to his feet. He told the story of his capture — giving it a coloring that would have seemed entirely original to Uncle Nathan. He told, with what articulation the sand had left him, how, after a most heroic defence, he had been overpowered. It was certainly wonderful how bravely he had fought the two prisoners, and how seriously he had, in all probability, wounded Uncle Nathan. The squad of soldiers marched back to the prison, listening to his thrilling recital.

Half an hour later, a small company of men marched rapidly up the hill in the direction of the scene of the struggle. Two negroes led the way, holding back by means of strong ropes a bloodhound — broad-breasted and dark. Long Bill led the way, his melancholy face glowing with something like excitement as he marched on ahead. The fat gentleman did not come. He stayed at the barracks to nurse his wounds and stir the patriotism of his comrades with his thrilling story of the conflict.

The company halted at the place where Uncle Nathan had given such a careful imitation of Stuart's mode of attack. The tracks of the prisoners were plainly visible leading off into the forest. The hound put his nose to the ground, and, with a low, deep sound, trotted off into the pines — on the trail. The chase had begun. The soldiers followed the dog with their arms ready for instant service.

Uncle Nathan and John ran as men run who see life held up before them as a prize. They had no definite route. Their great object was to put as many miles as possible between themselves and the stockade, and then by the aid of friendly negroes to determine their course. They well understood that they would be followed, and possibly caught up with, but they were determined never to be taken back. With the weapons they carried, a good defence could be made. On, on they hurried, as rapidly as possible. Through sand-beds thick with clinging briars, over fallen logs and stumps, through swamps and dense thickets, still on they pressed, for freedom lay before — death behind.

Uncle Nathan carried the musket. He had fastened the bayonet to the end, even though it impeded his progress. He was ready for immediate action. John carried the revolver, loaded and capped. He followed doggedly in Uncle Nathan's footsteps. He felt frequently for the letter under his vest. Archie was lying dead behind them, but Nellie was before, and he still pushed on, though his wounded leg tortured him at every step. Once, when they stopped to drink at a little brook, John examined his leg. It was badly swollen and was slowly bleeding. He bathed it in the cool water and drew the bandage tighter. Uncle Nathan watched him grimly.

"Can ye make it?" he asked, pointing off into the forest.

"I'll make it or drop," said John, between his teeth, and Uncle Nathan again pushed on, chuckling in his silent way at the "grit" of the men from "our town."

Twice they came upon dwellings. Hurrying on through a thick growth of young trees, they came suddenly to the edge of a large clearing, and stopped just in time to escape detection. It was a typical plantation; once prosperous and rich, but now, after three years of neglect, fallen to decay. The fields were grown up with weeds, the fences were down, and the stock roamed idly about. The old house seemed to have crept back under the trees, into the shadow and gloom, where it could brood over its sorrows in secret. An old, white-haired man sat on the piazza, with his head on his breast; dull, with the sense of his wrongs, without the energy or courage to repair the damages. It was a picture of utter despair — of lonely helplessness. As the fugitives halted at the edge of the clearing, two gaunt hounds, in full keeping with the rest of the picture, rose from beside the old man's chair, and looked eagerly in the direction of the disturbers. At a gesture from their master, they dropped slowly down again at his side. The fugitives crept back into the forest, and, skirting the edge of the clearing, again plunged out of sight.

A mile beyond the first house they came upon another plantation. They dropped under a bush to examine the premises. The house stood at quite a distance, but the negro quarters were close at hand. The same look of disorder and neglect pervaded the whole place. They were about to regain their feet and go back into the forest when the sound of a falling axe fell on their ears. It was apparently close at hand, and, after a moment's hesitation, Uncle Nathan pushed the branches aside and peered out in the direction from which the sound came.

An old negro, white-haired and bent with age, was cutting wood from a large log. To the desperate fugitives this poor old darky seemed like an angel. They did not hesitate to push their way toward him, and attract his attention. Uncle Nathan dropped the point of his gun and tried to bring his grizzled face into a smile. As the two ragged and desperate-looking men rose from beneath the bushes and moved toward him, the old slave dropped his axe and fell upon his knees.

" Go 'way," he muttered, " I ain't done nuffin'. I jes cuttin' wood fo' ole miss."

" It's all right, uncle," assured John as they neared the old slave. " We are friends — prisoners."

The old man changed his manner at once, at this announcement. He rose hastily to his feet and glanced around as if to assure himself that they were alone.

" Does you meanter say dat you is pris'ners? Dat you is Massa Linkum's men? I jes wanter look at youse." And the old fellow came nearer, and peered with dim eyes into their faces.

John told the story of their escape with simple directness. It seemed to him that he was talking to a child.

" What is our best road, uncle, and where can we get something to eat ? " he said at last.

The old slave shook his head uneasily during the story, and, at the question, looked hesitatingly about him.

" Is youse afeared of dorgs? " he asked, nervously.

"No, not a mite," growled Uncle Nathan, shaking his musket. "I won't run fer no dog."

"I is mighty glad you ain't," suggested the negro, "'case I *is*, an' 'case der'll be dorgs arter youse afo' morning, sho's yo' born. Dey will be arter youse wid de po'fullest dorg yo' eber seen, I reckon. Dorgs dat jes tar you all up. I's seed dem go by — I has. Dey is biz'ness dorgs, dey is. Dey is biz'ness work 'roun' yer when dem dorgs gits arter man, an' dey'll get arter you all fo' you knows it, I reckon" — and he looked nervously about him again.

"I tell you what, boss," he said, after a little thinking. "Ef youse is man 'nuff ter kill dat dorg, you is all right, I reckon. Ef you kin get shet ob him, I kin see you fru. I's got a boy hidin' to my cabin. He cum from whar dey is fitin' at, an ef you kin get shet ob dat dorg, you all kin go back wid him. Dey ain't no safe place fer you er me jes ez long ez dat dorg is on yo' track " — and he peered out into the forest, as if expecting to see the terrible animal approaching them.

Uncle Nathan was quick to see the sense of the old darky's advice.

"He's right," he said to John; "we've got to fight 'em, an' we might jest as well do it fust as last. You go home, ole feller," he said to the negro, "an' fix us up somethin' t' eat. We'll either leave that dog dead out yunder, or never come near ye agin," and he shook his musket, as if to add force to his declaration.

The old negro looked at Uncle Nathan admiringly. "You is a *man*, you is," he said, as he picked up his axe and moved stiffly away. He paused for a moment to give them some needed instructions. "When youse come back, yo' jes' stan' where dat big tree is at an' whistle, an' I'll send my boy out ter bring youse in. But done you come yer ontil youse kill dat dorg," and he hobbled off again.

He was soon lost to sight, for the light was rapidly losing itself under the trees. The darkness thickened and crowded in upon them as the fugitives made their plans. They sat for a few moments on the log, talking earnestly. Then they walked slowly into the forest, watching only for a good defensive position. They did not hurry now, for they were only anxious to meet their pursuers. Weary and faint with hunger and pain, John stumbled on unsteadily. Uncle Nathan seemed tireless. About half a mile from the log they came upon a place most admirably suited to their purpose. Under a great pine a cleared space gave ample opportunity for defensive operations. A high thicket of briars and heavy bushes rose in front like a wall. A little glade beyond made it impossible for pursuers to approach unobserved. Uncle Nathan placed his musket against the tree and glanced over the place with great satisfaction.

"We'll stand 'em off here, I guess," he said, grimly. "Might jes' well fight it out here as anywhere."

Had he been perfectly acquainted with the country he could hardly have selected a better place.

John dropped upon the soft pine needles, thankful for the chance to rest. He drew his revolver and placed it upon the ground beside him, ready for instant service. Uncle Nathan crouched in the shadow of the tree, with his eyes fixed on the space over which the dreaded bloodhound must come. What were they thinking about, waiting there in the solitude? Of the hateful prison, with all the horrors they had left behind them, or the home before, where the wife and the little girl were waiting? Is it not true that at such times, when we sit down with grim determination to wait the coming of our fate, when we feel that retreat is cut off, that the better, purer thoughts crowd into our minds, and the cruel, hateful past is dropped for the time? The moon came slowly up over the trees. It did not hurry over Andersonville as the sun had done. Its feebler light could not search into all the dark corners and push out the horrors that crouched there. Slowly and peacefully it sailed over the heavens, painting the earth with beauty, transforming hideous shapes, at a touch of its mellow light, into beautiful things.

The little glade, so eagerly watched by the fugitives, seemed, as the moonlight swept down into it, a very sporting place for fairies. The moonbeams danced right royally along the stumps and grasses. The thicket, behind which the men were sheltered, seemed changed into a row of hideous creatures, that scowled grimly over the little glade, and reached out with long arms to push back all intruders. The moonlight stole down behind the thicket. It glittered along the barrel of Uncle Nathan's musket, gleamed on the fixed bayonet, and touched the grizzled face of the stern sentinel into something like tenderness, for the same moon had looked into the faces of "the folks" at home. It was only for a moment that the ragged form under the tree was seen. Uncle Nathan crept back under the shadow, where the moon could not follow. For an hour they waited in silence. Then, suddenly, Uncle Nathan rose to his knees, and brought the musket to his shoulder. The bayonet flashed out in the moonlight. John grasped his revolver, and drew up under the thicket.

A slight rustle was heard on the other side of the glade, and, after a moment's hesitation, a man stepped out into the open space, and stood where the light fell directly upon him. He carried a package in one hand, while the other was held up above him. There were two things that caused the musket to lower. The face of the new-comer was the face of a negro. At his belt, the letters "U. S." flashed into view. Both were symbols of brotherhood to the fugitives. The man advanced a few steps, and again held up his hand.

"Halt! who goes there?" challenged Uncle Nathan, from his post under the tree.

"Fren'!" came the answer in the unmistakable accent of a negro.

"Advance, friend, and give the countersign," again came the hoarse whisper.

"Rations," was the answer, and the package was held up in front.

"Pass, friend, with the countersign," and the musket dropped, and John opened the thicket.

The man passed through this opening and stood

before them. A tall, well formed negro, wearing the pants, belt, and cap of the Union army. He carried a bag in his hand, which he threw on the ground beside them.

His story was quickly whispered. He was the "boy" of whom the old negro had spoken. A soldier in the Union army, he had left Sherman to visit the old folks. He was hiding by day, waiting for this very chance of guiding prisoners back to the Union lines. His father had told him of the adventure at the log, and, careless of the danger from the dreaded dog, he had followed them with a supply of food. He was ready to fight with them. He told his story simply, and then stood waiting for their reply. His race is inferior, they say. He never can lift himself out of his inferiority, and yet, what can we say when such men go to the very end of daring?

John and Uncle Nathan thought nothing of their new comrade's color. They shook his hand and welcomed him heartily. Sol — for such he gave his name — took Uncle Nathan's gun and advanced to the thicket, to stand on guard while the others ate the food that he had brought.

"'Tain't much, boss," he whispered, "but we git mo', I reckon, when we go back."

The repast was certainly a frugal one — a great corn-cake and a dozen baked potatoes. Frugal though it was, it seemed delicious enough to the hungry prisoners, and they ate greedily, on their knees, with the sack between them. The meal came to an end all too soon, and they rose for a consultation. At a sudden "hush!" from Sol, they all crept under the thicket to listen. The sharp ear of the negro had detected the approach of the pursuing party. He listened earnestly for a moment, and then gave the musket back to Uncle Nathan.

"Dat dorg done got away from dem," he whispered. "I fix him," and he drew a long knife from his belt, and crept through the thicket and across the open space. At the edge of the glade he halted, and, assuring himself of the dog's approach, he crouched in the shadow of a log to wait. Uncle Nathan cocked his musket and placed it in position. In a few moments the dog, entirely ignorant of the fate awaiting him, could be distinctly heard running through the bushes.

The squad from the prison had followed rapidly on the trail. The bloodhound made savage attempts to break away, but the strong keepers held him fast. He trotted with his nose on the ground, pulling impatiently on the cords that held him, and tearing at the muzzle over his jaws. Led by Bill, the soldiers followed in single file. The sun went down, but the party still pressed on through the pines. The moon gave them ample light for their purpose. All went well till the party reached the log where the old negro had been chopping. They halted a moment to rest and consult, when the dog, with one sudden and impatient bound, broke away from the negroes and sprang into the shadow alone. The keepers, fearful of the punishment due them, slid into the thicket, and hid from sight. The soldiers followed the dog, as best they could, though their course was but slow through the thick bushes. Thus it was that the dog came bounding on alone to the glade where Sol was waiting him. It seemed almost an age to the two men under the tree, before the hound burst through into the moonlight. The great ugly head fiercely thrust itself through the thicket, and halted for an instant, as if surprised.

Sol started from the shadow, with his knife in his right hand and a thick stick in his left. He advanced straight to the beast, with the club held before him, and the knife held at the side. John rose to his feet the better to view the strange combat. The fierce eyes of the hound glittered in the moonlight. He could utter no loud sound, for the thick muzzle held his jaws firmly together. Through his drawn lips the white teeth gleamed, and great drops of foam fell from his tongue. He drew back as the negro advanced, and like a flash sprang savagely at the club that Sol cunningly held in front of him. Sol stepped to one side, and, with one sickening blow, drove his knife into the dog's neck. The animal turned in its agony, and fell heavily upon its side. Sol sprang upon the hound, and plunged his knife again and again into the throat. The poor animal, muzzled as he was, could offer but a feeble resistance. In a short time he lay motionless. He had followed the trail to his death. After satisfying himself that the hound was dead, Sol came back under the tree where the others were waiting. He coolly wiped the blood from his knife with a bunch of pine-needles, and knelt in the shadow to wait the pursuing party, who now followed the dog.

Long Bill and his friends came at last. They

came crashing through the underbrush without the least attempt at concealment. The first intimation of the dire disaster that had fallen upon them was the mutilated body of the dead dog, which they found as they broke through the thicket into the little glade. Bill, who was leading, stopped in horror at this unexpected sight, and the others gathered about him where the watchers could easily examine them. There were nine in the party. Uncle Nathan covered Bill with his musket, while John took good aim at another; Sol grasped his knife, ready to spring into the crowd if necessary. Had the squad of rebels pushed on across the glade, a bloody fight would have ensued, for the fugitives, driven to desperation, would never have yielded. But Long Bill and his party never came by the dead hound. There was something terrible to them in this mysterious murder of the ferocious dog that had followed so many prisoners to the death. There he lay before them mangled and bloody. A few moments before he had been full of savage life. They had heard no outcry, no sound of a struggle. Some mysterious power, silent and terrible, had reached between them and their victims. They knew not in what dark shadow this terrible power might even now be lurking. They glanced nervously at the thicket before them. Long, eager arms·seemed to reach out to threaten them. They turned, after a short hesitation, back out of the moonlight. After a whispered consultation under the trees, they marched, with many a nervous glance, away from the fated ground where the dead dog was lying. They crept together in the darkness, and walked hurriedly on.

Back near the log where the great mistake of the expedition had been made, a badly frightened object rolled out in front of them. It was one of the negroes that had tried to hold the hound in check. Bill grasped the black keeper by the neck and brought him into the moonlight.

"Whar ye been hidin' at, ye nigger?"

The darky, never at a loss for a story, told with chattering teeth his imaginary version of the causes that led to the dog's death.

"You jes orter have seed him, boss," he said, with widely protruding eyes. "I done tole you dat he was a *man*. He jes grab dat dorg and shuck de life outer him, jes like I shake a rabbit. He was a *man* I done tole you."

Bill kicked the black story-teller to one side. It is not known whether the soldiers took the story for the truth or not. They certainly did not stop to discuss it. They marched sullenly back through the woods to Andersonville, and certain it is that the Maine men never set eyes on them again.

CHAPTER VIII.

THE NEGRO CABIN

THE fugitives waited under the trees long after the sound of the retreating footsteps had died away. They were not sure that this retreat might not be designed to draw them from their hiding-place. At last they crept cautiously from under the thicket, and followed the trail back to the log. Sol led the way, with his long knife drawn and ready. He could not help kicking the hated dog as they passed him. Uncle Nathan brought up the rear with his musket on his arm. At the log Sol left the others to follow the prison squad alone. He seemed to have the instinct of a hound, for he struck directly into the trail. In half an hour he returned with the joyful news that Bill and the soldiers had surely gone back.

"Come," he said, pointing over the log, "les go git supper."

John was weak and tired. His leg troubled him exceedingly. Even Uncle Nathan began to show signs of fatigue. They gladly followed Sol as he pushed off in the direction that the old negro had taken. A short walk brought them to a brook, into which Sol deliberately walked. The others followed him, and together they waded against the current.

"Fro' udder dorg off de track," said Sol shortly.

The others said nothing. They had resigned the leadership to the negro.

At a distance of a few hundred yards from the place where they entered the brook, the water suddenly spread out, forming a wide, shallow pond. Through this they waded, splashing through the shining water, coming out at last under a thick grove. Following Sol still, they passed on through the trees, over a meadow, up a sand hill, through a small corn-field, and halted at last before a little log cabin with a mud-and-stick chimney built at one end.

Sol stepped forward and gave three sharp raps at the door. In a moment the door partly opened and a white head thrust itself out.

"Is·dat youse, Solemon?" The voice was one that the fugitives remembered.

"Yes, I's here," said Sol. "Open de do'."

But the slight opening did not grow any wider. The old man wished to settle all questions concerning that "dorg" before he presented his visitors with the freedom of his cabin.

"Has youse killed dat dorg?" he asked with a tremor in his voice. "Ef he come snuffin' roun' yer, hit's sho' def fo' de hull gang."

"I reckon he's dead sho' 'nuff. 'Pears like he neber vote again," answered Sol as he pushed against the door.

"Is yo' *po'ful* sho'?" urged the old man.

Uncle Nathan came to the rescue.

"He's jest as dead 's a door nail. I'll warrant ye he won't do no more runnin'," he said, in his most assuring tone.

"Dat's all right! dat's all right!" apologized the old man, as he hastily opened the door and moved aside to make room for them to enter. "I is po'ful glad fer ter har it. I wouldn't have dat dorg snuffin' roun' yer for nuffin 't all."

The three men passed into the room. Sol closed the door and fastened it securely with a stout stick. The two white men looked about them with curious eyes. There was no light save that which came from a low fire in the chimney-place. This light was nearly obscured by the forms of two negro women who knelt before it, stirring the contents of several dishes that were cooking over the fire. The supper thus being prepared sent up a most delicious odor of fried meat and coffee. The two women at last moved away from their position in front of the fire, and the unobstructed light enabled the fugitives to view the room. The place was bare and rude, yet the light burst bravely out and did its best with the rough picture. It was a common negro's cabin — the home of slavery — yet it seemed the most like *home* of anything the two white men had seen for years. They felt that they were among friends who would die for them if necessary, and never ask for a nobler death. The great blindness of friendship and love will cover up many an imperfection that would seem bare enough in the house of a stranger.

The room was small and low. There was no plastering upon the walls, made of rough logs. The thin coating of whitewash that had once done its best to add respectability to the logs, had about given up the contest. It was discolored and rubbed, and in many places the original color of the logs grinned through its feebleness. The floor was full of great cracks, along whose edges barbarous splinters watched savagely for barefooted pedestrians. In one corner a board had broken in, and a wooden bench guarded the foot trap but poorly. The small windows were covered with wooden shutters, and the crack under the door was carefully covered with an old coat. The only circulation of air was that which entered at the cracks in the floor and found an exit through the chimney. The furniture was simple enough. Three chairs scattered about the room, a small table, and a bed made up the movable articles. A shelf for cooking utensils and dishes was fastened to the wall, near the fire. It was nearly empty, for most of the dishes had been placed on the table, which stood in the middle of the room. A sheet had been spread on the table, and the various tin dishes and cups placed upon it, in preparation for the meal. The light danced out from the fire over the shining dishes, and darted up on the dull walls. Like a brave friend, it made the best parts of the whitewash seem lighter, and kept entirely away from the bare places. It danced ahead of the old negro's bare feet and showed him the long splinters in the floor.

Uncle Nathan placed his musket behind the door and gazed about him with a satisfaction that was not in the least dampened by the odor arising from the cooking. The women, Sol's mother and sister, ducked their heads to the new-comers, and then went back to their cooking, again shutting out the greater part of the light. The best reception they could possibly give lay in the dishes they watched so carefully.

The old negro hastened to do the honors. He and Sol brought chairs for Uncle Nathan and John, and the tired men sat down at last with a great feeling of security. Sol brought water and bathed John's wounded leg, and placed the bandage securely. The old man hovered about, muttering and whispering his pleasure at being able to do something for Massa Linkum's men. This was the great event of his life and he meant to make the most of it. At last the women brought their pans to the table and poured the supper into the tin dishes. Uncle Nathan and John watched with hungry eyes. There was but little chance for conversation, for they all knew that a single loud word might betray them. The women, with a motion of the hand, indicated the fact that supper was served, and Sol and his father pushed the chairs up to the table and then stood respectfully behind their guests. Uncle Nathan motioned Sol to bring a third chair to the table and take a seat with them, but the young man shook his head. He knew or rather felt his place.

And Uncle Nathan, with a sweet memory of home in his heart, bowed his head for a moment, over the table, in thankfulness. The firelight flashed out over them. Over the grizzled soldier, who had fought so savagely, over the young hero who had felt the letter over his heart throb an answer to the prayer, over the worn old slave, childish and feeble, over the lion-like black soldier and the women, all thankful, though they knew not what the future might be.

No one can tell how the two soldiers enjoyed that supper. The fried chicken, the baked potatoes, the coffee, the corn bread, and the fried pork seemed most delicious after the long session of prison food. The old negro brought a pine knot from the fire and held it over them for a light. He muttered a few words of explanation as the meal proceeded. The coffee was such a great luxury that he felt called upon to expatiate upon its merits.

"Dat ar's sho' 'nuff coffy, dat is," he said, as he held the torch for Uncle Nathan to fill the tin cup. "Soleman brung dat coffy from way up yunder. We's been bilin' corn an' all dat, but dis yer sho' 'nuff coffy is worf a heap ob corn. Hit's po'ful strong, an' one pinch will build up dis yer play coffy mightily."

After the supper a short council of war was held. The four men talked in whispers while the women listened in the corner. It was at last decided to trust to Sol's guidance and make an effort to reach Sherman's army. They decided to start before daybreak, and, by a forced march, reach a place where they might rest in safety. They were to trust everything to Sol. This plan decided upon, the two white men lay down upon the bed to secure a short rest. Sol and his father, with the sleeplessness of the negro, watched through the night, with the musket and the revolver close at hand. How easily they could have secured their guests and turned them over to the prison guards. Many a white man would have done it, but these poor negroes, fearful and ignorant, still felt that these men had come to free them, and they would gladly have died in defending their guests.

It was still dusk when Sol touched the sleepers.

"Time fo' startin', boss," he whispered, as the tired men opened their eyes.

Breakfast was waiting them, and the three men — Sol joined them this time — made a hasty meal. The old man and his family probably went on short rations for some time to pay for this collation, but they were willing to fast in a good cause. With a whispered "good-by" the soldiers prepared to go. They were glad to shake hands with all the members of the family. The old man laid his thin hand on Sol's broad shoulder.

"Solemon," he said, "you wants ter be a good boy an' fite de bes' yo' knows fo' ole Massa Linkum. Done yo' neber do nuffin agin him. Hit don't make no odds about us down yer. We's mighty nigh fit out enyhow, I reckon. Dey kin kill de ole man, but dey can't neber break down dis yer ole flag. 'Pears like I want to see dat ole flag onct mo'. Done yo' ebber make me an' yo' ole mammy ashamed ob youse, Solemon. You is a good boy, an' I specks you kin do a heap of good ef you try."

The old slave patted his boy proudly and the old mammy kissed her son. The two white men watched this farewell. What white man with the spirit of chivalry bred into him for ages could have spoken nobler words than those which came to the lips of this worn old slave? What mother, proud of her honored name, could have blessed her boy as did this wrinkled, old, black woman? There is a proud feeling that cheers the heart when we send our loved ones out to fight for a cause that may send them back laden with honor and glory. How about this old slave who sent her boy to fight for a cause that bestowed no honor, no glory, upon such as her son?

Uncle Nathan noticed the old slave's shaking hand. He whispered hurriedly to John.

"Jest gimme that flag, will ye?"

John handed him the rude emblem, and Uncle Nathan thrust it into the old slave's hand.

"Thet's fer you, old man. Thet goes to the man that shows the best grit, an' I'll be darned if that man ain't you, if ye be a nigger."

The negro clutched at the flag quickly.

"Tanky, boss," he said. "I allus keep dat. I tink a heap o' dat."

The three men passed out into the morning. They crept through the corn, over the meadow, and into the forest. The day was spent at a negro's cabin, and at night they pressed on again. Slowly, under the guidance of Sol, they threaded their way through the country. Slowly they pushed on to the north, till one day, around a bend in the road, they caught a glimpse of a Union flag waving over a mass of blue uniforms. They were saved.

Sherman needed men, and so they shouldered muskets again and went marching in triumph on to the sea. Uncle Nathan wrote home, but John could not send Archie's letter; he felt that he must carry that to Nellie himself.

CHAPTER IX.

JACK FOSTER'S WELCOME

JACK FOSTER stood on the steps of the Sharpsburg court-house, and looked down the street. The steps were broken and fallen in decay. The house was covered with dull stains. It had looked down upon many strange scenes since it smiled exultingly on Jack's company marching away to battle. A melancholy sight it was that Jack looked upon. The long, silent street, the closed houses and stores, and the grass gnawing its way up over the very sidewalks, all told their sad story of suffering and despair. Jack could not help thinking of the pictures that had passed before these sad old houses since he left them. The pictures seemed to pass before him like a dream as he stood on the broken steps, with the sun in his eyes. The past crowded before him in sullen review.

A crowd of men gather about the court-house steps. Eagerly, with frantic gestures, they discuss. They shout and wave their arms, and fiercely shake their fists. They pass inside at last, and take their places on the rude benches. Old and young are there. Fierce, scowling faces, with eyes that glitter with hate. A gray-haired man calls the company to order. In passionate terms he alludes to the object of the meeting. Shall proud old Mississippi go out of the Union? Shall she cringe before the cowards of the North, or shall she stand up in proud defiance to protect her honor? He pauses, and a mighty shout goes up from the crowd. The scowling faces light with a sudden joy.

"Down with the Yankees!"

Jack himself seems to join in the shout. How confident they are! Defeat is impossible. How can the Yankee shop-keepers even stand up before gentlemen? But hark! A hush falls over the company. An old man, with a long, white beard, rises from his place and speaks deliberately against the proposition. They know him well. It is the old preacher whose words have guided them so long. He points his long, thin finger at the crowd, as he slowly says, "You are sure to be beaten in the end. You will see your homes desolate, your families in want, your country in ruins, and the ground covered with your dead, and yet not one point for which you contended gained. Be warned in time, and wait before you cry: —

"'Havoc, and let slip the dogs of war.'"

But a shout of scorn goes up from the crowd. The men are frenzied with passion. A rush is made at the old preacher. Crash — a club falls on the white head. A long, crimson streak darts out on the pale forehead, and he totters and falls. The State goes out of the Union — enters upon its weary and bloody pilgrimage.

A company of soldiers come marching down the long street. The sun glitters on the muskets. The uniforms are bright and new. Every man is full of enthusiasm. Every man carries a magnolia at the end of his musket. The new banner that the ladies have blessed waves proudly over them. The crowds cheer wildly. The ladies are waving handkerchiefs or casting flowers before the heroes. Sweethearts are smiling through their tears, mothers are blessing their boys. It is all life and enthusiasm. Victory seems assured. But behind the silent crowd of negroes that gather at one corner there seems to rise the warning figure of the old white-haired preacher. He shakes his head, and waves his hand sadly as the bright column moves on. The red mark on his forehead glows with a hateful color.

The streets are dull and deserted. The stores are all closed. The houses look grimly down through closed blinds. The grass grows over the streets. The trees droop dismally down to whisper their sorrow. Decay has laid its dreadful hand upon everything. A group of negroes and old men come straggling down the road. Ragged and dusty and feeble they march with implements of labor.

Grant is coming!

Out on the hills beyond the town, breastworks slowly rise. The workers are feeble and unorganized. A pause — and then a great wave of blue, with a crest that glitters in the sunlight, comes sweeping over the breastworks.

Grant has come!

The blue column forms on the hillside and comes slowly marching through the long street. Onward the soldiers come under the magnolias, white with fragrance. The trees will not bend lovingly over the invaders. The branches tremble with wrath. The flowers hang their heads in shame. They had grown in the hope of offering up their beautiful lives in garlands for their own brave soldiers. They would gladly withhold their perfume from these stern victors. The sun gilds the bayonets. The ranks rise and fall like the billows of a mighty ocean. The flag on high is faded and tattered. The stars gleam like proud eyes from their field of blue. Dusty and bearded and brown are the soldiers. There is no one to welcome them save a crowd of negroes who wait awkwardly at the corner. The silent houses frown down upon the army. The women and old men are inside, hid from sight, brooding over their country's dishonor. The officer at the head of the column touches his hat to the old flag that a negro waves. The soldiers halt in the square. They break ranks and scatter through the town. Over the picture rises again the figure of the old preacher. He bows his head in his hands. His prophecy is being fulfilled.

Jack could see all this as he stood on the broken steps. One by one the pictures passed before him. How true the preacher's words seemed to him now. The country was in ruins, he had seen the ground covered thickly with the dead, yet not one point had been gained.

His had been a sad journey from Georgia. Dishonored and stripped of all right to defend his country, he had come home. Home, the only place where comfort seemed possible. Home, where the strong and the weak, the humble and the proud, all must turn at last for comfort when all else fail.

He knew not how he would be received. It seemed to him at times that he had only to tell his story to convince Lucy that he had refused to shoot the Yankee simply because he loved her. At times he felt that she must see it as he did. But then he thought of her unreasoning scorn for all cowards, of his proud old mother, and his heart failed within him. He had not written since his disgrace. He still carried the letter he had written when death seemed to have almost touched him. He had determined to bear the news himself, and, as he slowly made his way across Alabama, he had proudly resolved to take the consequences like a man. He could not convince himself, after all, that he had done wrong. And here he stood at last, at home, waiting only for courage to tell his story to the ones he loved.

The street was almost empty. A few ragged negroes lay in the sun in front of the two stores that were alone left to do what little business the town required. Two old men stood leaning up against the door of the market. The sign that used to swing so bravely in the air had fallen to the ground, and no one seemed ambitious enough to put it back. The blinds were hanging loosely from their hinges. The building seemed to have grown prematurely old in watching the troubled scenes. The grass grew up almost to the sidewalk, pushing with its restless fingers the sign of trade and traffic away. A blighting curse seemed to have fallen upon all nature.

After some hesitation, Jack remounted his mule and rode slowly down the street. The old men in front of the market looked at him curiously, but he pulled his hat down over his eyes and escaped detection. The years had changed him and the old men had passed through so much trouble and seen so many strange and terrible faces, that they had almost forgotten how their friends appeared. They took this strange man to be in some way connected with the Yankees. Who else could be riding through their desolate town? No doubt they expected another raid, for they made haste to close the stores and take themselves out of sight. They could show just how the battles should have been fought, but when the foe came to close quarters they had no advice to offer.

Jack rode slowly past the deserted market. How well he knew the way. He reached Lucy's house at last, and, fastening his mule at the gate, walked hesitatingly up the walk. He had thought at first to find his mother before he saw Lucy, but somehow he could not ride past the place. Everything had fallen in ruins. The high weeds grew up to the walk, and narrowed it to a modest footpath. They had destroyed every curve, and strangled the feeble life out of the flower garden. Like true pirates of Nature they reached their hands exultingly over the narrow path, and threatened to push it out of sight. The railing of the piazza had fallen away, and one of the steps had broken down.

The magnolias rustled Jack a welcome as he came up to the broken step. He could not enjoy their fragrance. He was thinking of the scene that lay before him. What could he say — he the dishonored soldier — to this woman that he loved so well, and who had suffered so much for the cause? As Jack placed his foot on the steps, an old negro started up from the grass, where he had been sleeping. He rubbed his eyes open and stared at Jack for a moment in wonder. Then he ran stiffly to the back of the house, shouting, — " Massa Jack's come. Miss Lucy — Massa Jack ! "

Jack stepped to the door, feeling like a very guilty man. Two white faces peered in at him from the end of the hall. Jack recognized his mother and Lucy. An instant more and the two women came rushing down the hall to meet him. Lucy reached him first, and, with a glad cry, threw her arms about his neck and put her head on his breast. Jack could not help drawing her to him and kissing her. As he looked down into her eyes, he almost wished he had shot the Yankee.

The women led Jack into the parlor. How pale and thin they seemed. Their dresses were old and threadbare, and their hands roughened by the hardest work. They did not care for the ugly past now that the son and lover had come back to them alive and honored. Jack was surprised to see his mother in the town. He did not fully realize what a terrible desolation had fallen upon the country.

The negroes had done their best to butcher a living out of the land, but, left to themselves, they had grown idle and shiftless. The Union raids had run over the country so thoroughly, filling the negroes with an exalted idea of freedom, that Mrs. Foster had lost control of her former slaves, and when she came into town to find Lucy and her mother living alone, she had been easily prevailed upon to live with them. So the three women had lived there alone, saying nothing to Jack, and leaving the rich plantation to grow up to weeds and wilderness.

The women drew Jack to a sofa, and sat down on either side of him. Poor fellow; he hung his head like a guilty man, and avoided the eyes turned upon him so lovingly. He had imagined this scene many times, but, now that it had come, it seemed harder than he had dared to think. He knew that his story must be told, yet how could he tell it? The women noticed his dejection, and Lucy laid her hand on his arm as she asked quickly, — " Have they surrendered, Jack? "

The man raised his head proudly, —

" We never surrender. We will fight to the last man " — and then, suddenly remembering that he could fight no more for his country, he dropped his head sadly.

Lucy's eyes flashed proudly as he spoke. She was proud of her lover. Better this than victory purchased by dishonor. Jack's mother looked at him curiously. With a mother's instinct she knew that something was wrong. Her heart trembled, but she spoke slowly and coldly as she drew slightly away from him.

"Why do you leave the army without notice? Where is your uniform, my son? Are you ashamed or afraid to wear it? We women have boasted to the Yankees that if you had been here they never would have dared to insult us? Why do you not speak?"

His mother's words cut Jack to the heart. The utter helplessness of his position flashed through his mind. What could these proud women think of him — the dishonored soldier? Could he tell them that all their suffering, all their devotion had been for nothing? He covered his face with his hands and groaned aloud — he who had marched into the rifle pits at Gettysburg without flinching. Lucy put her arms about his neck to comfort him, but his mother rose proudly from her seat.

"Are you a coward?" she asked sternly. "Dare you not tell us why you are afraid to wear the uniform of your country? Come away from him, Lucy, and let him answer if he can."

The girl rose reluctantly and took her place at Mrs. Foster's side. She looked pityingly at Jack, and once she started to go back to him. The elder woman put her arm about Lucy's waist, as if to steady herself. Mrs. Foster looked sternly at her son, though her woman's heart was bleeding for him. Her gray hair had grown white with the terrible suffering of war. Her old dress hung loosely about her thin form, yet she stood erect and stately as of old. Lucy's under lip quivered, and she drew closer to Mrs. Foster.

"Speak, sir!" commanded the stern woman, with a slight gesture toward her son. Jack felt at her words a cruel, obstinate feeling rise in his heart. Had he been left to tell the story in his own way he might have softened the blow; but his mother's stern words goaded him to desperation. Was he a coward? He stood up straight and soldier-like as he answered bluntly: —

"I have no uniform to wear. It is all over with me, I reckon. I refused to shoot a Yankee prisoner, and I have been dishonorably discharged from the service."

It was a plain statement of fact, but if Jack could only have seen Lucy's quivering lip, he would not have answered so bluntly. When he answered he was looking straight into his mother's eyes, with all the pride she had given him. Had he struck the women a blow with his hand he could not have hurt them more cruelly. Mrs. Foster staggered to a chair, with all the proud scorn driven from her face. She lowered her head in her hands — this proud, stately woman. Her boy had brought dishonor upon them. Lucy's mouth stopped its trembling. She drew back from Jack with a shudder. For a moment she looked at him with flashing eyes — speechless with anger. Then with one wild burst her scorn found words.

"You a traitor? You refuse to shoot a Yankee? You bring back nothing but dishonor to us? Oh, if I could only be a man to shame you! They stood here, in this very room, and insulted your own mother. These wolves, that fight only women and children, cursed my sick mother when she defied them. And you did not dare to kill them — you who swore to be true to me. You are a coward!"

She stopped for a moment, fairly choked with passion. She could not see how anything could possibly justify a Southern man in sparing a Yankee's life. She only knew that the Northern soldiers had brought all the horrors and desolation upon the land. Before they came her life had been one long round of happiness. They were like wild beasts to her, and to think that the man to whom she had given her heart had refused to fight them nearly drove her frantic. She would listen to no reason now.

Jack turned to her with tears in his eyes. His mother's sternness had not touched him thus. If he could only let her know why he did not shoot the prisoner. If she could only understand that it was for love of her that he had lowered his musket. He held out his arms appealingly to her.

"My dear little girl," he began, but she waved him back and pointed to the door.

"Go, you coward," she sternly said, "never dare speak to me again. I will never look at you or speak to you again, so help me my God!"

She held her clenched fist above her as she spoke. Her other hand was pressed against her breast. She gasped and turned as pale as death, for she knew how well she loved this man. Jack knew she meant every word she had spoken. He offered no word of explanation. He turned proudly to the door, with a great pain at his heart. He could not even look at Lucy. His mother rose from her chair and tottered toward him. The mother's love is stronger than any.

"I will go with you," she said feebly; "you have dishonored your country, but you are still my son. Let me go home, my boy. Take me home, that I may die where no one can see my shame. I do not care to live now."

She threw her bonnet on her head and, leaning on her son's shoulder, tottered out into the sunshine. Lucy watched them with flashing eyes. They passed slowly down the path and out at the gate. She knew well that they would never come back, except at a word from her, and that she would not give. She watched them as they reached the gate and saw Jack's face as he glanced back. The anger faded from her eyes, and she threw herself upon the sofa in an agony of weeping. Her idol had been broken. Her knight had proved faithless.

CHAPTER X.

BROTHER HILL, THE PREACHER

As Jack and Mrs. Foster walked slowly down the street, they saw, ahead of them, an old man standing under the trees. His long white hair fell down almost to his shoulders, and his great beard swept his breast like a brush of snow. His clothes were old, yet carefully patched and brushed. He wore a wide straw hat. His head was bent forward, and his thin hands were clasped behind him. They could not see his face, yet Jack recognized him at once. Jack had seen him in that dim picture that rose before him at the court-house. Angry and humiliated as Jack was, he would gladly have turned back. He did not care to meet the old preacher when the evidences of the truth of his prophecy were so abundant. Those calm words seemed too true to him now. His mother pressed forward, however, and Jack reluctantly walked toward the old man. Their steps aroused the preacher from the reverie into which he had fallen. He glanced up, and then advanced with a smile of surprise to take their hands. No wonder Mrs. Foster had hastened to him for comfort. No wonder Jack hung his head in shame when that calm face turned toward them.

It was a beautiful face — calm and gentle and

dignified, set in a frame of hair of the most wondrous whiteness. The eyes were clear and calm, yet full of a soft, dreamy expression, as if they were looking far away from the present. The mouth was gentle, and yet there were lines at the corners that indicated a mighty will and a strong determination when some great occasion should demand it. There was one ghastly mark on the forehead, where a wide scar lost itself in the snow-white hair. It seemed as if some brutal finger had traced its protest against the gentle whiteness of the forehead. The pure skin showed whiter than ever above the scar.

Jack hung his head as the old preacher placed a thin hand kindly on his arm. Mrs. Foster grasped the thin hand as if it offered her some great comfort. It is not always the great, powerful clasp that brings us the greatest help.

"I must see you, Brother Hill. I must speak with you at once," she gasped. "We are going home, but I *must* see you first. We have changed, I know, but I must talk now, and you, my old friend, will tell me what I shall do."

She spoke wildly and leaned heavily on the arm of her son. It seemed strange that she should come at last to this gentle old man for help. For years he had spoken bravely against slavery, against secession, against everything that had led to the war. She had scorned him, yet now, heart-broken and helpless, she came to him for comfort. Perhaps some instinct told her how his brave, self-sacrificing life had given him the strength she needed.

The preacher spoke gently as he shook her hand:

"Come with me and you shall tell me your trouble — perhaps we can make it lighter."

He took his place at her side, and the three walked on together. He guessed at something of the trouble as they went slowly on. Jack's dogged, sullen manner, and the woman's wildness and feebleness, told him something of what had happened. He smiled sadly as he thought how this young man had laughed defiantly and tossed his musket in glee as he marched away a few years before.

The preacher at last opened a gate in front of a little cottage that stood back from the street, in a mass of vines and flowers. They followed him silently up the path and into the house. Jack helped his mother up the steps and into the study. She dropped into a chair and covered her face with her hands. Her pride, that had kept her tears back so long, was broken at last. The preacher with a gesture drew Jack from the room. They closed the door and went out to the front of the house.

"I do not know what has happened, John," the preacher said, kindly. "Perhaps I have no right to ask you what you have done, but you had better leave your mother here with me. I am an old friend, and it may be that I can say something that will bring her some comfort."

Jack held out his hand and grasped the thin fingers. His eyes were full, and he felt that great lump rising in his throat. Could not this gentle old man understand him when he told his story? Could not *he* see why it was better to be called a traitor than to shoot the Yankee prisoner? Jack felt so at first, but the cruel scar on the white forehead seemed to stand out more plainly into view, and he drove his purpose down.

"I will go, I reckon," he said simply. "I have disgraced them — they think — and I will take my mother home. I reckon I will ride out to the plantation and make it ready for her. I'll be back in a few hours."

The preacher shook hands again and walked back to the study, where the grief-stricken woman was awaiting him. Jack walked out into the street. His mule was still tied in front of Lucy's house. A negro boy brought the animal for him, and, mounting once more, Jack rode slowly away over the road he knew so well. He was anxious to get away — he cared not where — that he might think. Sad indeed were the poor fellow's thoughts as he rode toward his old home. Gloomily he stood at last in front of the old house and looked over the butchered plantation. He felt the letters he had read so often, under his coat. The two sentences came into his mind: "If you will only be *true*, I will love you forever." — "If you ever show them any mercy, I will never speak to you again." He knew that he had been true as life itself and yet he had shown mercy.

A short time after Jack rode out of town, an old man came riding through the street as rapidly as his sorry mule could carry him. He leaned far over the mule's head, as if to try and add to the animal's speed. His gray hair flew out behind him. His hat had been lost on the way, but his mission was evidently of too much importance to permit him to stop for such trifling mishaps. He halted in front of the post-office, where a small crowd had gathered to enjoy the sunshine.

"The Yankees are coming!" he shouted. "Another raid! Notify the town!"

By a vigorous application of his stick he pushed new life into his mule and rode on again to privately warn his own personal friends. The crowd in front of the post-office scattered like a flock of sheep at this danger call. They were mostly old men, who fought the home battles, and told how the real campaign should have been conducted. The few stores were hurriedly closed and the men hastened home to hide the few trinkets or the little money that former raids had left. Then one and all of the home guards "took to the woods," leaving the ladies to meet the Yankees with their more dangerous weapons of scorn and womanly abuse. There was little to choose between Grierson and Forest in the conduct of these raids. One took what the other left. Like Jack Spratt and his wife, they "licked the platter clean," without being hampered, as were the aforesaid distinguished couple, by any decided preference for meat of a particular quality.

When Grierson's cavalry rode into the town, an hour in the rear of the old messenger, they found a deserted village, with only one man — the postmaster — in sight. This government official was chained to his post by a disabled leg, which alone prevented him from taking a position in the front rank of the home guard. There was nothing of value in the mail bag. Just a great heap of letters from the soldiers. The blue-coats let them go, laughing now and then at some boasting sentence. The Yankees could not stay long. They must press on to the next town. Leaving a small guard on the main street, they scattered through the village in pursuit of plunder. The negroes hastened to meet them. Old slaves tottered out to shake hands with Massa Linkum's soldiers. Boys followed them about with open-mouthed wonder. Old women grinned and muttered in pleasure.

The soldiers were rough, good-natured fellows from Michigan. There was very little play or "fooling" about them. Three years of fighting had drilled some positive ideas into them and made them rough and sturdy. They had little respect for their foes, and the women who taunted them were sure to get a rough answer. No man was harmed who kept quiet, and most of the men were too far away for a sound to reach the town. Horses and valuable articles that could be easily transported were taken without ceremony.

A short time after the column halted, a heavy rap was heard at the door of the old preacher's study. There was no response to this rough notice, and the huge cavalryman who had entered the place pressed the latch and pushed the door open.

He stepped over the threshold, but something on the inside made him stop.

Mrs. Foster still sat in the chair into which she had fallen, with her face still covered with her hands. Her white hair had fallen about her neck.

The preacher was kneeling with his face toward the door, and his hand upon an open Bible that lay on the table. The red scar on his forehead seemed to fade away as he prayed. The soldier stood for a moment in silence. Then, with his cap in his hand, he stepped as softly as possible out at the door, and walked down the path, his sabre clanking as he went.

"It's all right, boys," he said as his comrades laughed at him. "It's all right. I s'pose like enough he was prayin' the whole Union straight into a hole, but that old woman looked just like my mother, an' I quit." The boys did not laugh at his explanation. They thought of their mothers at home, praying for them. It was something the roughest could understand. A few moments after the first soldier disappeared, another marched in at the gate. A young, boyish figure it was, with a clear skin and bright curls. It was his first campaign evidently. He marched pompously up to the door, drew his pistol, and walked in. The old preacher rose from his seat to meet the young soldier. He could hardly suppress a smile at the youth's importance.

"What do you wish?" he asked pleasantly.

"I demand the surrender of this house in the name of the United States Government, and I order you to bring forth any soldiers that may be concealed here," answered the young hero with a theatrical gesture.

The preacher answered with a smile, "We surrender most certainly to a superior force. March in and take possession at once."

The young man marched over the threshold, and began a sentence beginning, "Duty," when a little picture on the mantel caught his eye, and sadly broke into his eloquent speech. It was only a small tintype of a fair-haired girl. There was a hole cut in the top, as if some soldier had carried it about his neck. The boy — for he was nothing more — caught the picture hurriedly and closely examined it.

"Where did you get that?" he asked hastily; "that is my sister's picture."

"One of your soldiers left it here," said the old preacher calmly. "He was wounded just outside the town, and we brought him here, and cared for him till he died. We found this picture tied about his neck. Mary, I think he said her name was, though he could not talk intelligently."

The soldier's lip trembled as the preacher spoke. The martial air was dropped at once. The victor was ready to surrender.

"He was engaged to her, sir," he said. "He was like a brother to me, and we never knew where he died. Forgive me," he said, impulsively, "for coming in here as I did. I did not mean to insult you."

He grasped the preacher's hand as he spoke, and there were tears in the blue eyes. The bugle sounded far down the street, and he hurried away with the little picture as his only booty. One girl in the North will think kindly of the Southern man who cared for her lover.

It was late in the afternoon when Jack came back to the town. He had made a longer trip than he intended. With the help of an old negro he had put his mother's room into something like order, and set the hands to work at cleaning away something of the rubbish that had accumulated all over the place. He knew that his mother would prefer to be at home, where she could brood over her troubles. He came back to take her away from the town; but she was not to go after all. The preacher met Jack at the door with a very grave face.

"Your mother is very sick, John," he said. "You had better go in and talk with her, and if there is anything that you can say to set her mind at rest, you had better say it. You know what I mean, my boy; there must be something about this matter that will make it easier for her to bear. I know you too well to think that you have no defence to make."

Jack made no answer. He walked into the darkened room where his mother lay. An old negro woman sat at the head of the bed, fanning her old mistress. Jack sent her away. He took the fan in his own hand and drew a chair up to the head of the bed. Mrs. Foster had changed much since the morning. Her face seemed haggard and pale in the darkened room. She smiled feebly and held out her hand to her boy. All her pride had been burned away; she was only a weak mother now.

Jack, touched at the sight of her poor, thin face, kissed her and put his head on the pillow beside hers, as he used to do years and years before. She placed her hand on his forehead, and there, like a boy who comes to his mother to confess his sins, he whispered to her all the story. She did not ask him to tell it, but it seemed to him, for the moment, that he was a little boy again and that her smile could bring him comfort as of old. She listened in silence, brushing back his hair as he talked. She understood him now. A mother can always understand her boy when his wife or sweetheart could never read him. They remained there for a long time after he told his story, she still brushing his hair back from his forehead. Somehow he seemed dearer to her than he had ever been before. Somehow he seemed to forget his trouble and shame.

"You will promise me one thing," she said at last. — "You will stay here and live this down, won't you?"

"I will," said Jack, between his teeth. He knew what the promise meant, yet he could not refuse. She reached forward and drew his head up to her bosom. She kissed him very tenderly and then turned away on the pillow. Jack heard her sob, and she covered her face with her hands till the sobs died away. Jack knew that she was praying for him. At last she turned to him again and laid her hand on his head as she had done before. The light faded slowly out of the room and all the sounds of the twilight came on. The hum of insects, the rustle of the trees and vines, and the dim whisperings from the creeping shadows. The mother and son lay there without a word. The hand on Jack's head grew cold and clammy. He started up and threw back the heavy curtains. His mother was dead — dead with the first smile on her lips that had touched her face for many a day. Death had brought her the comfort life had denied. He could not weep and wish her back to life again, he knew that she was happier in death. He almost wished he was with her.

The townspeople came to the funeral, and many of them wept at the old preacher's sermon. Many an eye that the horrors of war had long starved of moisture was filled with tears. The congregation was made up mostly of women and old men. They recoiled in horror from Jack. It seemed to them that he had killed his mother. They magnified his fault a thousand times. He proudly kept the truth locked in his heart, where none could read it. Lucy would not listen to him, and he cared nothing for the others. No one spoke to him. He sat alone through the services. He walked slowly behind, as they carried his mother away. When he came to the side of the grave the people stepped back and left him alone. Lucy wept over the coffin, but she turned her back on Jack when he came near her. The old preacher tried to say a kind word, when the mourners came back from the grave, but Jack would not listen. He went back to the plantation, and never came into town. He worked on in a feeble, halfhearted way, shunned by his old friends, caring little what was done with him.

A few Union people of the place and the negroes soon got the idea that Jack was their friend. No one knew just what his crime had been. It was generally understood that he had, in some way, helped the Yankees. The negroes came from miles around to ask the news, and many of them expected Jack to arm and lead them out to attack a detachment of rebel soldiers that once wandered that way. Jack's heart grew very bitter that night, when he looked out upon the motley band of black men gathered before his house. There they stood in the moonlight, drawn up in savage strength. They urged him to lead them out to attack the men with whom he had fought. They tossed their rude weapons in the air, and told with savage glee of the brutal revenge they would take.

He lived aimlessly on till the dull years slowly dragged through to the end of the war. Then, a new bitterness was in store for him. The soldiers came back, and he saw yet more plainly what an awful gulf stretched between him and his people. He saw how it never could be bridged on this side of the grave. The cause of the Confederacy was to be held sacred by those who had suffered for it. It could not be otherwise. The busy, exulting North, in its great generous burst of triumph, could overlook, forgive one who helped the enemy. Not so with such as Jack Foster. His record will follow him to the grave. The soldiers came scattering along, sometimes one at a time, and sometimes in little groups. They came slowly and reluctantly. They had been beaten, when they had sworn to bring victory or die. The long years of agony and sorrow had gone for nothing. There was nothing to sweeten the memory of the dead, only the dull sting of defeat that would not lie in the graves of their loved ones.

Sad, indeed, it was to see these brave fellows, who had given all for what they thought to be their duty, come back in this way to their old homes. The towns were guarded by Union soldiers, the slaves were all free — impudent and grinning at their old masters. The country was in ruins. The beautiful homes they had left were fallen. Thousands of the friends with whom they had marched away were now sleeping on battle-fields from which they could bring no glory. The very color of their uniforms was a national disgrace. The flag they had worshipped was in the dust. They could bring no glorious words with which to bind up the bleeding hearts that waited for them. Women were waiting for their husbands, their sons, or their brothers. Old men were watching with sad eyes for the boys who were far away under the sod. What comfort could such sad hearts take from the bitter story of defeat? It is the saddest page of all history — sad, that such bravery, such devotion, should be wasted.

It was hardest for Jack, to see the way in which the ladies received these defeated soldiers. The people of the town never turned out to meet the soldiers. They came in sullen silence, and took up the bitter round of life as best they could. There were no reproaches. The women all knew that these men had done their best. There were flowers, and garlands, and tender words of encouragement, for the brave — brave and honorable, even in defeat.

For a time, the people waited in sullen despair. Labor was completely disorganized, and the country lay one great heap of ruins. There was but little incentive to work. The wounds were too sore, the hearts too bitter. The South sat brooding over her defeat. Jack tried at first, honestly, to win back the esteem of his old comrades, but it was a useless task. The people shunned him — he was a traitor in their eyes, and they could not forgive him. He lived a life horrible in its loneliness. His very associates seemed to drive him farther and farther from society. The negroes and white Republicans saw that his own people drove him aside, and they tried to bring him into their party. They promised him any office, and they were in a condition to carry out their promises. He never would go with them, yet they were the only companions he could find. His old companions, and the people with whom he had been raised, thought he had joined the despised party, and he fell lower than ever in their estimation.

At last, the people rose against the negro rule. For years they had fought against it, but now they rose with savage purpose to push it by one supreme effort out of sight forever. Stern, determined, desperate men, who felt that they were fighting for all that was sacred and true, rose against their former slaves, ignorant and incapable. Such a contest could have but one result — the weak went to the wall.

When the negro and "carpet-bagger" government fell like a rope of sand, the white people changed in sentiment and action. Many of the men who had joined the Ku Klux or the "Red Shirts" simply because they had been driven to desperation by what they considered a national crime went quietly about their business, and were the strongest supporters of law and order. A better feeling began to prevail.

Improvements were contemplated, for people felt that their homes and their property were safer. They considered Republicanism and negro government as surely dead. They knew little difference between the two, for they had always come to them together. After the horrors through which they had passed, they thought they were justified in taking extreme measures to prevent any return of the old days. As the times grew better, Jack began to gain a little of the confidence of his old comrades. They never quite forgave him, but the memory of his crime — for so they still called it — faded a little. But Lucy never would even look at her old lover. She always passed him without a sign, and his life was full of misery.

But for his promise to his mother, he would have gone away, but that promise held him to the scene of his sorrow. He worked aimlessly on, with a great hunger at his heart, thinking oftentimes of the prisoners for whom he had given so much.

CHAPTER XI.

BREEZETOWN'S WELCOME

THERE were stirring times in old Breezetown. It was a bright afternoon in May, and all Nature seemed to have put on a new dress in order to help out the celebration. The soldiers were coming home from the war. The long, cruel fight was over at last, and the old "town boys" were coming back under the brave old elms — coming back heroes — with the tokens of a wonderful victory. The news had come in the morning, and by two o'clock the whole town had gathered on the green to welcome the boys. The stores were all closed, and every house in the town had sent its representative. Even the gray old farmhouses clustered on the hills outside of the town had sent in their delegations. The old village flag, grown ragged in the cause of liberty, swung over the road in front of Sam Price's hotel.

The women and girls carried great bunches of flowers. Old Silas Plum and Eben Cobb, thin, white-haired soldiers of the war of 1812, with drum and fife, — honored by age and execution, — stood in front waiting for the signal to strike up with Yankee Doodle. They watched for the sign of the rising dust on the road far down under the trees. The men were gathered about the musicians, while a crowd of boys with tin horns could hardly be restrained from practising their part of the greeting. To a boy, a celebration of any kind can never be complete without a hideous noise. As we grow older we learn the value of the silent, heartfelt greeting. The crowd stood in eager anticipation. No one could say that old Breezetown was not willing to do all she could to welcome back her brave sons.

She had given her best and bravest — given them willingly. Forty-five men in all had gone from the old town. Some of them were dead, they knew — there were sad hearts in that waiting crowd — sad hearts that looked down the long lines of elms where the boys had marched away. How many were dead — they could not say. The prison doors had swung open at last, and the living were coming back. This was all they knew.

Six wagons had been sent down to meet the train. These, with the stage, would surely be enough to bring back the boys. So they stood waiting for the soldiers, with a brave greeting for those who came and a tear for those that death held back. There was no bitter feeling such as lay in the hearts of those who waited at the South for *their* boys to come home. Victory had been won, the glorious cause they knew to be right had triumphed, and the glory so nobly won drew out for a moment the bitter sting — hid for a moment the awful face of despair.

A great cloud of dust surged up under the trees far down the road. The watchers on the hills saw it, and came riding at full speed into town to prepare the way. The crowd formed in long lines along the street, where the wagons might pass between them. The Sunday-school children, dressed all in white, stood with bright flowers in their hands. The wives and mothers and sweethearts stood back of them, eager for a look at the well known faces. The friends of those who could not come from the grave turned away with a choking feeling, that they might not see how others were glad. Such happiness would only make their grief harder to bear. They looked up at the proudly waving flag, and the blow seemed lighter. Their loved ones found victory at least — the country had been saved.

The stage moves into view far down the shaded road. It does not move as rapidly as they expected. The old musicians strike up their tune and the men take off their hats for the cheer. But a hush falls over the crowd as one by one the wagons roll on through the dust. The eyes that strain for the first look at the dear ones can see that the wagons are empty. Many a cheek pales and many a heart throbs as the empty seats tell their sad story. Many an eye is filled with tears that mercifully hide the sad procession.

The stage halts in the crowd. The door opens and Uncle Nathan and John Rockwell step out. They turn and tenderly lift from the seats two feeble men whose great, hollow, death-like eyes fill with tears as the gentle arms of friends clasp them about. The boys have come home!

The cheer died away on the lips of the crowd. **Was victory so precious, then, that such countless** treasure must be paid for it? Did not the war "cost more than it came to"? The people fell back stupefied by the cruel blow. One little girl brought her flowers and laid them in John's hand. Dear little girl, her father had died in Andersonville praying to her mother's face.

The old men passed by in solemn procession to shake the soldiers' hands. The women turned away with quivering lips — all but two. Uncle Nathan's wife threw her arms about her husband's neck and clung to him. A tear stole down the face of the stern old man as he kissed her. He thought of the three brave boys who could never come back to their mother. A little woman dressed in black, with a face as white as snow, and her bright curls brushed back from her forehead, came timidly out from the crowd and put her two little hands into one of John's. And as John looked down into Nellie's eyes something told him that Archie had told her the story of his crossing the dead line.

The people slowly fell away at last, and John and Nellie followed Uncle Nathan and Aunt Susan to the wagon. The people went back to their homes. The celebration was over; but what of those whose friends came not? The Union was saved, the flag was whole once more, the victory had been won. But the aching hearts made answer — it cost too much; of what use is the Union when its life is the death of those we love? There could be no answer — only the flag rippled proudly in the air above them.

Uncle Nathan's horse and wagon came backing

out of one of the sheds at the rear of the meeting-house as they approached. The exit was slow and laborious, for old Whitey, who supplied the motive power, had seen his best days. Uncle Nathan patted the old beast affectionately, and was much gratified to see that the horse appeared to know him. The wagon seemed like an old friend, and he examined it with a critical eye. He shook one of the wheels and whistled softly.

"How long sense ye greased them wheels, Reuben?" he asked of the boy who had backed old Whitey out of the shed. This boy had done his best to do "chores" and take care of the "wimmen folks." Reuben felt hurt at this question. He seemed to consider this as an insinuation against his agricultural carefulness. He felt that he had done his best as a home defender to keep the fighting members of the family at the front. He did not propose that the value of the services of the home guard should be underestimated.

"I greased 'em this mornin', an' I've done jest as well as I could to keep things up straight. Just look at that hoss, will ye? I'll leave it to Aunt Susan if I ain't gone over an' above my stent."

"So he has, Nathan," urged Aunt Susan, at this juncture. "Reuben's ben a good boy, an' he ain't done no complainin'."

Good old Uncle Nathan hastened to set matters right again. He had seen this boy's father die like a brave man, and he thought — it is only a boy, after all. So he said nothing about a great scratch on the wagon, and he straightened a trace that had been twisted, and buckled a dangling strap, without a word.

"I know ye done yer best, Reuben, an' I stan' ready ter give ye full credit for it. Old Whitey there looks as slick an' clean as can be, an' I hear good reports of ye from all sides. Ye wanter be a good boy, now, an' alluz mind what's told ye, 'cause yer pa, he said to me, jest afore he died, that he set gret store by ye. But ye mustn't cry now; that won't do ye no good, ye know."

The boy, at the mention of his father's name, had dropped the look of pride that Uncle Nathan's words had aroused. His mouth twitched with a great sob, and he laid his head on old Whitey's shoulder. What was the victory to him? Old Whitey could sympathize with him at least. They had had many a quiet cry out in the barn. The old horse turned his head and rubbed his nose affectionately against the boy's shoulder. Aunt Susan, too, soothed the poor little home soldier.

"Ye mustn't cry now, Reuben — you're gointer be our boy now, ye know, an' we'll do by ye jest as we would by one of our own."

Her voice trembled a little as she spoke, and Uncle Nathan hid behind old Whitey's face. At last they induced the coat sleeve to leave the overflowing eyes, and the boy, with many a sob and choke, recovered his self-control. Uncle Nathan was bound to make the recovery as complete as possible. He pulled a ten-cent scrip from his pocket, and gave it to Reuben.

"You've ben such a good boy, that I'm gonter

make ye a present. You're pretty spry-legged, an' I guess ye can run home, an' then agin we'll pretty nigh fill up the wagon. Git ye some candy, if ye wanter, only remember," he added, cautiously, " be sorter careful what kind of a bargain ye make, 'cause money don't grow on every bush, an' it has ter be handled keerful to make anything out on't."

Reuben ran away to invest his capital, and Uncle Nathan and John helped the women into the wagon. It is safe to say that Reuben went home sweeter at mouth and lighter at pocket. Candy is to the average country boy what whiskey is to the drinking man. Not a country boy but will hoard up his pennies and leave the wholesome home sweets to purchase the uncertain mixture of sweets and disease found at the country store.

"We want you to go home with us, John, an' we won't take ' no ' fer no answer," said Uncle Nathan, as he climbed over the wheel.

John had not the least thought of saying " no " when Nellie looked at him as she did. Without a word, he climbed into the wagon and took his place on the front seat. Uncle Nathan picked up the reins and clucked to old Whitey, as an intimation that they were all ready to proceed. The patient horse had grown old and stiff during the years of war, and under the doubtful training of the " wimmin folks " and Reuben he had gained remarkably fast in laziness. It was only after several sharp applications of the stick that he could be induced to develop a rate of speed in any way satisfactory to the soldier. In thus forcibly starting the current of old Whitey's being, Uncle Nathan did not wish to be unnecessarily cruel. He selected a place on old Whitey's tough hide where the blows could be heard rather than felt. The old horse understood matters at once. They drove through the town, old Whitey keeping up his stumbling trot of his own accord, as if proud of his burden, and desirous of showing it off to the best advantage. The crowd had scattered and the green was deserted. The people had gone home to the gray old farmhouses, to take up the dull life again, and try to forget that under the joy of victory there crouched the agony of despair. A few loungers were gathered about the post-office, and the seats in front of the store were all occupied. Uncle Nathan pulled in his steed at the post-office, as was his wont to do. It seemed to him that he had just returned from a visit.

"Jest bring me my mail, will ye, Deacon Smith? I kinder hate to leave the hoss alone."

No one took an exception to this very flimsy reason for asking Deacon Smith to bring the mail. John and the "wimmin folks" did not feel in the least insulted. Deacon Smith and the rest of the spectators knew that it was the delight of old Whitey's life to be left alone in such a condition. The entire company understood the matter, so there was nothing to be said. Deacon Smith disappeared in the office and presently returned with a paper in his hand. He brought it out to the wagon and handed it to Uncle Nathan. He glanced over his spectacles at the two soldiers, as he nervously brushed the dust away from the wheel.

"Didn't see nothin' o' my boy, did ye, Nathan?" said Deacon Smith. " We ain't heard a word frum him sense you was took pris'ner. I wuz kinder in hopes you might have ben there when he died so'st we could know whether he died in peace or not. 'Twould be a great comfort to us to know how 'twas. His mother ain't ben well sense the news come. Gittin' sorter childish, 'pears ter me, an' I dunno as I wonder at it much."

Uncle Nathan reached down and shook the deacon's hand. That warm hand-clasp told more than his words ever could tell.

" We left him in that prison when we come out, deacon. He'd ben low then for quite a spell, an' I don't s'pose he ever gut up at all. We all set great store by him. He was one of the best boys in the whole company. He never shirked nothin' an' done his duty all the time — without a word."

"I'm glad to hear that — I declare I be. His mother'll be glad to hear it. I'm glad he done his duty — but 'pears to me sometimes jest as if I'd 'a' gin all the world ef I cud only see that boy agin. 'Pears ter me I'd feel better if he was buried here. It don't seem jest right somehow — I s'pose it is, though."

He glanced again over the spectacles, and still brushed the dust from the wheel.

" Ye mustn't feel that way about it," said Uncle Nathan bravely. " I know jest how 'tis myself; but ye wanter remember what's ben done — what's ben gained by the war."

The deacon's head sank lower as he turned away.

"Mebby so — I s'pose ye're right — I wish I could think so," he said, as he walked back to the sidewalk, and Uncle Nathan started the horse again.

Old Whitey jogged on through the quiet street, and out under the trees towards the country. A high sand hill that raised the road up into the free country air, soon gave him a chance to show his favorite quality — slow progression — to good advantage. Uncle Nathan kept his eye open to note all the village improvements that had been planned during his absence.

"Seems ter *me*, John, this grade to this hill ain't nigh ser steep as it wuz when we went away " — but he added critically — " they might hev done a good deal better job if they hed jest scraped that dirt up to one side an' put some sand on the brow of the hill. I don't s'pose, though, they felt much like fixin' things up when the heft of the pushin' men was away."

Uncle Nathan had been an honored town officer. Perhaps this fact had something to do with his criticism of town affairs. They had reached the brow of the hill by this time, and old Whitey stopped to take a good breath before pushing on again. Uncle Nathan stood up in the wagon to obtain a better view of the country.

"Wall, there's the old place," he shouted eagerly — "looks nat'rel, don't it, John? Git up there — we wanter git home an' see how it seems ter set foot on yer own sile. Git up!" — and he gave old Whitey a blow that started that good-natured piece of horseflesh into a trot.

"I guess I'll have ter git me a new hoss afore long," said Uncle Nathan as he seated himself. But he noticed old Whitey's frantic efforts to obey orders, and his heart softened. "I guess I'll keep this one too — we'll need him to do our runnin' round with."

Old Whitey kept up his pace so well that in a short time they pulled up before the gate at Uncle Nathan's place. John opened the gate — it was no easy task, for one of the hinges had rusted away — and Uncle Nathan drove up to his own door. He looked about him with a critic's eye.

"I s'pose like enough Reuben has done his best, but things looks pooty slack arter all. I'll git me a couple of scythes sharpened up an' mow them weeds the fust thing I do."

Uncle Nathan planned other needed reforms as he and John took the horse out of the wagon and led him to the barn. The old man went through the buildings, and looked over the stock. He laid out the work for the summer as he walked about the place, with his uniform laid away, and an old farm hat on his head. They went into the house at last, and the old soldier's cup of happiness seemed as full as possible as he drew his armchair up to the old place at the window. He looked out into the orchard, white with blossoms.

How pleasant it seemed, after the years of fighting, to sit there at home. His boys never could come back — he thought of that as he drew his chair up to the window — but they died like men — the country had been saved.

The old orchard just bursting into bloom, the

sandy road lagging past the old stone wall, the bare, hilly pasture rising beyond, with the rocks starting from it gray and moss-covered, made a beautiful picture to his eyes. The cows were coming down from the hills, with Reuben behind them. The red sun dropped behind the woods, so slowly that the gray hillsides smiled back in pleasure. A wondrous feeling of rest fell over the grizzled soldier's heart, as he looked out over the fields he knew so well. He had never seen anything more beautiful.

Aunt Susan and Nellie bustled about to prepare the supper. John sat and watched Nellie as she drew out the table and sliced the bread. She looked at him every now and then in a way that honest John could not understand at all. Every time she looked in that way, John felt a thrill run all over him, and he felt instinctively for the letter under his vest. Miss Nellie grew happier and brighter the more John looked at her. She pulled Uncle Nathan's hair and glanced at John merrily, as if she knew how he would go over the dead line again to have her pull *his* hair. She ran down cellar after the butter, singing as she had not done since the news came that Archie had been taken prisoner. That news had killed her mother, and she herself had almost lost hope when the months rolled by and brought no word. She had been nearer than a daughter to Aunt Susan all through the terrible days of suspense, and when at last Uncle Nathan's letter with John's postscript had told them how death had been cheated, the two women had wept tears of joy together.

Uncle Nathan and Aunt Susan looked meaningly at John as Nellie went singing down stairs. Perhaps they remembered something of their own youth. Poor John blushed like a girl, and the two old people smiled kindly at each other. Uncle Nathan forgot to watch the hills. He sat nodding his head as he thought — perhaps of the night in the Georgia forest. The table was ready at last and Aunt Susan brought a great smoking dish of baked beans from the stove. The family drew around the table, and Uncle Nathan, with a voice that trembled a little, spoke a few words of thanks and praise.

The meal was a pleasant, but not a merry one. The three boys who used to fill up the places at the table were gone forever. The new children, Nellie and John and Reuben, filled up the places, yet there was something lacking — something that might not perhaps be so plain in the future. They all realized what a change the war had made with them. It was not until John reminded Uncle Nathan of the meal they had eaten with Sol and his family that the conversation became general. The older man told the story of the escape, urged on by an occasional question from the others. Nellie and Aunt Susan shuddered as he told how Sol had killed the dog. John smiled, and Reuben — the "home soldier" — grasped his knife as if to show that he would like to face the enemy. Uncle Nathan told the story so well that almost before they knew it they found themselves listening so intently that they forgot to eat. All but Reuben. He felt bound to keep up the reputation of the family. He pushed a large doughnut into his eye. He had kept his eyes upon Uncle Nathan so carefully that he forgot the way to his mouth.

Aunt Susan quickly called the meeting to order. "Don't never neglect your vittles for stories," she urged, and her practical suggestion broke the spell, and they all fell back to their knife exercise with a will.

After supper, Uncle Nathan took his place by the window, in his favorite armchair. John found an old hat and coat, and went out to help Reuben do the chores. Nellie and Aunt Susan cleared away the dishes. It was growing dark rapidly, yet they did not light a lamp. Uncle Nathan did not care to read. He sat watching the two women as they moved about at their work. Aunt Susan was washing, while Nellie wiped and arranged the dishes. At last the work was done, and Aunt Susan hurried away to prepare a bed for John. Nellie brought a lamp to the table, but she did not light it, for Uncle Nathan spoke to her in a tone she had never noticed before.

"Come here, little gal, an' set by me. I wanter tell you something before the rest come in."

She brought a cricket and sat down at his side. He had always been her favorite uncle. She could hardly remember her own father, and this gruff, yet kind man had always made her his pet. Whatever Uncle Nathan said had always been a law from which there could be no appeal. She had always been his "little gal," and she had found a place in his heart that no one else — not even his wife — had ever found. She came and sat on the cricket, clasping both hands over his knee, and put her chin upon them just as she had done so often before. She looked smilingly at his face. They made a pretty picture, sitting there in the moonlight. The sweet little woman leaning so lovingly upon the grizzled old man, who stroked with his rough hand the hair back from her forehead.

"I wanter talk to my little gal," he began. "I wanter talk about Archie an' John. John can tell ye a good deal more about Archie than I can."

He spoke slowly, and stroked her hair as he talked. She raised her eyes and looked into his without a word.

"We all done our best for him, done the best we could, but John done more than any of us. He was jest like a brother to Archie, an' I've seen him time an' agin pick him up an' carry him along. The day Archie died, John walked right up to the muzzle of a gun, an' picked him a bunch of flowers. He done it for you, little gal. He tried to tell me how 'twas, but I heard Archie talkin' afore John went, an' I know he done it all for you. Now, little gal, when John gives you what Archie sent, I want you shud remember all these things. There ain't no truer man, nowhere, than John Rockwell is, if he was the widder Rockwell's boy."

Nellie listened, without a word, to what Uncle Nathan said. Her eyes glistened in the moonlight, yet, when she rose at last, she was smiling. She came, and leaned over Uncle Nathan's chair, and pushed back his stiff hair, and kissed him on the forehead, on the eyes, on the cheeks, and at last square on the mouth. The old soldier laughed, as he caught her by the ear, and pulled her face down to him. He kissed her, and then rose from his chair and guessed he'd go and see where Aunt Susan had gone. He chuckled and pinched Nellie's cheeks, as he gave this shameless reason for taking himself away. He discovered the whereabouts of Aunt Susan so well that nothing was seen of either of them for an hour.

When John and Reuben came in from the barn, they found Nellie sitting alone in the kitchen. She sat by the window, looking out into the moonlight. Her eyes were fixed upon the sandy road that swept like a silver ribbon up over the rocky hills. It lay like the track of an angel's finger before the house. Reuben was tired. The excitement of the day had been too much for him. He lay on a lounge in the corner, and in a few moments was fast asleep.

John brought in the milk, and strained it into the pans. He washed out the pail, and put it carefully on the shelf. He pulled off his great boots at last, and put on a pair of Uncle Nathan's slippers, and got into the soldier's coat again. Somehow, he felt braver in his uniform. At a gesture from Nellie, he drew his chair to the window, and sat in bashful silence opposite her. Poor John, he dared to face the rebel sentry, but the words he longed to speak stuck in his throat. Nellie looked up from the road at last.

"You have something for me, haven't you, John?" she said, almost in a whisper, while her eyes seemed full of the moonlight.

And John, without a word, placed the rough letter and the curl in her hand.

"Let me light the lamp," he said, with awkward politeness, but she motioned him to keep his seat.

She leaned up against the window, and slowly read the note. The moonlight was bright enough, yet she spent a long time over the little piece of paper. John sat there in the shadow, with a feeling in his heart like that of a man who has thrown his life into the balance.

How like an angel she seemed to him, as she sat with the moonlight streaming over her. She was looking directly at the paper, yet her eyes held a dreamy expression that told him she was not reading. What if she should speak to him as she did before? His heart grew cold, as he thought of such words, and he felt how awkward and rough he was beside her. And yet he felt that whatever she said must be right, and that he would abide by it.

Nellie folded the paper at last, and put it in her pocket. She did not take her eyes from the hills for a long time. She seemed to have forgotten that John was waiting there, — waiting with a terrible doubt in his heart for her answer. She was thinking as only a woman can think at such times. Her eyes followed the sandy road, white in the moonlight, as it climbed higher and higher up the rocky hill, to lose itself at the top in a wide space of glittering sand. The rough stone wall, gray with age and service, followed the road, and seemed to join it at the top of the hill. Nellie watched the two as they met. Who could read her thoughts? Who can tell what a woman thinks when the great question of her life comes up and demands an answer? She turned from the window at last, with a bright face. The answer had come to her, and she had dropped all her doubt and fear.

John's heart almost stopped its beating, as she rose and stepped to his side. A feeling he had never known before rose in his heart, as she took his great hand in both of hers, and whispered: "Dear John, I am so sorry I ever said what I did — I think I shall know you now — I am *sure* of it."

That was all there was of it. Why should I say more? Who that has one spot of freshness left in his heart cannot tell how John's thirsty soul drank of the water of life, as she brushed back his hair, and put her face against his as they sat in the golden moonlight, telling over and over again the old, old story, ever old, yet ever new. Why should I say that the weary years behind them seemed changed to brightness, and how the future seemed to them like a stair of gold? The dreams of youth are still the same. The moon smiled in upon them, and laid its kindly hand upon their heads with a loving benediction. Never had it seen greater happiness more truly won.

When Uncle Nathan and Aunt Susan came back, the lamp was lighted, and John and Nellie sat with the table between them; but the old people looked at John's face, and saw that the letter had been answered right.

When Uncle Nathan read the chapter that night, John listened attentively, and when the prayer was offered, who should kneel with the rest but the "widder Rockwell's boy"!

It was the first time in his life that John had ever been known to kneel, and Aunt Susan remarked it. She told her husband, after John had gone to bed, that she never knew before that John was a "perfessor." She hoped he wouldn't change his mind, for "them suddin' awakenin's is shaky."

Nellie blushed and smiled at the sage remark. She knew that John's conversion was a permanent one.

CHAPTER XII.

AFTER THE WAR

THE soldiers could not settle down to anything like regular work for a long time. There were too many stories to be told. So many reminiscences were constantly coming to mind that it seemed impossible to pick up the dull routine of country life at once. The whole North was one great blaze of patriotism. Sober work was well nigh impossible, while the excitement lasted. It was hardest for Uncle Nathan to forget the stirring days of the march to the sea. He read, with keen interest, all that the papers had to say concerning the state of affairs at the South. At some particularly startling news he would take hoe in hand and vent his feelings upon the weeds in his garden. The vegetables that year were noted for their excellence.

The old soldier was never tired of fighting his battles over and over. It will be noticed that these oft-repeated battles grow in vigor and importance as they are fought over. Any statement concerning a battle in which Uncle Nathan had taken part was enough to wind him up for an hour's talk — and he was always sure of an audience.

The village people listened, day after day, to the story of the escape from Andersonville, without tiring of it. They would sit with open mouths, as Uncle Nathan pictured the scene, or gave a practical illustration of the way in which he overcame the Confederate guard. Sol and the fat soldier came to be well known personages in Breezetown. One class of citizens, of which Reuben was a very good example, could not see why Sol had not done about as much to preserve the Union as old Abe Lincoln himself.

"Do you have any idee you killed that fat man, Uncle Nathan?" Reuben asked this question, after listening to the story for the fiftieth time.

"Wal, I never cud tell how 'twas. Ye see his head must 'a' ben putty hard or he wouldn't 'a' gin me the chance at him, but then, agin, I hit him a putty hard crack. I call it about a tie, an' I hope the chances is in his favor. One thing is sartin — I don't s'pose that dog never showed no signs of life agin."

It was much easier for John to settle down and forget the war times. He found himself quite a hero among the village people. Uncle Nathan was never tired of singing the praises of his comrade. He was glad to put John ahead, as an example of what "Maine men" could accomplish. There may have been something in the fact, too, that every brave act of John's introduced one in which he had figured.

"It tuck grit to do them things, an' there warn't no grittier soldiers in the army than them that went from the State o' Maine. I s'pose John, here, done about the grittiest thing that was done down there."

John would blush painfully at this glowing eulogy, prouder by far of the glad look in Nellie's eyes than of the whole chorus of, "I declare," and, "I vow, it beats all," and the admiring glances of the audience. He had told Nellie the whole story of the Andersonville violets, and she had complimented his bravery, in a way that made John wish he could find a chance to do the like again. They were speaking about it one Sunday afternoon, when Nellie suddenly said : —

"I wonder what made that man let you pass over and get the flowers?"

"I don't know," said John. "P'raps he had some one at home like you. That's about the only thing that would make *me* do it."

"Ain't you ashamed?" said Nellie, blushing with pleasure at John's honest compliment.

"Not a mite. I don't see nothing to be ashamed of."

Nellie did not seem to see anything either, yet, of course, it would not do to let John know it. After a long silence, Nellie spoke again : —

"I would like to see him, John."

"What for?" demanded John.

"Oh, because" — and she ended the conversation by brushing John's hair down over his eyes, and then running away. Neither of them knew how soon they were to see Jack Foster again, and learn the true reason of his conduct. Surely, these were golden days for John. He worked on Uncle Nathan's farm in a way that startled the neighbors. His heart was in the work, and he never knew what fatigue meant. Politics meant nothing to him: he was planning for Nellie's comfort. As the little woman grew rosy and bright with happiness, John grew away from his old awkward self. He grew to be a strong, earnest man, with but one idea, and that one the noblest that a man ever can have, — to give his life up to the happiness of the one woman he loves. So they lived on, drawing more and more of the rays of happiness to the old farmhouse.

In the latter part of July, John got a letter that produced quite an excitement in the little household. It was from the colonel of John's regiment — not the one in which he had served at first, for that had been swallowed up at Andersonville, but the one he had joined after the escape. In consequence of the free and easy style of marching adopted by Sherman's army, John had several times been thrown into close relationship with Colonel Gray. The officer, a warm-hearted Western man, had taken a great fancy to the sturdy Yankee, and after the war he had kept track of him. He wrote now, to offer John a position. Shortly after the close of the war, Colonel Gray had bought a large plantation in Mississippi. It was badly run down, and he bought it for a small sum, expecting to go himself and build it up. Like many Northern soldiers, he hoped to settle at the South, and take advantage of her great natural advantages. A proffered office in one of the Territories had tempted him to give up his farm operations, and he wrote to try and induce John to go down and practise a little Northern agriculture on Southern soil.

"The chance seems a good one," he wrote. "You

know how these cotton planters have abused their land, and what can be done in that country with regular, systematized work. You are just the man to go down and take hold of this place, and make it worth something. I am satisfied that you could make it a very profitable property, and help yourself in many ways. I do not look for very much trouble. Society may be broken up, for a time, to some extent, yet the war memories must be buried, since there is now nothing to fight about. The Northern men, who are flocking by the thousands to the South, will, in my opinion, with the aid of the negro, overcome the more turbulent class of Southerners. The soldiers of the rebel army will be glad, I think, to drop the contest, and develop the arts of peace."

At the close of the war it is probable that a good share of the thinking Union soldiers held about these ideas in regard to the state of affairs at the South. As slavery had been killed, they could not see why the North and the South could not be one.

This letter was a sore temptation to John. With New England thrift, he had made many a calculation as to what these plantations could be made to accomplish. He had figured many a time how, with one of these great farms at his command, he could make a fortune such as Breezetown's rocky hills could never know. He never made a single suggestion, however, when the letter came. He was sitting in the kitchen with Nellie that night when Reuben brought the letter from town. Uncle Nathan and Aunt Susan had gone to make a visit. Reuben, with his characteristic watchfulness, fell asleep on the lounge before

John finished reading the letter. John was not a great literary man, and he read the letter through slowly and carefully before he could get its real meaning. When he had finished he handed it to Nellie without a word. She put down her work and read it through with a troubled face. Her under lip quivered as she put the letter down at last.

"Please don't go, John," she said. "I could not leave home now."

John said never a word in reply. He folded up the letter with the air of a man who has just listened to some unanswerable argument. He smiled a little as he thought how utterly impossible it would be for him to go when she wished him to stay. Nellie watched him with eyes that glistened a little. She came and stood at the back of his chair and ran her fingers through his hair, and at last bent over and kissed him. She had read his thoughts perfectly. John could not have concealed them from her if he had tried.

"I know you would like to be rich and famous for my sake," she whispered to him, "but I don't mind. I know I can make you happy here, and that is better for us both, isn't it?"

John answered in a way that left very little doubt as to his sincerity, and Nellie went back to her work, happy again. John picked up the county paper. The first thing his eyes fell upon was a little poem in the "Poets' Corner." He had not read a line of poetry for years, yet he studied this poem out word by word — he knew not why. It was a simple little thing; there was not even a name to it.

>The sun went merrily up the hills
> That stood like sentinels grim and gray
>Between the vale and the busy world
> Where fame and honor and fortune lay.
>
>The shepherd wistfully watched the light
> Fade over the mountains far and dim.
>Could *he* but follow and find the place
> Where fame's bright mantle was waiting him?
>
>A soft hand tenderly touched his arm,
> A sweet voice spoke in his waiting ear:
>Fame lies over the mountain high,
> Love and happiness yet are *here*.
>
>The sun went over the hills alone,
> Touching the sky with a crimson flame.
>Men may long to be great, yet still
> Love is better by far than fame.

John studied away at the poetry until Nellie came and pulled the paper away from him. He woke Reuben and sent him off to bed, where he could slumber on a more economical basis. Then John came back to the table and thought the poetry over till Uncle Nathan and Aunt Susan came home. He kept the little poem in his mind, and studied over it for many a day. Nellie cut it out of the paper and pasted it into her scrap-book.

John wrote Colonel Gray a plain letter, telling him honestly the reason for declining the offer. The "little girl" that he praised so proudly looked over his shoulder and boxed his ears for daring to write what she loved so well to see. Why a woman will take such forcible and contradictory methods of indicating her pleasure, will always remain one of the mysteries of nature. Surely these were golden days for honest John, though at times the hours seemed to crawl by with lagging footsteps. At last the nights began to grow cool, and the first frosts bit savagely at the flowers and grass. The fall is the saddest season of the year. It is the season of death. To John, however, it was the season of life.

Thanksgiving day came at last, and John and Nellie were married. They tried to have a quiet wedding, but the village people would not hear of this at all. All Breezetown crowded into the weather-beaten church, and when John and Nellie stood up before the pulpit, every woman envied Nellie and every man envied John. Reuben drove them home in fine style to eat the great dinner that Aunt Susan had prepared. Even old Whitey entered into the spirit of the occasion. He kicked up his heels and fairly ran down hill, something he had not done since Nellie was a baby. It may have been Reuben's stick that taught old Whitey this complimentary caper, but let us not take such a practical view of it. Let us believe it was pure sentiment that pulled up the heels.

After dinner Uncle Nathan made a speech to the company. He closed with his old eulogy of Maine men in general and John in particular, and then, not knowing of any compliment strong enough to do anything like justice to Nellie, he kissed her, and then hurried out into the woodshed, ostensibly to get some fuel, but really to blow his nose. Many men like Uncle Nathan are obliged to relieve the heart through the nose. Would that there were more of them. The company had a very merry time with singing and games, till at last they went away with many a heartfelt wish for the happiness of the young couple. And John and Nellie standing at the door to bid their good friends good-night, he like a strong, rugged oak, and she like a tender, clinging vine, felt indeed that the world was opening before them bright and fair.

The days went by like sunbeams in the little household. Each day left a little of its brightness as a sweet memory. Reuben grew up under John's influence, into a faithful boy. Uncle Nathan grew more grizzled as the years went by. His eyesight began to give out at last, and even his spectacles failed to enable him to read all the political news, of which he was so fond. This eye trouble induced him to take a great interest in Reuben's elocutionary training. He pressed the young gentleman into the service, and, by means of promised help at the chores, bribed him to read aloud the long statements and interviews concerning the South that filled up the papers at that time. It was funny to watch the two politicians thrashing the grain out of the political stack — Reuben slowly and painfully struggling through the long words, skipping or widely guessing at the meanings, and glancing every few moments at the end to see how much there was left, and the gray old man listening patiently in his armchair, putting in a word now and then, or explaining with a theory of his own some intricate point.

If Reuben did not make a very strong Republican, it was surely no fault of Uncle Nathan's. Sometimes Nellie would take Reuben's place as reader.

This would make the audience larger, for John would come and listen — believing every word because she read it. Uncle Nathan and Reuben even carried their political discussions into the barn, where the old man went to pay in work for the reading.

"You said they give them niggers twenty licks apiece, didn't ye?" Uncle Nathan would ask, the more fully to digest some point of the reading.

"That's jest what the paper said," Reuben would answer stoutly. Printers' ink was to him but a synonym for truth. "They tied 'em up to a tree, an' licked 'em awful, an' they had something like white piller cases on their heads, an' sheets tied around 'em."

"An' them is the folks that fit us so hard," Uncle Nathan would answer. "I wish I'd 'a' been there with sech a company as we tuk outer here. It beats all," and he fed the young heifer with so much violence that that innocent creature started back in alarm at the force with which her food was presented. He would go muttering his displeasure at Southern outrages, down past the cattle. It was woe then to the unfortunate animal that kicked out at him. Such an action would force the kicker to act as a scapegoat for all the Ku Klux that Uncle Nathan had ever heard of.

But John and Nellie had no need to hire Reuben to read to them. John took no interest in politics. He always voted, but as far as discussing the questions as Uncle Nathan did, he felt that he had much better business in hand. What was it to him what the politicians thought, when there was something to do to make Nellie happy?

So the days went by, and after a few bright years had joined their hearts closer than ever, there came a new member into the family, to share the sunshine. It was a little Nellie, with the same bright golden hair and the same blue eyes. She grew into a sober little tot of a girl, with John's honest face and quiet ways, and Nellie's gentleness. The whole family grew wondrous proud of the little treasure. Aunt Susan would do her best to make the little thing sick by feeding it upon little cakes and other home confectionery. Reuben would even try to keep awake for the sake of holding the baby. Uncle Nathan would allow her to pull his nose and whiskers, without a word of complaint. The dear little baby would always pull her own hair just as hard as she pulled the whiskers, and then, finding how she must have hurt Uncle Nathan, she would kiss him to make matters right. No wonder he never complained. John was proudest of them all. The little girl would always come toddling out to meet him as he came in from work. She would often run in advance of her mother, that she might get the first kiss. John would lift her on his shoulder and carry her in triumph into the house. Every night, just before baby was put to bed, John would take her on his knee and ask her a series of questions, that might well take the place of many a prayer. The little girl was always tired and sleepy, yet she would always answer just the same.

"Do you love mamma?"—John would ask the

question as the little one nestled up to him, while Nellie would stop her work while she listened for the answer.

"Es, I does."

"And papa too?"

"Es, I does."

"Which do you love the best?"

This was always a tough question for the little girl to decide. Sometimes it had to be repeated before she would answer. At last, after carefully thinking the matter over, she would say:

"I love ou bof the best."

This was always most satisfactory to John, and he would explain the triangular bond that held them all together. During his explanation, Uncle Nathan would sit and smile over his spectacles at the loving group.

"I love mamma the best, and mamma loves me the best, and baby loves us both the best."

This explanation would satisfy all parties so well that when Nellie came to take the little girl away to bed, there was always a triangular kiss, where it was very hard to say which one had any advantage. John would go back to his work, thinking himself the happiest man in the world, and Nellie would sing beside the little one's bed the sweetest music human ears can ever hear.

The little girl changed John and Nellie in many ways. They felt that this little life had been given them to build up and develop. It seemed as if all the good in their lives had centred in this little one. The baby fingers pulled their hearts still closer together, so that while they loved each other even more than before, they had still a wealth of love to bestow upon the baby. As the little Nellie grew older and developed more and more of her baby graces, a feeling came to John and Nellie that all young parents probably experience. It was a desire to educate their little girl and give her every advantage of refinement and culture. They planned for her hundreds of things that they well knew the simple country home and the sandy farm could never provide.

By the time baby was five years old, John and Nellie had determined to adopt some plan for improving their circumstances. John had long since found the farm growing too narrow for him. He began to feel, as he told Nellie, "like a man workin' in a peck measure." Perhaps his ideas had broadened since the baby began to be so much like her mother. Reuben was now a young man, and fully able, with Uncle Nathan's help, to carry on all the farm work. There was a good living to be made on the farm, but no money with which to care for the little girl as they wished to do.

John and Nellie talked the matter over many times after baby had fallen asleep. They decided that they would make any sacrifice that might be demanded, so that baby might be helped. It was Nellie who at last proposed a plan that John had often thought of, yet never had spoken. They were standing one night at little Nellie's bed, looking at the little dreamer. Nellie had been quiet and thoughtful all day. John had noticed it. She bent down to brush back the baby's hair, and then suddenly turned and put her hand on John's shoulder. She was obliged to reach up to put her hand there, for the top of her head did not rise higher than John's heart. John looked down at her with a feeling in his heart that always brought the look into his eyes that she loved to see.

"Do you think we could have that place at the South now, John? I would be willing to go now, I think."

She whispered this slowly and glanced at the sleeping baby. John understood her. There was a strange huskiness in his voice as he said: —

"My *dear* little woman, what can I ever do to pay you for this?"

She looked up at him with a bright smile that told him how she could be paid. There was but little more said about the matter. Both knew what a sacrifice the little woman had made in thus offering to leave her home for the sake of baby. John wrote at once to Colonel Gray, and stated his case with Yankee honesty. The officer wrote an enthusiastic letter and urged John to go down at once. The plantation had been run by negroes since it was bought, and needed more than ever a good man to take charge of it.

"We hear, of course, a great many reports of violence in that country," he wrote, "but I think many of them are exaggerated. I feel sure that a man who will mind his own business and keep out of politics will be safe enough. In any event, they won't run an old soldier like you very far — and by the way," he continued, with a soldier's gallantry, " I wish you would kiss that little soldier of a woman and that little girl for me; of course I can't do it myself. I'm afraid of you. You are a lucky man, Rockwell, and I wish I was in your place."

It is needless for me to say that John carried out these suggestions to the letter, and fully agreed that he was a " lucky man."

And so they decided to go. John helped through the summer's work, and then went with Nellie on a short trip to bid all their friends good-by. Most of the old people shook their heads dubiously when they learned where the young folks were going.

" Better stop right where ye be. Ye're doin' well 'nough now. Ye're jest takin' yer life right inter yer han's when ye go down inter that country," dismally urged one old croaker.

Uncle Nathan always came to the rescue when such attacks were made.

" I'd resk my life in John's hands jest about's quick ez I'd put it anywhere, I tell ye," he would declare, stoutly. No one could give John a better character for carefulness than this, surely. It was very hard work for Uncle Nathan to advise John and Nellie to leave the old home, but he brought himself to do it at last. He knew how much of the home happiness and sunshine the little family would take out of his life, yet the noble old man knew just how John felt. He was willing that the last of his life might be darkened a little so that those he loved might come to him at last with brighter and happier lives.

"I dunno but ye're doin' jest what I shud do, John," he said bravely, "if I was in yer place. I can't blame ye a mite. That little gal comes about as nigh ter bein' an angel as I ever see. Looks jest as if the Lord hed picked out all the good pints you an' Nellie ever hed an' bundled 'em together so tight that all the bad pints got squeezed out. But you don't wanter make too much of an idol out o' her, John. That won't do, noway."

Uncle Nathan always began these talks bravely enough, but he never could finish without being forced to go out-of-doors to blow his nose.

At last the time came for starting. Who can describe the feelings that come into the heart when such a farewell is spoken? It is a sad scene, that haunts one for a lifetime. How the heart seems ready to burst, how the throat fills with something we cannot control, how the eyes *will* fill with tears, how doubly dear each old association seems, how the sweet home music rings in our ears. It is the saddest and tenderest picture of a life. It is cut into the heart, and long, long years after, we look back to it with souls that pine for the old home rest, and almost wish we had turned back at the trial.

It was hard indeed for the young people to leave the old home, where they had been so happy; but the thought of little Nellie kept the tears back, and strengthened their hearts for the trial. There was no great "scene" at parting, and they were all glad of it. A natural home picture is the best that one can take away at such a time. The stage was a trifle late, and they were glad to hear Sam Jones call out, "Hurry up, no time to lose!" In the bustle of a hurried departure, they might forget something of their grief. All the home people kissed Nellie and the baby and shook hands with John. Uncle Nathan gave him a great grip.

"I wish I was goin' with ye," he said; "I'm too old, I s'pose, but I'd like to go. Don't ever back down a might afore them fellers, an' don't never forgit whar ye come frum."

The old man held a shoe in his hand, which he proposed throwing after the stage for good luck. The stage rolled away at last in a cloud of dust. It disappeared over the hill, and the home folks went back to their work. The immigrants kissed the little girl that drew them away from home, and then resolutely set their faces to the future.

CHAPTER XIII.

A SOUTHERN TOWN

JOHN and Nellie reached Sharpsburg on Saturday. They stood on the platform of the station and looked about them with the peculiar feeling that every Northern person experiences on entering a Southern town. It is a feeling that can hardly be described. A mingled feeling of distrust, curiosity, surprise, and criticism. All the old stories that have been told concerning the country and people crowd into the mind, and the first impulse is to look about to see how much of the record appears to be true. The first impression is not generally calculated to put the mind at rest. Everything was different from the order of things at home. There was no great stir and bustle of business. A good crowd of people had gathered about the station, yet there was no excitement. Every one seemed to have plenty of time to think matters thoroughly over before beginning to work. A few white men stood listlessly about, watching the train with eyes entirely devoid of curiosity. Not one stood erect. Every one of them leaned against some convenient post or wall. On a platform opposite the station a group of negroes were busy unloading a bale of cotton from a wagon. The workers, mules, negroes, and all, had suspended operations to watch the train. A crowd of ragged darkies, with clothes that hung about them in tatters, swarmed about the steps or sat in a long row in the shade at the rear. The train seemed to have stopped in a most unpromising portion of the town. There was nothing to be seen save a few rough unpainted negro cabins, and a little blacksmith's shop, the most striking feature of which was a glaring mistake in the spelling of the sign. The white men stared curiously at John, but they stepped back and touched their hats as Nellie appeared.

As the passengers paused on the platform, one of the most ragged of all the little negroes ran up the steps and pushed his remnant of a hat up from his forehead by way of salute.

"Hotel, boss? Bes' in de city! whar all de gemmens stop at," he said as he caught at John's satchel.

John looked at the little fellow with a smile. He thought how easily he could carry the darky and the satchel, too. It seemed absurd for such a little, ragged shadow of humanity to offer to do work for a strong man.

"Show us the way to the tavern," he said, "an' I'll carry the bag."

But the boy pulled the baggage away, and, placing it carefully on his head, skipped merrily along before his patrons. John and Nellie, each holding a hand of the little girl, followed their conductor.

The newly arrived Yankees did not present a remarkably imposing appearance as they walked up the street from the station. The little walking ragbag that led the way trotted on with the satchel on his head. He balanced the burden with one hand, while the other was occupied in holding his various garments about him. His costume was of such a fragmentary nature that a good shake would have taken it entirely from him. The various fractions of garments were held together by a series of strings that met at a common centre as though to brace themselves for a strong pull. It was such a ludicrous sight that John and Nellie could not help laughing, though Nellie's first impulse was to offer to patch the garment that sinned most visibly. The walking rag-bag turned at the sound and joined in the laugh as heartily as any of them, though he knew nothing of the cause of the laughter. It was such a cheap exercise, and one so pleasurable to him, that he was glad to join. By a skilful movement, he changed the occupation of his hands without dropping the satchel or his clothes. Then he trotted on again. As they walked along, John could not help thinking how Uncle Nathan would have groaned at the lack of thrift and care everywhere visible. The town was built on a series of low hills, over which the streets lamely progressed. Great gulleys, worn out by the water in its effort to get out of the way of public travel, ran up and down and across the streets, like the wrinkles on the face of an old man. There was a most feeble apology for a plank walk that ran along the side of the street with about the spirit of a dog that had been caught stealing meat. In many places the earth beneath the walk had been washed away so completely that the foot passengers were in great danger of falling through. The houses were low, and most of them unpainted and dismal-looking. The yards seemed slack and disorderly. The fences were old and unpainted or built of barbed wire that seemed to reach out with its hungry teeth to cut into the clothing of the passer-by.

There was not a single white woman to be seen. A few men were in sight; most of them were sitting in the shade; many were asleep. Negroes were working listlessly in some of the yards. They all stopped their work to look at the new-comers, and many of them touched their hats with "Howdy, boss?" John, with New England friendliness, bowed to them all, which act of recognition caused the white men to look at him in wonder. What manner of man could this be, they thought, who would thus publicly recognize all the "niggers" he met.

The little darky who served as guide halted at last before a gate, and led the way through it up a long avenue of trees to a large white house. It was a massive structure, with a wide piazza in front. Years before, it had been the home of some proud Southern planter, but the fortunes of war had sadly changed it.

The rag-bag placed the satchel on the floor and went in search of some responsible person. John and Nellie sat on the broad piazza and looked about them with curious eyes. It is easy to pick out faults where one has been taught for years to believe they exist. Everything seemed strange because it was new. They could not imagine at first how people could become used to such an arrangement. The high, airy rooms pleased Nellie exceedingly, and the little cook-house at the rear seemed to her a great improvement upon the hot kitchen at home. John noticed how far the well was from the house — almost a day's journey, as he afterwards stated — and how carelessly the wood-pile was arranged. He would have had every stick of that wood in under a shed. Everything about the house seemed to him slack and unbusinesslike. He was yet to learn by sad experience that cheap labor was expected to make up for lack of conveniences. As they sat looking about them, a living poultry market in the shape of an old negro came up from the gate. He carried about twenty chickens tied about him by the legs. They were all over him, peeping out from under his arms, over his shoulders, and between the folds of his ragged coat. The old fellow hobbled up to the cook-house and began an animated discussion with the cook about the sale of a portion of his burden. The cook, after a long argument, bought several of the largest, and, there being no place in which to secure them, and evidently not wishing to spend his time and energy in chasing them about, he cut off their heads at once, much to the wonder of John, who was watching carefully. John wondered what the landlord could be thinking of to permit such a shiftless proceeding.

At last the mistress of the house appeared. A tall, dignified woman, with gray hair and a face that showed deep lines of suffering. The war had cut the lines into her face as plainly as it had cut the scars on the face of the country. She brought out a book, in which Nellie, who did the most of John's writing, registered. The old lady glanced at the names with a slight shrug of her shoulders.

"You are from the North, I see," she said, quietly.

"Yes, mar'm," answered John. "We come from the State o' Maine."

"Ah, indeed?" She spoke in a tone that gave John to understand that he might just as well have come from Germany, so far as his former residence concerned her. The landlady led her guests into a large room on the first floor, and then bowed herself away. It was not long before the bell rang for dinner, and the immigrants walked out to the dining-place. One long table extended the full length of the room. A swarm of flies were buzzing about the room. There were no screen doors or windows. Near the head of the table stood the little negro who had brought the satchel from the station. He held his clothes together with one hand while the other pulled at a string which kept in motion a series of paper frames, swinging over the table. The wind caused by this motion served to keep away most of the flies. A massive negro woman stood at a side table where the soup was to be served. She was barefooted and unkempt. The cook stood at the door of the cook-house, ready to pass in the dinner whenever it should be needed.

The grave politeness of the company at dinner rather disconcerted honest John. He had been used to the free-and-easy New England society, where one is perfectly free to try and find out his neighbor's business; where the strange thing about a newcomer would be his failure to ask questions. The grave courtesy of the men he met at dinner, and the cool way in which they evaded all his questions, was something entirely new to him. No one seemed to be able to tell him anything about the soil or the crops. He made but a poor meal.

Another thing that seemed strange to him was the fact that he was the only man in the company without a title of some kind. The rest were all captains, or doctors, or professors, and one tall man with a very red nose rose as high as "General." John was the only plain Mister, until the landlady, wishing doubtless to maintain the reputation of her table, addressed him as "Judge." He was known as Judge Rockwell thereafter, much to the amusement of Nellie, and the great embarrassment of John himself. Nellie hardly knew what to say to the ladies she met at dinner. She was almost as nervous as John, and could not seem to start a conversation. She had no common feeling with these people who seemed to look at her so sneeringly when she asked some questions in regard to the preparation of the meal. She did not know that these ladies knew almost nothing about cooking, and probably cared still less. All these points were to be learned in time.

There was only one thing that happened to make John and Nellie feel better. One old gentleman smiled at little Nellie, and came over to pat her on the head as he went out. The little girl's mother smiled so sweetly that he bowed as he passed her. John wanted to get up and shake hands with him.

Little Nellie was very tired, and soon after dinner she fell asleep. John sat and watched his wife as she soothed the child. The little woman's lip was trembling in spite of the song she tried to sing to the baby. John knew she was thinking of home. He carried little Nellie to the bed and laid her tenderly there; then he came back to his wife. She sat in a low rocking-chair by the window. He knelt on the floor at her side and put his head in her lap. She brushed his hair back from his forehead, and then, with both her hands, turned his face so that she could look straight into his eyes.

"What are you thinking about now, John?" she asked.

Her lip had stopped its trembling, and she smiled down at him, though John knew that her heart was wrenched with homesickness.

"My dear little girl," he broke out, "I know it is hard for you, but it won't be so hard when we have a home of our own."

The brave little woman tried hard to smile, but her lip quivered strongly, and before she could stop them, the tears came down over her cheeks. She had meant to comfort John and have her cry all to herself, but she was too tired, and the tears *would* force themselves out, and she covered her face with her hands and sobbed like a little child. And good, brave John, though his own eyes were wet, soothed his wife, and whispered comforting words to her till she stopped crying.

"I am so tired, John," she said, wearily.

"I know it, my dear little girl, and I want you to sleep now. I am going down town to find out something about the place, and while I am gone you must take a nap."

John kissed her, and went out. He sat on the piazza for a while, and then softly opened the door of the room and looked in. Nellie had fallen asleep. She lay with her arm thrown over the baby. John closed the door, and walked down the path to the street. As he passed through the gate, he met the old gentleman who had noticed the little girl at dinner. This new friend bowed and held out his hand, which John shook heartily.

"I am glad to see you, judge." The old gentleman spoke with an emphasis on the new title, that showed that he fully understood how John regarded it. "I am glad to see you — my name is Lawrence, and if I can be of any service to you I shall be very glad. You are a stranger here, and, if I am not mistaken, a Northern man."

John shook the old gentleman's hand again. "Yes, I'm a Yankee, I s'pose," he said simply. "I come from the State o' Maine."

He had determined to say as little as possible about his State or his former home, being convinced, as most Northern people are, before they come to the South, that the mere mention of his former residence would be used as an argument against him.

"Ah, indeed?" replied Mr. Lawrence — by this time they were walking together down the street — "I had some relatives in New Hampshire years ago, in fact, I came from that State, but it was so long ago that I expect they are dead long since. It is very hard, however, for one to forget those old hills."

John would not have been a Yankee if he had not tried to cross-question his new friend.

"You've been here a good while, I s'pose."

"A great many years. I have seen many changes, and many stirring times. You have come here at a very trying time, and you will find it necessary to do many things that you would not think of doing at the North."

"What sort of a country is it?" John asked the question a little hesitatingly.

"It is a country of magnificent possibilities — that is the best I can say. You will see what I mean when you are fairly at work. The strength of this land lies in the future — it will be strength or weakness, just as the present generation shall decide. There is no place in the land where the immigrant will find it so hard to become contented, yet there is no place where strong-hearted men and women can do so much for themselves and for their country as they can here. By the way, you were a soldier, I suppose?"

"Of course I was," said John, stoutly. This was one of the questions that he felt unable to dodge. The old gentleman looked at him keenly.

"You think the negroes are the equals of our white people, I suppose, that is, you think the government did right in giving them equal rights with white people?"

"Of course," answered John; "wasn't that what we fought the war for?"

His companion smiled sadly and shook his head.

"Let me give you a word of advice, my friend. Never give one of our Southern negroes to understand that you consider him as an equal. At home you would doubtless invite a negro to your table. Never think of doing it here, if you want to enjoy any of the privileges of society or business. You have come among a very proud and impulsive people. They have strong beliefs — stronger than your own in fact. They know the negroes are incapable of governing people who are superior in intelligence. You will see that this is true before long, and I must advise you as a friend to be guarded in your remarks. Nothing is to be gained by talking too much, and everything may be lost. I am an old man and I have studied this question carefully."

John felt that this was all true. It was about what Uncle Nathan had meant when he said: — " 'Twon't do ye no good ter spread yer idees round there too thick. People ain't gonter change their notions in a minnit. If they ask you where ye come frum, jest tell 'em and don't stop ter make no argyments ner excuses. They'll think a great site more of ye if ye mind yer own biz'ness. You jest stick ter work, an' let them run their own wagin."

"I've made up my mind to keep my mouth shut and mind my own affairs," John said, as they walked on toward the business part of the town. In a few moments they stood in front of the court-house, where they could command a good view of the main street.

It was a dreary sight to John, accustomed as he

was to the stir and bustle of New England. A group of men sat in front of every store. They were staring vacantly into the street, or talking in a listless manner, each word being obliged to fight its way out through their jaws. Before several of the larger groups a few sidewalk orators were holding forth in thrilling style. The stores seemed to be kept for the most part by Jews. They stood in the doorways with that peculiar smile and hand motion for which the Jews are famous the world over. A line of sad-looking mules, some saddled and others attached to wagons, stood along the street. They hung their heads down as if trying to appear as lazy and spiritless as their masters. Surely a man is known by his mule or dog. Near a small tree that was making a brave struggle for existence on a high clay bank, John saw a horse standing in a crowd of mules. The degraded animal seemed heartily ashamed of himself at thus being forced to associate with mules. If he had straightened up proudly or even pranced a little, he would have appeared finely in the crowd of lazy creatures about him.

A yoke of bony oxen had hauled a heavy wagon up near the village well. One of the animals lay contentedly upon the ground, while the other stood patiently holding the whole weight of the yoke. The driver, a long, lean, yellow-faced man, with hair, face, and clothes all of the same color, stood leaning against the wagon, holding a long whip which he cracked at intervals in the direction of a group of negroes. The stores were low and discolored. One felt that trade must be cramped and dwarfed before it could enter them. The sidewalks were broken and dirty. There was little paint to be seen. What little there was seemed creeping into the dirt for protection. A few white men were at work, but most of them sat in the comfortable chairs and gazed at the street. The negroes supplied most of the life in the picture. It was Saturday, and they had gathered from all sides for a general holiday. In all stages of costume, from a few rags held together by a strap, to a gorgeous combination introducing all the colors of the rainbow, they stood or walked about talking and laughing as though the chief end of life consisted in manufacturing all the fun possible. In one corner a crowd had gathered about a ragged musician who discoursed sweet music from a mouth-organ. The crowd stood about in openmouthed attention, often beating time with their hands or feet as he played. The driver of the ox team listened until " Rally Round the Flag " roused him to action. That melody evidently brought the old times back to him. To drive them back into the past, he cracked his long whip over the crowd, in such close proximity to the player's head, that the tune came to a very abrupt termination. The company broke up with mutterings and head-shaking. The ox-driver drew in his long lash and placed himself in readiness for another shot.

In a vacant lot near the street a negro orator was selling various bottles of a "Kunger" medicine of his own manufacture. He was dressed in a bright uniform of red and yellow. He wore a tall white hat from which floated several black feathers. He was addressing a crowd of open-mouthed negroes, and eloquently stating a series of the most remarkable physiological facts that ever came to the light.

Several refreshment stands were placed along the street for the benefit of the darkies. There was nothing princely about these establishments. An upturned dry-goods box or a board laid across two barrels served for a counter. A basket of small cakes, a great, shapeless piece of pork, and a pile of biscuits formed the stock in trade. An old crone with gray hair and a face twisted into a mass of wrinkles presided over the stand near where John stood. She was smoking a long pipe directly over the great piece of boiled pork. A big negro approached and laid a dime on the board. The old woman cut a large block of meat from the mass and laid it upon one of the little cakes. This, with one of the biscuits, formed the ration. The negro grasped his food eagerly and crouched on the edge of the sidewalk to devour it. A rival establishment near by was doing a fine business in fried sausage. A small oil-stove supplied the heat, and a battered tin pan held the food. It was cooked in great balls in a rusty frying-pan, and turned about with a jack-knife. The purchasers received the meat directly into their hands.

CHAPTER XIV.

COLONEL FAIR

As John stood watching the negroes, Mr. Lawrence touched his arm, and at the same time beckoned to a tall man who had just left one of the groups of white men.

"My friend, Colonel Fair — Judge Rockwell," he introduced, as the tall man came near. "Colonel Fair is a Northern man; he lives near your place and can doubtless give you some information concerning it. Now I must bid you good evening, for I am obliged to go. I leave you in good hands. I shall be glad to see you again," — and with a shake of the hand and a stately bow Mr. Lawrence walked down the street to the place where his horse had been tied.

"Nice ole man," said Colonel Fair, abruptly. "Doc. Lawrence is a nice ole man, but he ain't got much sense."

John looked curiously at the man who spoke his ideas with so little reserve. A tall, thin man, with long, bony hands. The skin on his face seemed to be drawn so tight that it pushed his eyes into undue prominence. He wore a thin, short beard, and his hair was just in the struggle of turning from gray to white. His mouth was strong and firm. He was a trifle round-shouldered, and carried his head a little in advance of his body. He looked keenly at John, and held out his hand in a sharp, businesslike way.

"Glad to see you, judge," he said. "You're gonter take the old Bell place, I reckon. I'm glad you be — you'll be neighbors to me."

"Yes, an' I'm gonter move right out," said John, "but, look here — I ain't no judge at all. They give me the name up to the tavern, but I dunno how they come by it."

"That's all right," the new friend laughed. "You'll git used to that after a while. Everybody here has to be somethin', when, right down to business, they ain't nothin'. Somethin' like the two fellers up here to Memphis."

Colonel Fair cleared his throat and coaxed his face into the self-satisfied expression that comes to announce a good story.

"A couple of these fellers — lawyers they was — went up there to tend court. They got to talkin', an' at last one of 'em says, 'By the way, I've been told that I look jest like the poet Byron — do you reckon there's any truth in that story?' The other feller looked at him sorter sharp, an' then says, 'I reckon so — you do look jest like him, I reckon.' The talk went on till after a while the second feller says — 'By the way, a heap of my friends say that I remind them of Thomas Jefferson — what do you reckon about that?' The first feller looked at him pretty sharp, and then says, 'Well, sar, I can't see no resemblance at all.' The second feller he drawed off an' said — 'No, sar, and you don't look no more like Byron than my old mule does.'"

John laughed heartily at this story, and Colonel Fair went on to apply it.

"Now look at them men settin' in front of that store," — and he pointed to the nearest group. "There's a cap'n, two majors, a doctor, and two colonels, an' I'll bet there ain't two of 'em that's got any real hold on his title. They just set there and carry out the play. Them fellers jest set there all day long an' tell how many slaves their fathers used to have, an' cuss this free-nigger labor. While they are wearin' the paint away from them chairs, the niggers are wearin' out their arms for 'em."

John was a little surprised at this plain talk. This man was evidently not in the least afraid of being shot.

"What sort of a country *is* this any way?" He asked the question to draw out his new friend. Somehow he liked these blunt sentences.

"The country's all right if the people only had some git up to 'em. They jest lay right back and make the niggers do all the work. How many white men do you see a-workin' on this street? You go through the country an' you'll find it jest so all along. When a man comes down here ready to dip in an' work, he'll do fine. This country won't be much till these boys grow up. I tell 'em that all these old fellers have got to die off before the country kin come up. These old chaps live 'way back yonder. They fight every new idee."

Colonel Fair talked rapidly and earnestly, pointing down the street as he talked. John listened in surprise. He hardly expected to find a man talking this way right in the very heart of the South. He indicated his surprise at this very plain talk.

"I ain't a bit afraid of 'em," said Colonel Fair, "and they know it. I've been here a good while and they know who I be. They know I don't know how to run worth a cent. I'm a Democrat — always have been. Down in this country you've got to be either a Democrat or a nigger. You ain't got no idee yet what a nigger is. Wait till you have 'em to work for ye an' all around ye. That's the kind of men that runs this country " — and he pointed to a group of men gathered in front of one of the stores.

"They set there all day an' do nothin' but talk politics, an' yet there ain't one of 'em that can tell ye what Protection means. I'll bet ten dollars I can go up to that crowd an' ask 'em what the news is, an' every man will say 'not a word to-day ' — come an' try it." And he drew John along with him.

They reached the group after a short walk. Colonel Fair introduced John as Judge Rockwell. He shook hands with some of the men, and with a sly twinkle in his eye asked, "Well, gentlemen, what's the news?" The men looked sadly at one another and mournfully replied, "Not a word — you got any?"

The men regarded John in sullen silence. At last a good-natured-looking fat man, who appeared to be the proprietor of the store, seemed to realize that John was in an awkward position. He kindly came to the rescue.

"I reckon you'll like this country, sar," he said,

as he pushed his hat up from his face. "Good country, I reckon. Mighty easy fo' a man to make a livin' down yer. Right smart of chances, I reckon."

"That's jest what ails the country," broke in Colonel Fair. "It's too powerful easy to make a livin' here. If you fellers had to scratch a little harder you'd be better off. But it's just as I tell ye — you've all got to die before this country can come up any. You all know it, an' there ain't no use tryin' to dodge it."

John was surprised at the way the crowd took this verbal attack. He fully expected to see them start up and attack the blunt speaker. Not a word was said, however. The men all glanced sullenly at each other, but made no audible reply. After a few ordinary remarks John and Colonel Fair walked on down the street. As they passed away John caught a glimpse at the downcast faces of several of the white men. They must have hated his companion intensely. Colonel Fair noticed his surprised look.

"I reckon they hate me," he said, "but it don't make no odds. I've got a good place, out of debt, an' money ahead. I don't owe 'em nothin', an' a heap of 'em do owe me. They can't run me out, an' they've jest got to stand up an' hark at what I tell 'em. You're a stranger here, an' don't know what's goin' on. You'll find out quick enough, an' I'll be glad to help ye all I kin."

They stopped at the bank, where John was introduced to several other Northern men. They were all quiet, determined, marked men, who looked him straight in the eye. They all seemed glad to see him, and were ready to give advice and information. John easily obtained the needed knowledge in regard to his place. It was close to Colonel Fair's plantation. That gentleman invited John to stay at his house until the place could be cleared up.

"I reckon it's nothin' but a nest o' niggers now," was Colonel Fair's opinion.

John gladly accepted the invitation. He promised to come out on Monday for the purpose of looking over the place. He shook hands with his new friends at last and started back to the hotel. He began to fear that Nellie might need him. As he passed by the store where they had spoken with the group of loungers, the fat proprietor smiled with so much good-nature that John stopped, Yankee-like, for a talk. The crowd of lazy men had departed in search of more comfortable seats, and the fat man was able to reserve the best chair for his own use, and give John the choice of all the rest. John sat down beside his portly friend and glanced curiously up and down the street.

"I reckon we have a heap mo' niggers than you all does," said the fat man, as he saw John's look of curiosity.

"I guess you do," said John cautiously. "We don't have only here and there one."

"I don't reckon you knows what the nigger is. Down yer whar we have 'em all around us, we understand 'em. You all has ter come whar they is befo' you kin know much about 'em. The nigger" — here he waved one lazy hand in front of him — "ain't never a-goin' to be nothin', an' he don't know how ter learn. He's sorter like a pinter dog. He can read an' write, but the mo' he learns, the mo' devil he gits inter him. You'll see jest how it is befo' you've ben yer a year. You give the nigger his schoolin' an' ye spoil him to wonct. He wants ter go right ter teachin' or preachin'. He don't know nothin' an' he never will. There they be to-day. I don't reckon there's a dozen in this town that knows what they come in fer. They spend their time an' money on some little trick that ain't got nothin' to it, an' there they be."

At this moment two negroes came up to the store to make a purchase. The fat merchant was obliged to close his argument while he attended to the wants of his customers. During his absence John walked away. He had listened to some curious views surely. It seemed as if all the men he met eyed him suspiciously — all but the Jews — they smiled, and invited him to walk in. The negroes all bowed or touched their hats. John returned all these salutations, much to the scorn of the white men who watched him. He reached the hotel to find Nellie and the little girl sitting on the piazza. Sleep had driven all the homesickness away, for the time, and they were eagerly watching the curious things about them. John brought out a chair, and, taking the little girl on his knee, told them all about his adventures in the town. Nellie was anxious to move out to the plantation at once, and John decided to go out on Monday to look the house over. As they sat talking, a man came out of one of the rooms that opened into the hall. He looked cautiously about, as if to see that no one was watching him, and then walked up to John with his hand held out, as he introduced himself.

"My name's Battle — I live up in Ohio — don't make no odds jest where — I come from York State when I was a boy, an' I'll be dogged if I ain't glad to see a Northern man — only 'twon't do ye no good to say I told ye so," he added, as he glanced behind him. "Of course I ain't no special friend of these folks, an' I ain't got no notion of gittin' 'em down on me — but jest you an' me a-talkin' — I'm dogged if I ain't glad to see ye."

John shook hands with the cautious stranger, and introduced Nellie. Mr. Battle brought a chair from the hall, and placed it so near John that he could talk without the least risk of attracting attention to himself.

He was a short man with a stoop in the shoulders, and a head almost completely bald. A slight rim of gray hair ran just above his ears and under his chin. It seemed as if his bare head had been pushed up through a woollen bag, and that the edges of the bag had fallen over. He had a large, good-natured-looking mouth and nose. His eyes were small and partly hid by shaggy eyebrows. Mr. Battle held out his hands to little Nellie and made up a face that was intended to show that he was ready to play with her. After a little urging the little girl left her father and went to Mr. Battle's chair. He pulled out his watch and held it to her ear a moment, and then began a careful examination of his pocket to see if the piece of candy was still there. These pleasant advances captivated the little girl, and she climbed on his knee, taking care to show John and her mother that this was only a temporary arrangement.

"Jest gut in, ain't ye?" said Mr. Battle, when the little girl had settled in his lap.

"Yes, we come in this mornin'. I s'pose you've ben here quite a spell, ain't ye?" John answered cautiously.

"Wal, no, I ain't been here no great sight o' time, after all. I just came down to sorter look up a little property, like. My wife's mother, ye see, has considerable property, like, an' sence I quit farmin' I ain't done much but sorter run round an' look after it. I've been sorter lookin' round fer a spell, an' I'm jest about done now — an', jest me an' you a-talkin', I won't be a mite sorry when I get outer this country agin."

John said nothing, but let the old gentleman talk on as he pleased.

"I've alluz heard a good deal about this country, an' I'm glad I've had a good chance to sorter look it over. A feller can't tell nothin' about what the prospects is till he comes and sorter sees for himself. Now you take these niggers" — and he looked carefully about to see that he was alone — "they don't seem ter have much *man* about 'em, do they? I'll be dogged ef they don't 'pear ter be a sorter shiftless set like. 'Pears ter me, ef I was down here myself, I'd hate to have 'em a-runnin' me. Now we've gut niggers up where I live, but they gut some *man* to 'em. They 'pear ter be right up onto business, right straight along. These fellers here is alluz leanin' up agin a house. I'll be dogged if *white* folks 'pear ter have much more life in 'em. Jest look at the sidewalks they gut in this town. I jest wanter take me a hoe and go ter scrapin' 'em off myself. I've ben out in the country, an' I'll be dogged if it don't beat all how they farm it. Great big houses — all entry an' doors — no tools, an' a great crowd of lazy niggers, jest eatin' their heads off."

At this moment the supper bell rang, and Mr. Battle put the little girl down and beckoned the others to follow him into the dining-room.

"I guess we'd better sorter fill up our places, hadn't we?" he said as he led the way from the piazza. "Don't it beat all, though, what they give us t' eat here? I'm dogged ef I know what I'm eatin' half the time, but I jest shet my eyes an' risk it."

He was not entirely satisfied yet, for he stopped John in the middle of the hall to whisper, " Of course I don't know who you be — don't make no special odds what my politics is, you understand — that's jest me an' you talkin'."

The supper was a pleasanter meal to John and Nellie than the dinner had been. Mr. Battle was a great help. He talked to every one and asked question after question. The boarders seemed to regard him with a pitying scorn, but he never noticed it.

"What's them?" he asked, as the waiter handed him a new dish.

"Grits," was the answer.

"What be they made of? I'm sorter new here, ye

see, an' I wanter be able to answer all questions when I git home. I expect I'll be in the wetness stand for quite a spell."

The supper came to an end at last, and John and Nellie went to their own room. Here they were followed by Mr. Battle.

"I s'pose you folks is singers, ain't ye?" he asked, after a short conversation. "Because if ye be, there ain't no reason why we can't have us a good sing. I sing bass myself — I do. There's a sort of an organ like into my room, an' pears ter me we might sing a tune or two without no trouble."

They all adjourned to Mr. Battle's room, where the "sort of an organ like" proved to be an old-fashioned melodeon. With Nellie at this instrument and John and Mr. Battle to sing, they began. In a short time one after another of the boarders dropped in, and quite a large choir was formed. This little "sing" did them all good. When they stopped at last and John and Nellie went to their own room, Mr. Battle seemed to feel that he ought to say a word to cheer the young people. Perhaps he feared that his own dismal view of Southern society might make them homesick.

"I s'pose like enough you may feel sorter homesick, Mis' Rockwell. Ye mustn't do that, 'twon't do ye no good. My folks to home is sorter alone, I expect, but I sorter fixed things sos't they'll git along. I went out an' gut 'em a ham, there's milk an' bread comes right to the door an' all these things. I expect they'll git along fust-rate."

CHAPTER XV.

THE MAN AT THE DOOR

SUNDAY morning found our friends up bright and early. Mr. Battle took his station on the piazza within sight of the dining-room door. When John appeared, the old gentleman at once picked up the discussion of the night before.

"How's all the folks this mornin'?" he asked, as he shook John's hand. "Beats all how holler a feller gits in this climate, don't it?" he added as he glanced in the direction of the cook-house. "If I was runnin' this place I'd had them niggers rousted out long afore this. It beats all how these niggers lives, don't it?" Mr. Battle dropped into his confidential tone again. "I gut me a hoss t'other day an' rode out inter the country a piece. I kinder thought I'd go inter one of these cabins jest ter see how they looked. They told me it was jest as they have it in winter. Don't never fix nothin' up. I could take me a pile of boards an' throw 'em into a better house than them folks had, easy. Big cracks under the door, an' holes in the sides big enough for me to shove my hand through anywhere. There they live, jest like that. I could see jest how 'tis. What's your idees about 'em?"

John was getting a little nettled at the old gentleman's talk. He could not help remembering what

Sol had done for him years before, and how that despised negro cabin had seemed like home to him.

"My idee is," he said stoutly, "that the darkies would come out all right if they only had a chance. They're gonter do jest what the white folks do. If white folks shirk an' loaf around, ye can't blame the darky for doin' the same thing. I ain't gonter be ser quick ter give this thing up till I see some of 'em have a fair chance."

This was a long speech for John to make, but he meant every word of it, and Mr. Battle made haste to put himself in a position where he could reach either side of the question.

"Like enough that's so — like enough they ain't had no fair chance. You train 'em up an' give 'em a chance an' they might do fust-rate. I ain't gut no idea that I'm a-gonter stay here an' try it myself, though."

He was about to answer Mr. Battle in a very forcible manner, when Nellie — who had probably heard part of the conversation — came from her room. When she came John forgot all about the argument, and Mr. Battle entirely forgave the late cook as he played with little Nellie. He got a chance at John again as they went into breakfast.

"I dunno who you be, of course, but I'll be dogged if I don't like ye. If you ever come 'round within gunshot of me, I want you to hunt me up."

It did not seem like a Sunday morning breakfast to John and Nellie. There were no baked beans on the table. It is a fact that the true New Englander sadly misses this toothsome evidence of the day of rest. The bean worshippers are sincere in their religion — how sincere they themselves do not know until they go into the land of "hog and hominy." After breakfast John and Nellie walked through the town and out to a hill that rose just behind an old church. They left Mr. Battle discussing religion with one of the boarders.

The streets were dull and deserted. The stores were all closed, and, save a small group in front of the court-house, there were no white men to be seen. A barber's shop was open, and a number of negroes lounged about in the sun. Out on the hill they sat under a large tree and looked down upon the village. They sat there and talked as only such a family ever can talk — words of sympathy, of strength, and of tenderness — till the bell on the church below them began to ring out the first call to worship. The sound of the bell seemed to carry their thoughts back to the gray old church at Breezetown. They could see the old home picture as they sat in the sunshine looking down over the dull town.

The white-haired sexton was pulling slowly and heavily at the bell rope. The rope coiled and twisted about his feet as though seeking to trip him up. The church stood open, and the bright sunshine was working its way up over the battered pews to the pulpit. The little organ was opened. The choir had been practising. It would take a wonderful amount of practising to fill the gap caused by the loss of John and Nellie. The rough farm wagons, laden with worshippers, were crawling lazily over the sandy road. The flowers in the minister's garden were nodding brightly in the sun. The birds were singing in the little grove back of the church. There would be a vacant space in Uncle Nathan's pew that would make many a heart sad and add a tenderness to the minister's prayer. It was the hardest hour in the lives of John and Nellie — worse than the parting at home. They began to realize at last how far they had gone from the old life, and what a lonely, heart-breaking work it would be to grow up into this new one. But they never doubted and never questioned. They looked at the little girl and then at each other, and were satisfied.

The bell brought them to their feet, and they walked slowly back to the hotel to prepare for church. The very thought of worship seemed to give them comfort. Just as the sound of the bell carried them back, in thought, to the old home, with all its cherished associations, so the very thought of going to church seemed to strengthen them and drive the homesickness away.

They were indebted to Mr. Battle for facts concerning the religious condition of the community. Mr. Battle had spent the morning in drawing out his fellow-boarders. He had obtained much valuable information, which he made haste to condense for the benefit of John and Nellie. He was on the watch for them, and, on their return, he followed them into their room and carefully shut the door.

"Where ye goin' to church this mornin'?" he asked. "It would be a good thing for ye to go, I s'pose. Give ye a good chance to see how folks looks, an' then agin it'll show folks that ye're all ready ter chum right in with 'em. Guess we'd better go 'long, hadn't we?"

"I'm gonter find my church, an' go to that," said John, simply.

"What church is yourn? I guess I kin tell ye somethin' about that. I've kinder talked things over with some of the folks."

"I am a Unitarian," said John.

"Oh, you be?"

Mr. Battle had not the least idea in the world what "Unitarian" meant, and he made haste to change the drift of the conversation a little.

"I guess ye're sorter like me. I don't favor no 'special church. I go to 'em all, so's ter show that there ain't no feelin' agin 'em. Can't nobody say I've ever slighted any of 'em. You folks ain't gut no church here. The Methodists an' the Baptists 'pear ter have the crowd in this place. Them Presbyterians seems ter be sorter strong, but they're sorter split up like. That makes 'em sorter weakenin'. I guess we'd better go 'round ter the Methodist this mornin', hadn't we? I've sorter figgered it out, and 'pears ter me that's our best holt. Our landlady here is a Methodist, an' that might make a little difference on board. Then, agin, there was a feller this mornin' said he'd kinder like ter have us set up in the choir. I s'pose he heard our music last night. Like enough he heard me singin' bass. Guess we'd better go 'round, hadn't we? Ye see they're buildin' a new church now, sos't they hold services in the court-house. Sorter give ye a chance o look 'round that, too."

As Mr. Battle was talking, the lady of the house came to the door and invited John and Nellie to attend her church. Her invitation had more effect than Mr. Battle's arguments, and the young people gladly accepted. They soon started for the courthouse under the pilotage of Mr. Battle, who seemed to feel that they were under his immediate charge.

"They's one sorter cur'us thing about this church business," remarked the guide, as they reached the street. "The niggers don't go to the same church that the white people do at all. They sorter git off by themselves, an' have preachin'. As nigh as I can come at it, from what they tell me, the Methodist church sorter split like when the war bruck out, an' they ain't never come back, except that the niggers is sorter in with the Northern end, whilst the Southern end sorter hangs out. P'raps I ain't gut it straight, but 'pears ter me the niggers an' the white Methodists up North forms one sorter church, an' the folks here is sorter in another click. Beats all, don't it? They say these niggers ain't got no idee of religion at all. They jest go off by themselves, an' folks say it beats all what they do an' say."

John studied a while before he made any answer. Such talk made him think of the matter as he had never done before. He looked at several groups of negroes that passed on their way to church. The men were neatly dressed, and the women were radiant in many-colored costumes. At last he said, slowly: —

"It 'pears to me that that's jest where these folks makes a big mistake. They send these darkies 'way off somewhere, where there ain't nobody to show 'em what's right, an' then blame 'em because they don't do as well as white folks. I don't s'pose that the common run of these darkies has got much sense, but it ain't agoin' to give 'em any more to send 'em 'way off by themselves. You set a fool to teachin' fools, an' you'll raise fools faster'n ye can take care of 'em."

This was a new line of thought to Mr. Battle. He could only say, "Like enough that's so." By the time he had found any other answer they had reached the court-house.

A small group of young men stood about the door. These stood back as John's party approached. Once inside, a tall man at the end of the room rose and beckoned them to a place at the front. After taking their seats, they looked carefully about them. They were in a large, high hall. The walls were discolored in many places, and a colony of industrious spiders had left their marks all over the corners of the ceiling. A light railing marked off perhaps one-third of the room — drawing the dividing line between lawyers and spectators. The seats were low and rough, and many an industrious knife had used them for an autograph album. The men sat on one side of the room, while the women filled the other. Behind the bar, at one side, sat a line of old, white-haired men, with their heads bent forward upon their canes. At the other side, the members of the choir were gathered about a small organ. The singers were mostly bright, young girls, there being but three men to hold up the masculine portion of the music. Mr. Battle went up and took his seat with the choir. He tried to get John and Nellie to follow him, but they preferred to stay in the congregation. The preacher sat on a little platform at the extreme end of the room. It was the place usually reserved for the judge. Just over his head stood a small statue of "Justice." By some accident the bandage over the eyes of this image had been broken, and one eye looked carefully at the scales held in the hand. The dust of time and neglect had done its best to take the place of the bandage, but it was not much of a success. The eye still kept upon the scales.

The church services were conducted with spirit and dignity. There was nothing about the sermon that could not have been said at the old church at Breezetown. Many of the expressions seemed odd to the New England people — as, for instance, the preacher spoke of giving a great "dining." In making an illustration of the freedom of salvation, he said: "Suppose you were all invited to attend a great dining. You would all go, I reckon. The man who gave the dining would come out of his house and say, 'You are all free to come. This is for you. You are all free to attend this dining.'"

John had somehow expected that the preacher would allude to the political situation in his sermon. There was nothing of the kind to be observed. The sermon was simply a plain, earnest talk, and John felt better after hearing it. The hymns, in which Mr. Battle's bass did yeoman service, were well sung. There was one deep alto voice in the choir

that swept like a flood of melody through the hymns.
At the last prayer the people all knelt together.
The sun shone brightly on the white-haired group at
the side. The old men prayed earnestly, with their
arms thrown over the railing. Kneeling there at
their side it did not seem possible to John that he
had fought these men, and that these women had
cursed him so terribly.

One thing happened that caused John a great deal
of study. As he entered the building he had noticed
a man of about his own age standing near the door.
This man stood in a humble, lifeless attitude, with
his hat pulled down over his eyes. John could only
see a portion of the face, but there was something
about it that made him stop in surprise. He could
not tell what it was — he was ashamed of himself
for stopping — yet when Nellie pulled at his arm he
went on into the court-house, trying to think where
he had seen that face before. It seemed burned
upon his memory, and yet he could not tell where it
had looked into his life. The man at the door did
not notice John at all. He pushed farther into the
corner, but his eyes were bent upon a young woman
who came slowly up the steps just behind John
and Nellie. He kept his eyes on the ground as
she came in the door, only now and then glancing
up at her face. She walked proudly past him, without
even looking in his direction.

She was a small woman — about as large as Nellie.
Her hair was black as jet, and her face pale and
pinched. Her eyes seemed to flash as she passed by
the man in the doorway, and her mouth came firmly

together as she turned her head away. The man hung his head still lower as she entered the room. He came in at length, and sat on the end of the row where she was sitting. He kept his eyes straight ahead, and never looked at her until she bent forward during the last prayer. Then he watched her with a wistful look in his eyes. After the service he walked slowly out with the rest. He seemed to be alone. Few people spoke to him, and John saw him at last mount his horse and ride slowly out of town.

John and Nellie talked about him as they walked home from church. Mr. Battle stayed behind. He wished to practise with the choir, and there was a good prospect of his being invited to address the Sunday-school. John was greatly puzzled. He could not bring himself to remember where he had seen that face, and yet he remembered it well. Nellie laughed at him. She had only noticed that the strange man was dreadfully in love with the pale woman in black. She was glad John had noticed the man, for now he could tell just how *he* had looked on a certain memorable occasion. John laughed at this and said he was sure he had never looked quite like that; but Nellie was sure of it, so he said nothing more about it, though he still studied away to try and see if he could not tell where he had seen the stranger.

As they walked slowly onward, a man came briskly behind them. John turned aside to make room for passing, but the new-comer did not seem at all disposed to hurry by. He seemed so evidently desirous of speaking that John nodded and at last held out his hand. The stranger shook the proffered hand heartily.

"Mr. Rockwell, I reckon," he said.

"Yes, sir: that's my name," answered John.

"I'm mighty glad to see you, sar," said the newcomer, as he shook hands again. "My name is Bond — David Bond. I come from Iowa. I heard that you come in last night, an' I wanted to speak to ye after preachin', but somehow I didn't like to bother ye. My wife thought I'd better step along an' invite ye to come round an' eat dinner with us. We ain't gut no great show, but, such as 'tis, we'd like to have ye come an' eat."

There was a bluff heartiness about this invitation that pleased John and Nellie greatly. It came nearer the home style of doing such things than anything they had found since they had left New England. They accepted at once, and followed Mr. Bond up a side street till he stopped before a little cottage that stood back from the street in a perfect mass of vines and trees. "This is my place," said Mr. Bond, as he opened the gate for them to pass through.

Mrs. Bond stood at the front of the house to welcome them. She was a thin, sickly woman with a sweet, patient face, that told of strengthening suffering. She greeted the new-comers so pleasantly that Nellie could not help kissing her. This act tended to bring out the best possible feeling among the whole party. John and Mr. Bond, of course, had to shake hands again, and Mr. and Mrs. Bond had to kiss little Nellie, while John gathered about him the small army of little people that came trooping out of the house. Nellie afterwards told John that it seemed just like meeting "home folks."

After a short talk Mrs. Bond excused herself. The dinner was well under way, and she was obliged to superintend it. Nellie went too, though Mrs. Bond tried to make her remain on the piazza. She did not like to ask her visitor to work, but Nellie was determined to help. Most of the children followed the women, and Mr. Bond and John were left to talk.

John simply asked a few questions and let Mr. Bond talk. He had listened to so many different opinions that he hardly knew what to say. Mr. Bond seemed glad of the chance of telling his story. It had been locked up in his heart too long. It seemed to take some of the bitterness away to relate it to friendly ears. He talked so long and earnestly that both of the men were surprised when the crowd of children came rushing back with a loud call for dinner. The two men rose and followed the little army of hungry mouths back to the dinner-table, where the two women were waiting. The baby — of course there had to be a baby in such a well ordered family — was staring from the arms of a little negro boy as they passed through the hall. David caught the little end of the family on his shoulder, and carried him in triumph into the room. When they sat at the table, baby sat on his father's knee in order to save room.

The dinner was a very merry one. To be sure the table was small and the company was a large one, yet the two families were on such good terms that a little crowding did not hurt them at all — in fact it did them good. The little negro boy, with one or two of the smaller children to help him wash dishes and spoons, did nobly as a waiter. The children who helped him sat at the ends of the table, in convenient places for sliding in and out of their chairs without giving a serious shock to the whole company. Sometimes they took part of their dinner with them and ate with one hand while they helped with the other. The dinner was a great success. There was nothing elegant about it, but everybody, down to the baby, had enough to eat. The guests felt that they were being handsomely treated, and the host and hostess knew that their friends enjoyed themselves. How could a dinner be more of a success? When it was finished, David showed John about the little place. By hard work and study the few rough acres had been turned into a garden. There was a small vineyard, a little orchard, a good garden, and a pasture for the cow. Below the garden fence was a rough hillside, cut with great gullies that seemed to have turned red with the blood of murdered agriculture. On the other side of the fence was the neat garden. It seemed as if some monster had gnawed its way up to the fence and then turned back in rage before the careful culture that dulled its cruel teeth. The red gullies had been closed up and every foot of land inside the fence was doing its duty. David pointed out the difference to John.

"Five years ago," he said, "it was all just like that land below that fence. Now you see what a little work and mother-wit have done. They told me all along that I couldn't raise grapes or apples or peaches in this country. They all said this land would wash out. Here it is, an' it don't look like it was goin' to wash much this year. You can raise anything you want in this country. People hang onto cotton an' won't touch nothin' else. They buy their meat an' corn an' pay three prices for 'em. They can raise every ounce of meat an' every peck of corn right in this country, an' they have got to do it or leave for some other State where the land ain't wore out. They have got to pick up Yankee farmin' an' the Yankee style of doin' things, whether they want to or not."

As John and Nellie walked back to the hotel, they talked over the events of the day. Mrs. Bond had told Nellie her side of the life during the "Radical rule."

John studied away in silence for a moment. Then he said, suddenly:

"Are you sorry we came down here?"

"Not a mite," said Nellie, brightly. "We shall get along all right, I'm sure — only don't say a word about politics, John. It won't do us any good and it might hurt us dreadfully."

They found Mr. Battle waiting on the piazza.

"Where you folks ben?" he asked, as they came up. "I've sorter lost run of ye sence the preachin' — ye orter stayed an' heard what I said to the Sunday-school. They 'peared to like it first-rate."

"We've ben makin' a visit," said John.

"Where'd ye go? — beats all how you folks pick

up friends, don't it? There was a feller like to invited me home ter dinner, but somehow he didn't git round to it. Beats all how these folks sorter hang off an' never come up when ye want 'em. Goin' to preachin' agin this evenin', I suppose, ain't ye?"

John and Nellie decided to stay at home, and, after further talk, Mr. Battle went alone to contribute his bass to the volume of the choir's music.

CHAPTER XVI.

RUN TO RUINS

As soon as breakfast was over, Monday morning, John went to the livery stable to secure a horse. A sleepy negro was the only business occupant of the stable, and, while this individual was caring for the horse, John walked slowly up the main street. He felt so full of energy that he could not sit down and wait. There were very few people abroad. The Jews were all in their stores, and a few men sat along in front of the buildings, smoking their pipes as if the week could never be properly opened without an extra flood of smoke. They smoked with great seriousness and kept their eyes fixed upon the ground. There was no energy about their pleasure. The smoke crawled lazily out of their mouths, as if caring little what its future might be. A melancholy individual was standing in front of the store where John had talked with the fat merchant — a tall, thin man with a yellow face and hair of the same color. The face was long and thin — the cheeks hollow — and the eyes were small and dull with a heavy, boiled appearance. The forehead receded as if in haste to meet the tangle of hair that looked as if the thin man had placed a quantity of poorly cured hay under his hat. The face looked as if this hay had been steeped and the water permitted to slowly trickle down to the chin. The man was clothed in a suit of jean of a most uncertain color. His clothing hung about him with about as much grace — as John expressed it — as the week's washing hung on the clothes-line. A pair of great shapeless shoes covered his feet. He had evidently just driven into town, and was resting against a rickety wagon before which stood two stunted oxen, leaning against each other for support. The man held an empty bag in his hand.

As John came nearer, this melancholy individual started from his position near the wagon, and walked slowly and despairingly into the store. The fat proprietor met him at the door, and John followed the two, curious to see what the mission of such a melancholy specimen of humanity could be. After a long discussion the customer bought a peck of corn and a great lump of salt pork. He looked longingly at other provisions which the proprietor temptingly displayed, but they seemed to be too expensive for him. He walked back to his wagon at last — walked wearily, as if the rust had gathered on all his joints. After packing his supplies away in the wagon, he started his gaunt oxen into activity, and walked down the street at their side, cracking his great whip as he walked. It seemed like a perfect picture of agricultural despair.

The portly merchant, rendered affable by his early sale, smiled as he glanced at John's face.

"Mighty hard way ter live, I reckon," he said, as he nodded in the direction of his gaunt customer.

"He'll go out till he eats that meat up, an' then he'll come back for mo'."

"How do you git yer pay?" asked John.

The customer had paid no cash for the goods, and John could hardly see how such a looking man could secure credit. At home, a merchant would not have trusted such a man with a box of matches.

"Oh, that's all right, I reckon. We don't lose no pay scarcely. Them things is all paid for now, ye might say. We jest take a lien on his crop, an' when he brings it in we run up his account an' start him off agin for next year. Such fellers as him don't raise nothin' but cotton. We keep 'em in corn an' meat an' take their crop to pay for it. They might raise every pound o' meat, I reckon. Folks uster could befo' the war, but that ain't none of my business, I reckon. Them fellers don't never git nothin' ahead. They ain't gut no pluck, an' they won't never be nothin'. I reckon they'll all have ter move out for Texas, some day. I'd hate powerful to see 'em go, for there's a heap of money to be made tradin' with 'em."

"Where do ye git yer pork an' corn?" asked John.

"Right smart of it comes from Chicago. It costs a heap to git it yer, too."

"Couldn't ye raise the heft of it here?"

"I reckon so. I reckon we cud raise it all if folks warn't so powerful lazy."

John walked back to the stable, thinking over what he had seen and heard. If this farmer was a fair type of the men who were to be his neighbors, he would certainly have very little in the way of society. The facts concerning the provisions pleased him exceedingly. With keen Yankee thrift he saw at once the key to the situation. With these thousands of people raising nothing but cotton, and buying such a large proportion of their meat, the meat producer or stock grower would be in a position to reap an abundant profit.

Colonel Gray had given John unlimited authority. The officer knew nothing of agriculture, and he had the utmost confidence in John's wisdom and ability. He stood ready to supply any reasonable capital, and place the entire management of it in John's hands. John was acquainted with but one style of farming, and he was not the man to experiment with the property of others. The first principle of agriculture, as he understood it, was to supply as much as possible of the food used at home. On the thin, rocky farm in Maine, he had raised almost all the provisions needed in the family. Those that could not be raised at home were bought with the money obtained from the sale of extra hay or stock. This was the only style of farming that John understood, and the more he saw of the South, the more he became convinced that the system could be made very successful on a larger scale.

John rode slowly out of town, over a lonely country road that went crawling lazily over little sand hills and low, level places, as if it had been left to pick out its own way. John rode slowly. He was painfully aware of the fact that he was not a graceful rider. He preferred to let the horse select its own pace rather than urge the animal to a rate of speed that would betray his own awkwardness. The animal he bestrode was of such a very mild disposition that the arrangement suited him exactly. He went on with a long, swinging walk, peculiar to the Southern riding horse, tossing his head slowly up and down, to show how well this pace suited him.

It was not a cheerful ride. The country seemed, somehow, to be covered with a shadow. The woods were green and beautiful, the flowers were springing by the road, and the sun came sparkling in right good humor — yet there was something, it was hard to say what, that seemed to deaden and chill what should have been a beautiful picture. No doubt if John had never seen the hills and lanes of New England, he would have been satisfied with this prospect. No doubt the picture was more magnificent than any he had ever seen on his gray old rocks at home, but he could not appreciate it. Most of the land near the road seemed dead and wasted. A few scattering fields of corn or cotton showed green and beautiful in the sunshine, but the vast tract of land stretched back from the road, dull and gnawed by great waste patches that disfigured its surface, disappointing the visitor. There was only a rank growth of weeds or worthless grasses to cover its nakedness. In the great agricultural prize fight it had been soundly whipped.

The fields were not even used as pastures. In New England every acre would have been dotted with cattle or sheep. Here, the only stock to be seen were a few work horses or mules, and some angular cows that kept close to the house, as if for society. In place of the great smile of hospitality that seems to light up the front of a New England home, a pack of savage dogs came tearing out at almost every yard to snarl and bark the sentiments of the family. No wonder the country seemed dreary and lifeless to John. There was no life and bustle of industry. All nature lay idle and wasted. There is nothing but work, or the evidence of it that can put true beauty into a landscape.

There were but few houses to be seen along the road. A few negro cabins, rough, and broken, and disorderly, each with its little patch of cotton or "truck," stood at wide intervals. At longer distances, the house of some large planter would start gloomily out from its little grove of trees. Most of them were massive structures, with wide piazzas and great pillars in front. They all seemed neglected and gloomy. The paint had been worn away, and never replaced. The grounds, planned in the days of magnificence, before the war, had never been kept up. Now, the weeds and grass ran over walks and flower-beds, and choked out the beauty of the original design. The fences were ragged and unpainted. All things bore the mark of some terrible blight that was still eating its way to the heart.

John was directed to his own place by an old negro, who sat sunning himself in front of a cabin. This old fellow pointed, with his stick, a short distance down the road, to a place where a broken gate admitted a side track into a small grove. John rode on in the direction thus indicated, and halted at the gate for a first view of his new home. The gate had fallen directly across the road, and several teams had evidently been driven over it. Some of the slats had been cut off for firewood. The fence was falling in many places. The road wound gracefully up through the little grove, to the front of a large white house, inclosed by a low picket fence. The house looked dingy and dirty. The paint had peeled away in spots, and the blinds hung broken and unjointed, or stood up against the house. Many of the windows were broken, and the door that opened into the wide hall was off its hinges. It stood helplessly up against the side of the hall, leaving the open door to grin over its victory. There were great dingy spots of decay about the door and windows, like the dark lines that gather about the mouth and eyes of a sick person. The little yard in front of the house was foul with weeds and vines. It looked like a face on which is growing a two-weeks beard. It is too short to be picturesque, and too long to be tidy.

As John rode in from the gate, he found a negro working by the side of the driveway. It was John's first view of Southern haymaking, and he watched the process with a curious mixture of feelings. The negro had gathered his hay into a number of small piles. He was engaged in carrying it to some point behind the house. He had a broken wheelbarrow, which he placed at some central point. Then, with a long-handed shovel, he made a trip to each little pile, returning with a shovelful to the wheelbarrow. When about one-fourth of an ordinary "forkful" had been collected in this vehicle, he started leisurely with his load, stopping to "rest" at short intervals. John watched one of these trips without a word. When the negro came back, he ducked his head, with, " Howdy, boss?"

"Why don't ye use yer fork an' take a good-sized load?" asked John.

" I ain't gut nary a one, boss," was the answer, as the negro stopped work to lean on his shovel and scratch his head.

"What'd ye cut that hay with?" asked John, as he dismounted and fastened his horse to a tree. The ground from which the hay had been cut looked more like a shingled roof than the smooth mowing ground at home.

" I reckon I done cut it with a hoe, boss."

The negro spoke as though he considered the only surprising thing connected with this fact to be the thought that a white man should not know what tools were in use.

As John was speaking, two men came riding along the road. At the gate they separated. One came up the driveway to the house, while the other rode on down the road towards the town. John knew the first to be Colonel Fair, while the other was the strange man he had noticed at the court-house the day before. Colonel Fair rode up and fastened his horse to a tree. He shook hands with John.

"Glad to see ye, judge. I thought I'd ride over, an' show ye round a little. Them niggers have jest about run things into the ground, I reckon. Here, you, Jim," he said, sharply, to the black haymaker, "go git me some water; bring it into the house."

Jim dropped his shovel, and at once started for the well, while Colonel Fair led the way into the house. John groaned aloud at the weedy garden and the dingy house.

The house was in wild disorder. In what was once the grand parlor the negroes had heaped a great pile of cotton. Most of the furniture had been removed. The walls were discolored, and the floors blackened. John wondered what Nellie would say when she saw the dirty rooms.

An old negro woman sat sunning herself on the back porch. She was smoking a short clay pipe, which she removed from her mouth as the two men came through the hall. After some discussion, she was induced to stir from her comfortable position and kindle a fire under a large kettle that hung between two posts in the yard. John was determined to begin operations at once, with a liberal application of hot water to the inside of the house. The black haymaker was detailed to assist the old woman; and leaving the two at their new work, the white men started out to look over the plantation.

It was a sad-looking sight to a thrifty farmer like John. Not one-tenth of the land was under cultivation in any form. A few fields of sickly cotton and consumptive corn, and some few truck patches around the negro cabins, comprised the entire agricultural system of the place. Great barren fields, covered with weeds, and cut and slashed with great red wounds, stretched away on every hand. There was only one small shed to serve for a barn. The only stock to be seen ran swiftly away at their approach, — a small drove of long-nosed hogs, and two bony cows; old tools, sticks, and litter of all kinds were scattered about. A gin-house stood at some little distance from the shed, and a pan for evaporating sugar was built near the well. The plantation had evidently been once owned by a large slaveholder. The negro cabins were numerous; they formed a little village just below the house. A few negroes were at work in the cotton fields, while a small army of little blacks ran about the place or played under the trees. John and Colonel Fair walked down to the little hill back of the gin-house, where they could look over the entire plantation. Never had John seen the literature of idleness, mismanagement, and lack of thrift written so deeply upon a farm. Here in this beautiful country, with every natural advantage, this grand old plantation, with all its wonderful possibilities, was running to a desert. He did not feel in the least discouraged. He had perfect confidence in his own ability. He knew what land could be made to do. His life had shown him what honest work could accomplish.

"What be they thinkin' of, to run a farm this way?" he asked, as they started back to the house. "I see that feller in front of the house loadin' hay with a round-pinted shovel. That beats all the hayin' I ever see."

"You'll see plenty more jest like it afore you git done here," said Colonel Fair. "They don't know no better, an' a heap of 'em don't care nothin' about learnin'. A heap of the white folks jest leave their farms to such niggers as you've gut here, an' then growl because they can't make nothin' at farmin'. The great trouble with this country " — he stopped in the shade of the gin-house to put a rivet on his argument — "is jest what I told you in town. There's a heap of old fellers here that jest live to keep this country back. I've lived here a good many years, an' I've studied these fellers like a book. I've done well here — mighty well. I started with nothin' an' now I kin show the best place in the county. I'm well fixed, but I ain't satisfied. There ain't nobody here for me to talk to as I wanter talk. It's worth a heap ter live up North among them people, I reckon. I'm mighty glad you've come in. We ain't had much for neighbors afore now. Old Doc. Lawrence is a nice old man, but he ain't gut no sense at all. Sorter cracked, I reckon. Foster over yunder ain't no company. Sorter slack, he is, an' yet, come to git him to work, he might do somethin'. We must work together an' try to fill this country up with Northern men. If we kin get a hundred families in round us here, we won't want no better thing at all. We can run the county an' fix things to suit us. I sorter like you. I reckon you've come here to stay. We can work together on a good many things."

As they walked in from the gin-house, John told all of his story that he thought advisable. He told enough to show Colonel Fair what he meant to try and do. His new neighbor showed much interest in the plans.

"You're gut jest the right idee," was his comment. "You kin turn every one of them rough-looking fields into a pasture. Don't try to raise nothin' but cotton. That's a good crop to raise, jest like they raise wheat at the North. Make it the surplus crop an' you've gut 'em."

They reached the house to find the cleaning operations suspended for the time being. The fire under the kettle had gone out while listening to an animated discussion on religion, that had been started by the haymaker and warmly taken up by the old woman. The two debaters stood by the side of the kettle, talking and gesticulating with such earnestness that they did not notice the approach of the white men. When they looked up to find that a new and critical audience had assembled, they dropped the debate and fell upon their work with a vigor which would, if kept up, soon have finished the job. The haymaker dropped upon his knees and put his breath to a more practical use, by blowing fresh life into the fire. The old woman hurriedly stirred the water, as if that process would hasten its heating. Colonel Fair smiled at John's expression of disgust. "That's all right," he said, "you've got to stay right over 'em an' *make* 'em work. That's jest nigger-like, an' you can't change it at all."

John did "stay over" them with a royal good will for the rest of the forenoon. He even took off his coat and worked with them. With an old broom and a bucket of hot water, they scrubbed out the hall and two rooms. John tried to find a scythe with which to mow the weeds that had formed a dense mat in the little yard. Such an implement was unknown on the plantation. The little hay that had been secured had been cut with hoes. John hunted out a negro who brought a great clumsy hoe with which he slashed the weeds. There was no such thing as a pitchfork on the place.

Colonel Fair rode away, on some errand of his own, shortly after John began work. At noon he came back and insisted that John should go home to take dinner with him. John was glad of this invitation. There was something about this blunt neighbor that he liked. Leaving the negroes at work, the two men rode out at the broken gate and down along the road over which John had come.

Colonel Fair's house stood about half a mile from John's gate. They were neighbors, as the two plantations joined. The house stood back from the road, in a beautiful group of trees. Everything about it was neat and orderly. The paint was fresh, the fences were well kept, and the lawn was clean and well arranged. It was a beautiful picture of thrift and comfort. There were no dead and wasted-looking fields in sight. Everything was covered with a beautiful cloak of green — Nature's bridal color.

"Looks sorter nice, don't it?" said Colonel Fair, as he reined in his horse at the gate. "It was wuss-lookin' than yours is when I fust took hold of it. It takes work, an' an almighty stout heart, to git along here, but it's sure to count in the end."

Colonel Fair's family consisted of his wife and two young boys. They all greeted John very pleasantly. The boys seemed a little strange to John. Born at the North and inheriting Northern sentiments and tastes, they had been brought up at the South, with all the peculiar influences that affect the Southern youth. They were different from Northern boys, and yet unlike the boys born at the South. Colonel Fair touched upon this very point when, after dinner, they drew their chairs out on the piazza.

"I'm mighty sorry," he said, "that I can't bring up my children at the North. It's mighty bad to have children, boys 'specially, come up here amongst these niggers. It spoils a smart boy to bring him up here where he kin git a nigger to breathe for him if he wants. The nigger was born to work an' he knows it. These boys understand jest how 'tis an' they are goin' ter shirk all they kin. You notice now in these Southern families, an' see if it ain't jest as I tell ye. The girls are the smartest every time. Nine times out of ten, the brains an' the 'git up' of the family will be found right in the girls. The woman of the next Southern generation will run things. Now you see if that ain't so."

"But what makes 'em let things run so ter ruins?" asked John. He could not bring himself to understand how men with ordinary common sense could live as most of the people were evidently living.

"They're sorter lazy, an' then agin they all wanter be boss. They kin all talk some big scheme about doin' things in a hurry, but you talk to 'em about usin' a lighter hoe, or ploughin' deeper, an' they won't listen to ye. Some like the story I heard a feller tell once about General Scott. They was fightin' the Mexicans, an' old Scott had his hands about full. Jest when the fight gut hottest, there riz up a cloud o' dust about a half a mile back of Scott's headquarters. Nobody knowed what 'twas. A squad rode back to look things up, an' when they come near they see a crowd of men markin' time in the road — jest kickin' up a big dust. The officer called out 'Who are ye?' One man stopped markin' time and yelled back, 'A regiment of Kentucky kernels come to reënforce Scott!' There warn't a private in the whole crowd — nobody to obey orders, and there they stood markin' time."

As Colonel Fair finished his story, and before he could make any application, a horseman came riding slowly in at the gate. He directed his horse up the driveway, and when within a short distance of the house stopped and held up several letters to indicate that he had brought the mail. John recognized the horseman at once. It was the man he had seen at the court-house who had watched the pale woman in black so closely. John knew he had seen that face before, and yet he could not tell where. He was glad to follow Colonel Fair down to the fence. He hoped to get a better look at the horseman. He followed so closely that an introduction was absolutely necessary.

The two men shook hands and glanced closely at each other. The name of Foster brought no intelligence to John. He knew he had never spoken with the man before, and yet there was something in the face that seemed natural. Jack Foster — for it was surely he — looked down into John's face with a puzzled expression. Where had he seen this tall Yankee before? He started once, as if about to speak, but at last, after a few commonplace remarks, he turned his horse and rode slowly back to the gate. Half-way down the road he turned back for another look at John. He nodded his head and closed his mouth firmly, while a bitter look crept over his face. Every movement of that little drama that had so rudely broken his life had been burned deeply into his memory. That famine-stricken face, looking up from that terrible Andersonville, rose in his mind again. He knew that John was the desperate prisoner. The man for whose sake he had killed his own happiness had come to live near him.

"Maybe he's come to bring me good luck," he muttered grimly. "He can't bring any more bad luck, I reckon."

"There's a man that orter make a good neighbor if somebody could only stir him up a little," said Colonel Fair, as Jack Foster rode away. "They don't like him fust-rate 'round here. They've gut somethin' agin him that dates 'way back to the war. He done somethin', I can't make out jest what it is, that they can't never git over. He went back on 'em some way. He ain't no coward, for I've seen him fight. But there's somethin' wrong an' they don't trust him. He won't never say nothin' about it to me. He's a good sharp feller, but somehow he ain't gut no ambition to fix up his place an' be somebody."

As John started back to work at his own plantation, Mrs. Fair came and invited him to bring Nellie and stay until his own house could be arranged. Colonel Fair seconded the invitation so heartily that John accepted at once. He rode back to town, stopping only for a moment at the plantation, to see that the work of cleaning was still going on. It was "going on," but so slowly that he saw it would never be finished until he superintended it in person. The negroes were applying the hot water as tenderly as they would have applied it to their own bodies. It is wonderful how laziness cultivates pity. The lazy man always seems to feel that the object upon which his work is exerted is in danger of being seriously injured.

John rode into town and had a busy afternoon. He bought a pair of horses and a wagon and such tools as he needed for immediate work. The little luggage that he had brought from New England was at the depot. With Nellie's help he selected enough furniture to furnish a few rooms of the great house. John was glad to be at work again. He worked with an energy that fairly surprised the natives. The men who sat in front of the stores watched him with sneers.

"He works mighty brash, don't he?" they muttered. "He'll git over that afore he's ben here long."

John gave his social standing a staggering blow before he went home. On his way to the hotel he stopped at the village well for a drink of water. An old, white-haired negro, bent and twisted with age, came hobbling up just as John reached the well. The old fellow caught hold of the rope to draw the water. He was pulling feebly at the heavy weight when John took the rope out of his hands.

"Let me pull it, uncle," he said. "I s'pose I've gut more muscle than you have."

Of course he should have waited and made the old fellow pull the weight alone, but John had curious notions with regard to gray hairs. He pulled up the water and then actually filled the cup and handed it to the old negro before he drank himself. The old fellow pulled off his hat in his great pleasure at this compliment. He did not take the cup, but motioned John to drink first. When John walked up the street, the old fellow stood watching him with admiring eyes.

After supper John sat on the piazza and told his wife and little Nellie all about the day's adventures. Mr. Battle was greatly interested in the story. He followed the party from their room, and questioned John very closely with regard to his plans and the value of the plantation.

"I s'pose you've gut quite a place out there, ain't ye? Must be worth a hundred thousand dollars, I expect."

"I don't know," said John, cautiously. He was getting a little tired of this constant questioning.

"Wal, call it seventy-five thousand — it must be worth that, I s'pose — ain't it?"

"I don't know," was John's only answer.

"Wal, say sixty thousand — there ain't no doubt about that, I s'pose?"

"I don't know how 'tis."

"Wal, say fifty thousand — it can't be no less than that, can it?"

John did not know, and Mr. Battle very accommodatingly reduced the price to twenty-five thousand. This had no better effect, and at last he changed his tactics a little.

"I s'pose you're somethin' like a feller that lived in our town a number o' years ago. He was a good, honest feller, but somehow or nuther he didn't seem to git along fust-rate. Folks sorter made fun of him. He couldn't go nowheres but he'd be the fool of the crowd. Gut so at last that he went away, an' folks sorter forgot him. After a year or so, back he come, an' I tell ye folks didn't make no more fun o' him. He'd done fust-rate in some new country, an' I s'pose he cud buy an' sell 'em all."

Mr. Battle might have produced other facts concerning his friend, had not the sound of the melodeon attracted his attention at this moment. He was pulled out of his chair by the music.

"Better come in an' sing, hadn't ye?" he asked, as he rose to go.

John and Nellie excused themselves. They were tired, and they wished to talk over the events of the day. So Mr. Battle went alone. In a short time they heard his bass forming a strong combination with the instrument. They were glad to see him go. They wished to talk alone.

John and Nellie sat and talked till the little girl fell asleep on her mother's lap. Then the little family went to their room.

"Do you know, John," said Nellie, as they stood watching the child asleep, "that I feel, somehow, that we are going to meet the man who let you get those flowers in that prison!"

"And I believe I've seen him already," said John, quickly, and he told her about Jack Foster and how he knew he had seen the man before.

"What if it should be him?" he asked suddenly.

"I hope it is; I shall be very glad, for I want to say something to him."

"What is it?" demanded John.

"Oh, you must wait and see," and the little woman reached up to kiss her husband.

CHAPTER XVII.

THE GERMS OF A NEW MANHOOD

THE rest of the week was packed full of work for John and Nellie. There was more to be done than they had supposed. After looking the house over carefully, John decided to make some extended repairs. This work would take some little time, and Nellie decided to stay with Mrs. Fair rather than try and occupy the house before it could be finished. She came to the plantation every day and helped John arrange for the future. John worked hard and thoughtfully. Acting upon Colonel Fair's advice, he determined to clear out half the negro cabins and turn them into stables or shelters for stock. Most of the negroes were working "on shares." He was able to arrange with them to leave when the crops should be gathered. Load after load of lumber was brought out from town, and John worked early and late to complete his arrangements for stock-growing.

Like most Northern men, John made a mistake, at first, in dealing with the negroes. He was too easy with them, and he expected them to do ordinary work without direction. He soon found that they took advantage of his lack of firmness. They became so familiar that he was obliged to be very strict with them in order that they might know their place. They were like great children in many things. Careless and good-natured, they would laugh and sing, or lie about in the sun and play some simple game. Well superintended and kept in good spirits, they did fair work, but the great majority of them were unable to plan their own work to any advantage. After John came to understand them, he got on better with his work than he did at first. He found, after many sore trials, that about the only way to succeed with the present system of negro labor is to give the negro to understand that he cannot enter the white man's place. Such, unfortunately, is the present idea. There are in every community a few clear-headed and dignified negroes, but the great masses of black workmen are ignorant, and cannot be governed as one would govern men of intelligence.

As John studied the matter, this question came up in his mind: "What shall we do with this mass of workmen when they learn, as they surely will, something of the dignity of manhood?" It will be impossible then to treat them as they are treated now. To say that they will not improve and grow out of their present ignorance, is to say that all history is a lie. John brought himself to believe that behind the negro's mask of ignorance and carelessness there lie the germs of a new manhood that will surely push to the outside. To be sure, the most of his negroes were lazy and careless. They were shockingly immoral. He was obliged to admit that he could not possibly allow them to eat at his table, or appear in his family, except as servants. Yet there were keen-minded and thoughtful negroes. Even his careless workmen, when they thought they had his entire confidence, showed that there was a little something of sober manhood hidden behind their black faces. That manhood will be developed — slowly, it may be imperceptibly — yet it will grow, and must, in time, assert itself.

A common impression prevails at the North that the Southern man treats the negro cruelly. The few old cases of slave-whipping or starving are quoted as being fair examples of the way in which the negroes were treated before the war. This idea is not a just one. The Southern man aims to treat the negro kindly, and to see that he does not suffer. There is no thought of a possible equality. He is simply dealing with a "nigger," who is treated kindly or affectionately, just as one would show affection for the family horse or the family cow.

People do not even blame the negro particularly for the part he took in the "Radical" government. The blame is laid upon the "Radicals," who organized the negroes, and supplied the brain power of the movement. The negro is regarded generally as harmless when left to himself, and treated as a valuable animal would be treated — kindly but firmly. He was simply a tool in the hands of designing "carpet-baggers." There was no particular reason why he should be greatly blamed for what had taken place. When we consider the condition of the ordinary negro, and the course of treatment that has placed him in his present position, we can understand why he is treated as he is, and what a disgust fills the heart of the Southern man or woman at the bare suggestion of living on terms of equality with former slaves.

John fought through the war with the belief that the sole object of the struggle was to free the slaves. Such was the real object, though it was covered for a time by questions of political economy. John came to the South with the idea firmly fixed in his mind that all the negro needed to make him a good citizen was a little encouragement and practical example. He had common sense enough to see, after a few weeks, that Northern arguments and theories would not work on Southern soil. While the Northern theory of negro advancement and intelligence might work to perfection in Pennsylvania or New York, it was destined to make a complete and ridiculous failure at the South at the present day, for the simple reason that there was no one to help the negro develop himself. He must do the work alone. Surrounded as he was by men and circumstances so directly opposed to his rapid advancement in intelligence and dignity, it was absurd to suppose that strange men, having only a theorist's idea of his nature and capabilities, men who could not even command the entire confidence of the communities in which they live, could deal with him as they would have dealt with ignorant workmen at home.

As matters stand to-day — with the brains, the money, and the majority of his party hundreds of miles away from him — the negro must work out his own social and political freedom. He can do it only by showing himself worthy to be called a man. He can do it only by writing a man's record on the pages of history. It will be a long and heart-breaking work, but the work will only develop a truer and nobler manhood. The white man can assist his black neighbor as a child might be taught — not by assuming that both are upon an equality, but by patient yet firm teaching — better yet by practical examples of industry and manhood.

It was a little awkward at first for John and Nellie to assume the roles of master and mistress. They had done all their own work so long that they hardly knew, at first, how to direct the labor of so many childish people. No doubt they made mistakes at first, but after a little study the mantle of authority fell easily about them, and they were able to direct the work with dignity and decision.

The first day that Nellie came to the plantation, as she came up to the little gate before the house, an old negro woman, bent and wrinkled, came hobbling down from the steps. The poor old creature peered with her dim eyes at the new-comers, and turned aside into the grass that they might pass her. Nellie hurried forward to open the gate. She stood beside it, and smilingly invited the old woman to pass through before her. Bowing and ducking with pleasure, the old creature came through. She paused to peer into Nellie's smiling face.

"You *is* pooty, honey — I 'clare you is," she said, as she dropped a courtesy that seemed like the starting of a rusty machine. "You is po'ful pooty, you is."

Nellie blushed with pleasure at this direct compliment, and John seemed to appreciate it, too. The old woman started mumbling away when she caught a look at John's face. She stopped and held one withered hand before her eyes, that she might examine him carefully. She raised her stick and pointed it at him as she spoke, slowly: —

"I know youse — I reckon you done stop at de ole cabin in Georgy when you all kill dat dorg."

As she spoke, a tall negro, black as coal and straight as an arrow, came walking past the corner of the house. The old woman looked at him proudly.

"Dere's Solermun," she chuckled; "I reckon youse 'member him, sho' 'nuff."

John looked earnestly at the negro for a moment. The black man stood like a statue before him.

"It *is* Sol," said John, as he sprang forward and held out his hand. It was the black soldier who had led the fugitives through the woods from Andersonville. A gleam of pleasure spread over the negro's heavy face. He took off his hat and shook John's hand with — "Howdy, boss? I's po'ful glad to see you, boss — I reckon I is, sho' 'nuff."

Sol took little Nellie and raised her high in his strong arms. She was not in the least afraid of him. She laughed merrily, and when he settled her upon his shoulder, she wound her little arm about his woolly head. She had listened to the story of

Sol's bravery many times. To her childish eyes he was not simply a poor "nigger," but a man who had saved her dear father's life.

"Did you help my papa an' Uncle Nathan when they were lost in the woods?" she asked, pushing up his face so that she could see him.

"I reckon so, honey," was all Sol could say.

"I love you, then,"—and the dear little girl bent down and touched his black forehead with her rosebud mouth.

"I love you"—the words sank deep into the soul of that black man. "I love you"—simple words from a little child that knew nothing of the great gulf that opened between her race and the man she kissed. "I love you!" What a hopeless love it was, and yet who shall say that these simple words were thrown away? Who can say that they may not kindle into flame a spirit of chivalry as pure as that of the days of old romance?

Nellie took Sol's great hand in hers and thanked him with the tenderness that belongs to such a woman. He looked at her curiously, and his lips came closely together. He did not rub his head and laugh, as most negroes would have done. He stood erect and firm—like a man. The old negress had been watching the group carefully. She tottered up to Sol's side, and patted his arm affectionately.

"You is a good boy, Solermun. I done tole you dat we's sho' to come out all right. I is Solermun's mammy," she added to the rest. "Aunt Jinny dey calls me allus. I is po'ful glad to see you all, bekase I tinks a heap ob you all sence my ole man done gib me dat little flag."

They all shook hands with Aunt Jinny, much to her delight, and then John led the way up to the house. Sol came last, carrying little Nellie on his shoulders. John brought chairs to the piazza for the company, but Sol would not sit down. He stood erect, holding his hat in his hand. He seemed to feel the difference between himself and his former comrade. Aunt Jinny sat on the upper step and took little Nellie in her lap. The old slave crooned and rocked with the little girl until the latter laughed out in glee.

Sol told his story simply and with few words. He went back to the old plantation after the surrender, intending to settle down and work for his parents. He did not lose his head, as many of the negroes did during the period of reconstruction. He kept honestly at work, and tried to keep out of politics. The negroes obtained control of affairs, and for several years held the offices. Then came the days, or rather nights, of the Ku Klux. Sol's father, a harmless old man, who had no weapon but a loose tongue, was taken from his house and whipped. Sol came upon the whipping party and with his axe knocked two of them senseless. His father died and Sol was obliged to run for his life. After a month's absence he came back by night and brought his mother away.

No one could tell how the two had wandered all through these years. Up and down through Alabama, through Mississippi, moving on aimlessly from year to year. They would work through one crop and then wander on to some new place. It is hard for the negro to build a new home without help. Once driven from his old home, and he wanders about aimlessly unless some stronger mind can direct him. Sol had heard that a Northern man had settled in the neighborhood. His mother had urged him to come and apply for work. The old woman had a reverence for Northern soldiers, that nothing could destroy. So Sol had come. When the negro finished his story, John rose and shook hands with him again.

"I want you to stay here, Sol," he said; "you're jest the man I want to help me."

"Tanky, boss. I'll do de bes' I knows," said Sol as he looked anxiously at his mother.

Nellie understood him at once.

"She must stay here too, Sol," she said quickly. "We will make her comfortable and take good care of her."

Aunt Jinny looked up as Nellie spoke.

"You *is* mighty pooty, honey, you is, sho' 'nuff. I is old and mighty nigh def, I reckon, but I kin work yit, an' I'll take car ob little honey de bes' I kin."

And so the wanderers found a home. One of the cabins was repaired and Sol and his mother moved in at once. In their great gratitude John and Nellie were almost ready at first to treat the negroes as they would have treated white people; but Sol never stepped out of what he deemed to be his place. It was only in private, where he knew he had John's confidence, that Sol would ever drop the negro and speak and think like a man. When other white people were about he was only a respectful servant.

Colonel Fair called Sol a "likely nigger."

"You're a good boy, I reckon," he said. "You wanter behave an' keep away from these night meetin's. Jest keep to work an' keep out o' politics. Such fellers as you be never gut no office, did ye?"

"I reckon not, boss," was all Sol said. There was not a movement of his heavy face.

CHAPTER XVIII.

THE ANDERSONVILLE SENTINEL

THE more John thought about Jack Foster, the more thoroughly he convinced himself that Jack was the sentinel who had spared his life at Andersonville. He hardly knew what to do in the matter — whether to go to Jack and speak at once, or wait till some chance should open a conversation on the subject. He decided at last to wait. They did not see Jack again until the next Sunday, when they spent the day with Mrs. Fair. After dinner Colonel Fair and John sat on the piazza, when Jack Foster came riding slowly from town. They had been talking about him but a moment before, and when he came in sight Colonel Fair hailed and beckoned him to come up to the house. After a moment's hesitation he turned his horse in at the gate and rode up to a tree, where he dismounted. Then he came up to the piazza.

"Come in and have dinner," said Colonel Fair. " I reckon you're hungry after your ride."

Jack declined this invitation — he was not hungry, he said. Lucy's pale face at church had driven all the hunger into his heart. He drew a chair up to the others, and tilted back on it against one of the pillars of the piazza. He looked at John keenly for a moment, and studied his face carefully. Then his eyes turned away and a dark look passed over his face. John longed to thank the man — to do something to show how he felt, but that dark look forbade such a thing.

The three men talked of the crops, the weather, and general agriculture, until at last they drifted into a discussion of politics and the general condition of the country. Colonel Fair was pronounced and bitter in his denunciations of the people. Jack Foster listened attentively and at times answered some statements that seemed to him too strong. He talked like a well informed man, but he did not enter into the discussion with any heart. His eyes kept wandering down the road in the direction of the town. There was a longing look in them at such times. John had little to do but sit and listen to the others.

"I claim — as I always have claimed," argued Colonel Fair, "that this is a mighty good country. I reckon there's room enough here for a heap o' them poor folks up North, but they can't never do nothin' here till a heap o' these old fellers dies off. There's too many folks up there that care more for a home than they do for money. That's jest the kind o' folks this country needs, an' it's jest the kind o' folks that ain't comin' here, because they can't git no society. They keep on goin' out West, passin' by this beautiful country, till it's too late to bring 'em here. They've gut to come in crowds an' settle in colonies, an' if they do that they'll have a fight on their hands right away. They'll rally the niggers jest as sure as you live, an' if they do that you've gut to do jest as ye did along back, or else let the niggers have a show. Now ain't that so, Foster?"

"I reckon a heap of it is," said Jack slowly, "but I don't reckon there's any way of helping it. There's a heap of folks here in this country that's lazy and don't know how to work. They are too proud to learn of you Yankees, and I don't reckon there is anybody else to show them how. If you all could come down here and be like us, and not stir up our niggers, we might get along well enough after a while. If a man comes down here and minds his own business I won't say a word against him, but it's no more than natural that I should remember that I was whipped, and that we just ground our noses in the dust for ten years. Folks judge you all by the men that came down here after the war and ruined our niggers. I know there are good men at the North that perhaps ought to be here. We need them — I admit that — but I haven't got much heart to welcome them. I know very well they are different from our folks, and I don't see how they can make themselves feel at home. It's no use trying to get people in here that will be discontented and then want to quit. If I should go up into your country and say what I think and what I know about the niggers, and about the war, I don't reckon I could make as many friends as you have here."

The two men talked on in this strain for some time. John could not help seeing how little they had in common after all. There could be but little confidence or concert of action between two such men.

There was something about Jack Foster's manner that repelled John. There was no chance to say the words he longed to say. Jack rose at last to take his leave. The conversation had drifted into a discussion of the real ideas that held Northern and Southern men apart. John never forgot the last words of this discussion. Jack stood with his foot on the upper step as he said slowly: —

"I did a thing for a Yankee soldier once that I don't reckon I could do again. It saved him, but I reckon it about ruined me."

He looked directly at John as he spoke. His voice was hard, and there was a bitter look on his face. As he turned to pass down the steps, Mrs. Fair and Nellie with the little girl came from the hall. Jack was introduced to the ladies. He almost started at the sight of Nellie. How much like the "little babe" she looked. He glanced at John uneasily, and after a few words took leave of the party. Mounting his horse, he rode slowly down to the road, with his head hanging on his breast.

This little golden-haired woman, he thought, must have been the sister of that sick boy at Andersonville. Suppose he had shot this Yankee, what would she have done? And then the thought of the long years of suffering and of Lucy's scorn pushed the better feelings out of his heart. It seemed hard to think that this man was living so happily, while he, who had spared the life on which so much happiness depended, was so miserable.

John told Nellie all about what Jack had said to him. The little woman was much concerned over the matter. She was anxious to show her gratitude to Jack, and yet she could not tell how to do it. They felt so awkward and strange in their new position, and there seemed to be something about Jack Foster that made it impossible for them to approach him. It was evident that he recognized John, but it was yet more evident that there was something so very unpleasant about the matter that he would not speak of it, or willingly give them an opportunity of telling him what they wished to tell him.

Just as the new life began to settle into its regular groove, a terrible feeling of homesickness came to John and Nellie. The excitement of preparation, and the novelty of the new life, had kept their thoughts away from their real condition for a time, but at last they were brought face to face with it. They longed with a terrible heart-hunger for the old familiar faces — for a glimpse of the old home. Their great house seemed desolate with no friends to share it with them. They had no one to take into their confidence. People seemed to view them with suspicion. Every face seemed ready to curl itself up into a sneer.

John and Nellie fought hard and bravely against this homesickness. They had set their faces to the task, and they would not turn back now, though the work was harder than they had expected. They did their best to comfort each other, yet there were times when it seemed as if they could not stand the awful longing for home. Night after night they would stand and watch the little girl as she lay asleep, and then their hearts would grow stronger as they thought how their work was all for her. Little Nellie cried sometimes for the old people at home, but her grief was short-lived. There were so many new and pretty things to take up her mind. She became greatly attached to Aunt Jinny, who followed her about and told her strange stories that pulled the blue eyes open in wonder.

There were very few visitors. Colonel Fair and his wife came over frequently, but the other neighbors made but one visit. John did his best to get acquainted with those who lived near him, but there was something, he could not understand what, that kept him from talking to them as he could talk to the neighbors at home.

Their first entertainment of visitors was not a complete success. They were both at work one day, Nellie in the house, and John at the new barn, when a carriage rolled up to the gate. This vehicle was a trifle rusty and decayed, but it bounded up and down on its old-fashioned springs, as if determined to keep up its share of the family pride. The two worn old mules were driven by a negro, who opened the door with a tremendous flourish. A stately old lady stepped from the carriage and advanced toward the house. She held an eye-glass haughtily to her eye, and glanced over the smooth lawn and the painted house with curious interest.

Nellie saw the carriage stop, and hastened to receive her visitor. She hastily dried her hands, and took off her apron. She sent little Nellie out to bring John in, and then went forward just as the lady's card was brought out by Aunt Jinny. When John came in, he found his wife sitting uneasily in her chair, with the old lady examining her critically. John did not add much dignity to the household. He wore his old working dress, and his clothes were covered in places with sawdust. The end of a carpenter's rule peeped curiously out from his breast pocket. Little Nellie had done her best to brush his coat, but her hand was small and she had not succeeded as well as one could wish. John knew that he had entertained visitors at home in a much worse suit of clothes.

The old lady made a very short call. She was very polite, but the young people could easily see that she was horrified at their appearance. She went away at last, much to Nellie's relief. John rubbed his head ruefully, as he saw the old carriage roll down the road. They had done their best, but they felt after all that they were only plain country people. This was the only call they received for a long time. People seemed to have decided to let them entirely alone. Colonel Fair laughed, when he heard of this adventure.

"Don't worry about that," he said; "they'll all come round in a year's time — jest as soon as ye make a mark on your plantation. Then, ye can pick and choose yer company. I don't know but you'll be something like me," he added, slowly; "I've ben here some years, an' I've picked up mighty few of 'em yet."

But John did not wish to live as Colonel Fair was

living. He wanted to be on good terms with all his neighbors.

John's farm operations opened most successfully. He bought a mowing machine at once, and drove the shovel-and-wheelbarrow method of haymaking into a permanent retirement. He bought a small herd of cows, and a few sheep and hogs. He determined to plough up the old cotton fields and get them into pastures as quickly as possible. Sol was of great help in this work. He seemed to have a white man's head with a negro's strength and endurance. John was soon able to trust much of the rougher work to Sol's judgment.

John had something to sell from his place in a very short time. Nellie's butter had been famous at home, and she determined to gain a like fame at Sharpsburg. John took a package of delicious golden rolls into the town, to see what market could be secured. After much bargaining, he sold his load to one of the Jews, who promised to take all that could be made.

"I knows a good ting ven I sees dot — dot vas von of de segrets of my peesness," the Jew said, rubbing his fat hands together, and nodding his head at John. "Dere is too much of this cotton-seed butter in dis goundry. Dey feeds de cows on de cotton-seed, an' dot chust won't melt in your mout wid dot dellegate flavor dot is de life of good butter. De butter peesness in dis goundry vas chust like all oders. Dere is no system und no push in dese men. People say dot dey can't find out how dese Jews vas suckseed chust like dey does. It is chust good peesness management — dot's chust how it vas. Ve vorks, und dey sleeps. Ve manages, und dey let tings go mitout any system."

At this moment, the Jew was called off by a customer. He went behind the counter to give a practical example of his " peesness ability." A tall man had been listening to the conversation.

"I reckon a heap of what he says is true," he said, as John passed him. "Them Jews is jest suckin' this country like an orange. They come down here an' sell goods so cheap that they drive white people out of business. They can live on nothin', I reckon. They don't never pay no taxes, scarsely. They keep all their money in cash, and they ain't gut no idee of building up the country at all. They hurt our niggers bad, I reckon. A Jew will put his arm around a nigger's neck, for the sake of sellin' him a nickel's worth of goods. They sell their goods and make money, because they know how to manage."

By this time, the Jew had finished his business. He came back, smiling at the bargain he had just made, and the tall man moved away. The Jew seemed to have marked John out as a profitable man to cultivate.

"You vas goin' do de speakin'?" he asked, as he moved his fat hand in the direction of the court-house.

John's eye followed the gesture, and noticed a crowd of negroes and a few white men gathered about the court-house.

"Dere is some speakin' over dere," announced the Jew, noticing John's questioning look. "I vas a

Demograt, of course," he remarked, complacently, seeming to imply that it would show very poor "peesness management" to be anything else. "I vas a Demograt, but I likes to see fair play all de vile. I drades mit dose Republicans, an' always dreats dem chust de same. If you go to dot speakin', you vill find blenty of fair blay. Eferybody has a good chance to say chust what dey pleases. Now, chust look here vonce." A sudden idea seemed to seize him. He drew John to one corner of the store, and, after looking carefully about, whispered: —

"You vas a Northern man, so I dells you somedink. I gives you von or dree boints. You chust hang right onto your broperty in dis coundry chust as close as you can. Don't you get discouraged. De time is coming when all dese lazy people must all git avay. Dere is blendy of dese farms dot is mortgaged, and de capital dot holds dem is from de North. Northern men will never buy land unless dey means to improve it. Den de niggers begins to see dat dey must vork for demselves."

The Jew would have said more, but at this moment a small wave of custom rolled into the store, and floated the proprietor away. John walked out on the street, and stood for a moment watching the crowd by the court-house. He had a strong desire to pass over and see for himself how the political meeting was being conducted. At home he would have cared nothing about it; but here he was beginning to be deeply interested.

"Who's speakin' over yunder?" he asked of his

friend, the tall man, who stood leaning against the building.

"There's a heap of 'em," was the answer. "Two Radicals an' some good Democrats. They always give everybody a fair hack — jest go over an' see if that ain't so."

Thus urged, John walked across the street and into the court-house. A large crowd had gathered to listen to the discussion. They were mostly white men, who sat solemnly on the rough benches and listened with sober politeness. A few negroes sat on the back seats, and as many more peered in at the windows and doors. The speakers sat in a row behind the bar, while in front of them sat the presiding officer — a short gentleman, with a red face and long, white beard.

As John entered, one of the speakers was just taking his seat. The audience applauded in what seemed to John a spiritless way. The men stamped their feet, and gave a series of cat-calls and yells. John found a vacant place on one of the front benches. As he took his seat, a man rose from the line of speakers and came down to the rail. There was no effort at applause. The white people looked at the speaker with scowling faces, while the negroes bent forward to listen carefully.

The speaker deposited a package of papers on a little desk, and then put on a pair of spectacles and looked calmly over the audience. His scrutiny ended, he removed the spectacles and placed them on the desk by the papers. He was a tall, determined-looking man. His mouth closed firmly, and his eyes were covered with great, shaggy, gray eyebrows. He did not show the slightest fear or hesitation. He announced himself as a Republican, and went on to state his reasons for being one.

"I carried a gun all through the war," he said, "an' done my best for the South. I was an almighty big fool to fight the last two years, I reckon. We was whipped, an' we knowed it. When the war was over, I made up my mind I'd wait an' sorter see what was comin'. We all know what we expected. What did General Grant say? He said, 'Let every man have his hoss an' mule to go home an' make him a crop.' I reckon there ain't nobody could have said more than that. I says, 'That's good enough fer me, I reckon.'

"I tuck my mule an' made me a crop in North Car'liny, an' then I worked on yer to Mississippi. I married one of the loveliest of Mississippi's daughters, an' yer I've been ever sence. I says, we're whipped — the other side's on top, an' they're gonter have the call. It ain't no use ter buck agin 'em, for we had ter give it up an' take our lickin'. So I says, let's all turn in agin an' sorter straighten things out. General Grant, he spoke mighty fair, an' I says, that's good enough fer me, I reckon. I come out an' joined the Republican party. I've been thar ever sence, an' I reckon I'll stay there fer good."

There was no sign of applause at this bold announcement. The white men sat in grim silence, and the negroes nudged each other, though their faces never moved a muscle. One rough-looking man on the seat in front of John shook his head in a satisfied manner, and bent forward to listen more carefully as the speaker went on.

"There was a heap of men, as you all know, that said they never would surrender. They went off to Mexico, an' Europe, an' all these other places, an' it warn't long before they had ter send home for help. What did General Grant do? He sent a ship all 'round, an' picked 'em up an' brought 'em home. I reckon we'd 'a' ben better off to-day if a heap of 'em had kep' away. But come down in a little closter an' see what the Republican party done. We give ye yer free schools, we built up yer buildin's, an' we give ye a start all along. That didn't satisfy ye. What did ye do? You killed niggers an' stuffed ballot boxes till ye gut things back where they started from. But it didn't do yer nigh ser much good as ye thought it would. It was just like a dog gittin' a taste of a sheep. You stuffed folks *in*, and I'm dogged ef ye didn't learn the trick of stuffin' folks *out* agin. It's a mighty poor rule that won't work two ways, I reckon."

Here the speaker produced his package of newspapers. He read a series of wordy articles, in which the State administration was most violently attacked. "The most corrupt administration ever known," "a despotic ring power," and other violent epithets were used in abundance. "That's the way some of your Democratic friends talk," said the speaker, as he laid down his spectacles.

"Now, I ain't no nigger. I'm a white man, I be. I fit as hard as any of ye till I gut licked, an' then I quit. I'll be dogged if I don't hate to see ye hangin' 'way back yonder. Why don't ye come out of yer shell an' be somebody? You go up where the Republicans is an' you'll find that they've got all the big men an' all the likely fellers in the country. Why don't ye jine hands with the best men up thar, and git some help in buildin' up this country?

"It needs help, I reckon. You can buy land here fer a song. Bad's I kin sing I cud git sum fer a solo. The same land up in the North would be worth ten times as much. There ain't no folks comin' in yer, but there's a heap of 'em goin' out. All yer likely young men are startin' out fer Texas — ain't that so? What's the matter with this country? You folks have give it such a name that people don't dare to come here. That's jest the size of it, an' you know it."

The rough-looking man in front of John brought his great foot down on the floor with a stamp of approval. There was no other applause. A little Jew, encouraged by the stamp of the foot to make an effort to secure the Republican trade, started to clap his hands, but he seemed to realize the lonesomeness of his position in time, for the hands never came together. The white men bent looks of the fiercest hate upon the speaker, while the negroes never moved.

"Another point I'm goin' to talk about is, where the Republican party stands on protection. I'm gonter make it so clear, that I reckon even a way-down, back-country farmer can understand it. You put up a cotton factory in this town, an' I'll guarantee that your farmers will build up a home market for all the pertaters an' fruit an' such like they cud raise. We want a cash business in this country, an' there ain't no way to git it, until we git up a new market."

We cannot follow the speaker all through his talk. I have given enough of his exact words to illustrate his arguments and mode of expression. He spoke fearlessly and forcibly for about an hour, and then took his seat. There was not a murmur of applause. A look of relief seemed to come over the faces of the white men. They seemed glad that a disagreeable duty had been performed. They had listened to these words to show that they were perfectly ready to allow "fair play."

The next speaker was a tall, elegant gentleman, who rose with much dignity from his seat, and came down to the rail. He was greeted with loud applause. The white men struck the floor with their feet, and yelled loudly as he bowed to them. He had the sympathy of his audience from the very first sentence.

"I deny the right of this man who has just taken his seat, or, in fact, the right of any Republican, to speak words of advice to the white people of Mississippi. Don't you remember, gentlemen, how, but a few years ago, these very men, with their army of ignorant plunderers, had the intelligent *white* men of this country down on their very backs, with a death grip on their throats? Don't you remember, gentlemen, those dark days when we hung our heads in shame before our ladies, for allowing this crime to remain unpunished? You cannot forget it. It is burned into the heart of every Southern man. It is a dishonor that galls our very souls with its remembrance. Will you ever follow the advice of one who turned his back upon his bleeding country in her hour of need, who helped to fasten this chain upon us, and who now comes before you as an office-holder — a blood-sucker — pleading only for more of your life?"

A mighty chorus of "never" demonstrated the feeling of the audience. The speaker might have spared himself all further talk. As it was, he spoke on for an hour and a half, and, to John's mind, simply repeated his opening sentences over and over again. John was anxious to stay and hear what the Republican speaker would have to say in reply, but he knew that Nellie would be anxious if he waited, so, after listening to an hour of this oration, he went away to try and digest a few of the theories that had been advanced so liberally.

He collected his load as rapidly as possible, and at last rode out of town towards home. About a quarter of a mile out of the village, he came upon a foot-passenger, whom he recognized as the rough-looking man who had occupied the seat in front of him at the court-house. John stopped his horses and invited the pedestrian to ride with him. The man glanced curiously at John for a moment, and then, without a word, stepped into the wagon.

"You're a Northern man, I reckon," he said, after a moment's pause.

"I s'pose I be," said John cautiously.

"How'd ye like that speakin'?" The man had a

rough, hard voice, that was as unpolished as his face.

"Wall, I s'pose I've heard better," said John, who did not care to commit himself.

"I reckon *so*. Speakin' don't do no good down here, I reckon. Folks sorter goes through all the motions so they can keep a good holt on the offices. Old Byrox talked pretty brash there to-day, but it don't do no good. We uster have speakin' here that tore things all up, but it's all one way, now."

"How long have you been down here?" asked John.

"I come down here right after the war. I went out on a cotton plantation an' made two or three crops, an' then I moved in here. We had big pickin's then. I built a court-house over in the next county. Charged 'em my own price for the work. They hed a lot o' niggers on the board of supervisors, and they done everything I said. Mighty lively times them was, an' money was plenty. But I'll have to leave ye here. I left my horse here when I come in."

John stopped the horse before a little white house, and his new friend jumped out. The two men shook hands, and John started on toward home again. If the talk of the afternoon had gone to show him how far he was from the people, events had been transpiring at home that promised to bring him closer than ever to one of his neighbors. As he turned in at the gate, he saw Jack Foster sitting on the piazza, holding little Nellie on his knee.

This sight was enough to make John stop his

horses in surprise. There could be no doubt about it. It was surely Jack Foster. As little Nellie saw her father, she ran down to meet him, while Jack Foster turned to his former prisoner with a curious expression on his face.

CHAPTER XIX.

BOB GLENN WANTS HIS PAY

THE first trouble John had with his neighbors was caused by a dog. The dog is a perfectly harmless animal so long as he is left to prey upon his own species, but when he comes in contact with live mutton he often causes much trouble. John bought a small flock of sheep just after coming to the plantation. They had always kept sheep at home, and John believed these woolly servants to be the most perfect farm scavengers known. There were but few other sheep in the neighborhood that he could find. Even Colonel Fair shook his head at John's purchase.

"Too many dogs here," he said. "Every nigger and every poor white man has got a dozen curs hangin' 'round. You'll have ter watch them sheep all the time. There ain't nothin' but a good charge of shot that'll ever cure a dog of sheep-killin'. The law allows ye to kill all dogs found huntin' round a flock o' sheep. Jest kill a dozen or so, an' they'll all keep clear of ye."

A few days after this talk, one of the best sheep was found dead in the pasture. A big, gray dog had been seen prowling about. John gave Sol instructions to shoot all dogs found on the place, and so well was this order heeded that the next day the gray dog lay dead in the pasture. He had been caught in the very act of chasing sheep.

Nothing more was thought of the affair until the next day, when a most unwelcome visitor came walking in from the road — a long, lanky, beardless "poor white." He walked up to the little gate in front of the house, and there stopped to lean lazily upon his gun while he surveyed the premises. His colorless clothes were ragged and limp. There was nothing but a cruel slit, stained with tobacco juice, and a pair of little, fishy eyes that gave any character to his face. Sol was at work near the corner of the house. The new-comer watched the negro for a moment, and then called, in a thin, rasping voice:

"Look yer, nigger, call out yer boss an' tell him I've cum round yer to get pay fer that dorg you all done killed."

Sol walked straight to the barn, where John was working. "Dere's a man out dere wants to see you, boss," he said. "I reckon it's 'bout that dorg I done killed. You better take you' pistol when youse go, I reckon."

"I don't want no pistol, I guess," said John, as he put down his hammer and started for the front or the house. Sol did not consider the hammer such a useless implement evidently. He caught up the tool and hid it under his vest, and followed John. The visitor still stood in front of the house, leaning on his gun. John walked up to him, and, nodding with the New England idea of politeness, said: "Howdy do?"

"I'm tollerble, I reckon," was the answer.

The long individual looked curiously at John over the muzzle of his gun.

"Your nigger killed my dorg," he said, at last. "I've cum round yer ter git my pay fer 'im."

John was as near to being angry as he often got. Things had gone wrong all the afternoon, and Nellie was at Colonel Fair's house. The man before him was such a miserable specimen of humanity, and he spoke so insolently, that John grew obstinate at once.

"I ketched your dog killin' sheep. I've gut the law on my side, an' ye can't collect nothin'."

"I don't care a shuck fer the law. I've come ter git the pay fer my dorg. Your nigger killed him. You Yankees needn't a think ye're comin' down yer to kill my dorg."

There was a wicked look on the dog-owner's face as he straightened up and raised his gun from the ground. He had sadly mistaken his man, however, if he expected to frighten John. An old soldier does not forget his military experience so readily.

"Don't yer pint that gun at me!" John said as he stepped forward. "I warn't brought up in the woods ter be scart by no owls. Stand back an' clear out."

John found himself well supported by Sol. The negro quickly drew the hammer from under his vest and stepped to the side of the stranger.

Before the gun could have been raised, Sol could easily have broken the dog-owner's skull. This latter gentleman seemed to appreciate the situation.

"You've got the drop on me, I reckon," he said, as he lowered the point of his gun; "but it's my turn next."

He turned and walked slowly down the path toward the gate. He did not go far, but sat down under a tree and examined his musket. Then he sat with his weapon across his knees and watched the house. John grew uneasy at this watching. Every time he turned from his work, he could see the unwelcome visitor still sitting under the tree. At last he went down to the little gate and called to the man to "clear out."

"I want the pay fer that dorg," was all the answer he could get.

Late in the afternoon Colonel Fair brought Nellie home.

"What ye gut down under them trees, judge?" he asked, pointing to the visitor.

John explained the matter, much to the amusement of Colonel Fair.

"Look out he don't burn yer gin-house some night," he said.

As Colonel Fair drove back to his own house he stopped near the seated figure under the tree.

"What are ye doin' here?" he asked sternly.

"I want the pay fer my dorg," was the sullen answer. The man had but one idea.

"You'd better quit now, an' keep the rest of yer dogs to home, I reckon. That man up yunder don't waste no words at all. I expect he's killed a dozen men. He says if you don't go mighty soon, he's comin' out on the porch an' jest use ye fer a target.

He can snuff a candle at ten rod, he can, an' you'd better quit afore he comes out."

The man was evidently moved by this address. He called out the object of his mission once or twice, and at last shouldered his gun and walked slowly out of the grounds. He paused for a moment at the gate, as if about to return and insist upon the payment, but John's reputation as a marksman was too much for him — he walked off along the road, looking back at intervals to see if John appeared on the porch.

This incident troubled John and Nellie considerably. They were afraid the man would return and make more trouble. The days went by, however, and nothing was heard from him until the day that John went to town and attended the political meeting. Late in the afternoon of that day, little Nellie determined to go down to the gate to meet her father on his return from town. Her mother was busy in the house, so the little girl induced Aunt Jinny to go down to the gate with her. The old negress was always willing to do whatever " little honey " proposed, so the two started on their pilgrimage. The old woman hobbled painfully along with her stick, but the little girl danced gleefully all over the road. She would run far ahead, and then dance back to help Aunt Jinny along.

" You is mighty spry, you is," said the old woman, as little Nellie danced back to take hold of the stick and thus increase Aunt Jinny's rate of progression. " You is mighty spry. I reckon it ud take a po'ful big piece of sunshine fer ter keep ahead o' youse."

Aunt Jinny sat down under a tree near the gate, while little Nellie climbed on the fence to obtain a better view of the road.

"There comes papa," she shouted at last, pointing down the road. Far in the distance, just coming over a little hill, she saw a wagon that looked exactly like her father's. She did not examine it closely, but, child-like, jumped to the ground at once to run and meet it.

"Come, Aunt Jinny," she shouted, "come and ride back with papa."

Aunt Jinny rose stiffly and followed the little girl down the road. Little Nellie did not stop to run back now. She danced on ahead, eager to meet her father. She was quite a little distance ahead of Aunt Jinny when a man started up from under a tree by the road, and shouted to her: —

"Hold on, thar!"

She stopped with her eyes wide open in wonder at this command. The voice was so hard and rasping that it frightened her. It was the same man that had troubled John. He picked up his gun from the ground and walked out into the road. He scowled fiercely at the little girl, and growled out his old demand: —

"I want the pay fer that dorg."

Little Nellie was badly frightened. Her finger went up to her mouth, and the little eyes filled with tears as the brute lowered upon her. Aunt Jinny did her best to reach the spot, but she was old and stiff. She hobbled on with a firm clutch at her stick, and shouted as best she could: —

"Let go dat chile — drop dat, yo' po' white trash."
The man pointed his gun directly at the old woman.

"Fall back, nigger," he growled, "or I'll blow ye inter rags."

Aunt Jinny never halted, but pushed on right up to the face of the gun.

"Drop that gun, Bob Glenn, or I'll blow the daylight right through yer head!"

It was a man's voice, sharp and clear as a bell. The dog-owner seemed to know it well, for he dropped his gun in an instant, and turned his face savagely toward the speaker.

Jack Foster stood in his wagon, one hand holding the reins, and the other pointing a bright revolver. It was he that Nellie had seen down the road.

"Pick up that gun and put it in my wagon," said Jack, sternly. "You know me," he said, as the man hesitated. "I always do just what I say I will, and I'd just as soon shoot you as eat."

The man sullenly picked up his weapon and carried it to the wagon.

"Now, clear out. If you want that gun again come up to my house, and if you come inside my gate I'll shoot you without warning."

Bob Glenn seemed to feel after this speech that he might just as well bid his gun a long farewell. He gave one last glance at it, and then slunk into the woods like a whipped cur. His sting had been taken from him. He was no longer dangerous.

Jack put his pistol back into his pocket, and got out of the wagon to speak a word to little Nellie.

The poor little girl was crying bitterly. She had been badly frightened. Aunt Jinny sat on the ground, holding the baby in her arms, and rocking to and fro with her.

"Nebber mine, lille honey," she muttered, "he done gone away now, I reckon. Yo' papy he come mighty soon now, sho' 'nuff."

"Don't cry now, little girl," said Jack, as he knelt on the grass beside her. Jack had always loved children, though of late years, in his silent and solitary life, he had seen but few of them.

Little Nellie looked up at him and smiled through her tears. She sprang away from Aunt Jinny, and put her arms about his neck and kissed him.

"I know you," she said, eagerly. "You are the man who didn't shoot my papa. I heard papa and mamma talk about you, and I love you."

She kissed him again, and at the touch of her lips Jack felt all the bitter feeling he had held toward John Rockwell pass from his heart.

That kiss came into his lonely life like a beam of sunshine into a prisoner's cell. He drew the dear little thing close to him and kissed her again and again, until she dried her eyes and laughed merrily. Jack placed her on the seat, by his side, and even helped Aunt Jinny into the wagon.

They drove on and reached the gate just as Nellie and Sol came hurrying down from the house to seek for the wanderers. Nellie had missed the little girl shortly after she started from the house. Jack Foster told the story in a few words. He handed the little girl down to her mother, and, after a short conversation, gathered up his reins to drive on. Nellie noticed how her little girl clung to him, and it seemed as if his face had lost that hard, bitter look it had worn before. A sudden impulse led her to say, as he reached for the reins: —

"Won't you come up to the house for a moment? *Please* do, for I have something I *must* say to you."

The little woman wondered at her boldness, after she had spoken. The invitation pleased little Nellie greatly.

"Please tum," she said, and tried to climb again into the wagon. Jack hesitated a moment, but the little face looking up at him was more than he could stand, and he dropped the reins again and jumped to the ground. He helped Nellie into the wagon, and put the little girl at her side. Then he drove slowly up to the house. Aunt Jinny, poor old soul, had not been able to climb to the ground at all.

Jack tied his horse to the post, and then walked slowly up to the piazza, where he took his seat. Little Nellie ran at his side, and, when he had seated himself, climbed on his knee. What a flood of memories swept through the heart of this lonely man as he looked down into this sweet little face. How true he had been to that one woman he loved better than his life. How the beautiful eyes of this child seemed to touch his very soul, and clear away a great weight that had rested on his heart for years. His eyes were dim with the mist of tenderness, when the little thing put her arms about his neck, and whispered again: "I *do* love you."

Nellie left Jack on the piazza, and went straight

to her own room. The thought of what she had
done, and what she was going to do, frightened her.
She wondered what John would say, and yet she
could not stop now. She unlocked her trunk, and
drew from the very bottom a little wooden box that
her mother had given her years before. It was the
most valuable thing that Nellie owned, yet there was
nothing in it but the long yellow curl that John had
cut from Archie's head, and the letter that had found
its answer so well.

Nellie held this little box tightly in her hand, as
she walked slowly back to the piazza. How *could*
she show these sacred tokens? No one but John
had ever seen them, and yet — but for this man —
she could not finish the thought.

She drew her chair to Jack's side, and told her
story simply, while Jack sat with the little girl's arms
about his neck, and her great eyes looking into his
very soul. She told her story as only such a woman
can talk. She did not cry, but her heart was in her
words. Her voice trembled, and her lip quivered,
but Jack, looking down through a strange blindness
into the great eyes before him, did not think that she
was only a poor, weak, simple woman.

Nellie told her story bravely, but when it was finished her woman's heart gave way, and she could
not keep the tears from her eyes. Little Nellie left
Jack and climbed into her mother's lap. She brushed
away the tears with her little hand, and kissed all
traces of them from sight. Jack waited till Nellie
had composed herself, and then he handed back the
little box. His face was strangely bright, and his
voice was gentle with tenderness.

"Mistress Rockwell," he said, " I must thank you for speaking as you have to me. I have carried a load in my heart for years. It is lighter now. I have never told my people here why I refused to shoot your husband. I have lived a lonely and awful life for years. I knew that no one could understand why I did not do my duty; but I reckon *you* can understand it, and I will tell you.

" When I went to the war, I left a little woman at home — almost as sweet and tender as you are. I loved her then, and I love her now a great deal better than I love my life. I reckon I'd die for her in a minute. I'd been reading her letters when your brother died, and when your husband came after the flowers. I couldn't drive that little woman out of my mind. I couldn't kill him for doing just what I would have done myself.

" People called me a traitor — and they had a right to, I reckon. It killed my mother, and my little girl has never looked at me since I told her I let your husband live. I couldn't tell her just how it was, and I reckon she hates me now. I've lived all these years here alone. God knows what I've suffered, and yet I can't bring myself to regret having spared that life. I am glad I did it."

And so Jack told his story. His head sank on his breast, as he told of Lucy's anger and his lonely life, and his eyes wandered wistfully down the road towards the town. It was the first time he had spoken of his trouble, and he hardly knew how to frame words for his story. Little Nellie came at last, and climbed on to his knee again. It was thus that John found them as he rode home.

Jack rose, and walked down to the gate to meet John. He held out his hand in silence, and John shook it heartily. Not a word was said about the matter, but the two men understood each other. Men with weaker minds would have stood and talked for an hour about it, but these two strong-hearted men could not find words to express what they felt. They knew that Nellie could explain far better than they ever could.

Jack could not take supper with his new friends. They all understood why. They all needed to think and talk over the new order of things before they could meet as they desired to. So Jack bade them good-by. He kissed the little girl, and gave John and Nellie a great hand-clasp, and then rode away down the road through the twilight. His heart was lighter than it had been for years before. It was filled with a strange tenderness too. Somehow, there seemed to be a hope for him at last. Of course, Nellie told John the whole story. John seemed very thoughtful that night as they stood watching the sleeping baby.

"What are you thinking about, John?" she asked, as she reached up to pull his face down so that she could look into his eyes.

"I was thinking how much better *you* are than anybody else in the world," said John, honestly.

Then it was Nellie's turn to be thoughtful, and John had to ask her the same question.

"I was wishing that we might do more for *him*," she answered.

CHAPTER XX.

JACK FOSTER'S TROUBLE

LIFE seemed pleasanter to John and Nellie, after the talk with Jack Foster. They had felt before that he hated them, and now that they knew his story, and how much he had suffered, they longed to offer their sympathy and help. They could understand his position exactly.

"Suppose you had been a traitor, John; or suppose I *thought* you had been," said Nellie, as they were speaking of Jack's case, one night.

"Well, would you have married me?" asked John.

"No, indeed," said Nellie, stoutly.

"But would you have stopped loving me?" and John caught his wife's face in both his hands, and held it where she could not look away from him.

She looked up at him almost sadly, as she answered slowly: "I don't think I could have stopped loving you, John, though I never would have let you know it. I don't think a woman ever can drive love out of her heart as a man can. She must stay at home and keep it in her heart."

It was some time before Jack Foster came to the plantation again. He seemed to realize that his friendship would help the new people but little, and perhaps the sight of the happiness of John and Nellie made him think of what might have been his own.

At last, John, at Nellie's suggestion, found an errand that took him over to Jack's plantation. Both men understood all about this errand. Its object was hardly mentioned after the conversation opened. The two men talked long and earnestly, and the visit was ended by Jack's coming back to look at John's stock and improvements. They walked about the place, discussing agriculture and politics. It seemed now as if they had known each other for years. They were surprised to find how much they had in common, when they were once brought into anything like confidential relations. Nellie would not hear of Jack's going home before supper, so he stayed until after dark. They all sat on the piazza and talked. It was the merriest time Jack had known for years.

After this Jack came to the plantation quite frequently, often making errands as transparent as John's first one had been. He seemed to enjoy talking politics with John, though there were few points upon which they could agree. He was never tired of holding the little girl, and it seemed impossible for him to go to town without bringing her back a present of some kind.

In all their talks, John and he never discussed their first awful meeting. It seemed to be understood between them that this topic should not be mentioned. They spoke of the war, of the various battles in which they had fought, of reconstruction and its results, but not a word was ever said of the day when John walked up to the dead line and the musket dropped.

Jack Foster was about the only friend that the New England people could find. There were plenty of people in the town who treated John civilly, and were glad to trade with him, but it always seemed as if there was a feeling of distrust behind it all. No one invited him home or asked him to bring his family to call. Their manner gave him to understand that he was on trial, and that he must prove his honesty and respectability before they could take him into their families. There seemed to be something — he could not tell what it was — between himself and the rest of the people. He was to find that this feeling would in time wear away, to a certain extent, yet he never could feel as he had felt with his neighbors at home.

No one came to call upon Nellie for a long time. A number of men came to look over the plantation and see what John was doing with it. They seemed like sensible, practical men. There was a very noticeable lack of energy about most of them, and a tendency to make great schemes rather than to suggest any practical way of working such plans out. Some of these visitors were ready to admit that farmers were raising too much cotton and too little corn and meat, yet they were every one of them doing this very same thing. They seemed to understand that a change must be made, yet they had neither the patience nor the energy to go through the slow process of development. They looked over

John's plantation carefully, examined the stock, looked at the new barn, and all the genuine Yankee contrivances that John was building, and noted the great preparations that John had made for pasturage and the grass crop. Some laughed outright at what they called John's foolishness.

"Cotton is the only thing you can raise here," they said. "You'll ruin yourself in two years, and then go back and curse this country."

Others concealed their ridicule or doubt behind a stolid face; they went away and told others of the Yankee's foolishness and sure failure. There were still others who frankly admitted that John was right in his ideas of farming. They shook their heads sadly, however, as they said: —

"You all kin do these things, but I don't reckon we ever kin. We're lazy, I reckon, by nature. You all will git lazy before you've ben here five years, an' then you kin see how it is with us."

And John, not knowing what laziness meant, and not appreciating what lives these men had lived, would justly set his neighbors down as being the most shiftless and indolent set of men he had ever seen. In New England the lazy man of the community was so rare, that he was picked out to serve as a terrible example for the boys and girls. Here the energetic men were as solitary as were their lazy brothers in Breezetown.

If there was a lack of agreeable society, there were many things about the new life that John and Nellie enjoyed. The weather all through the autumn was beautiful. Instead of the early frosts and cold nights of New England, there was a succession of beautiful sunny days, and nights so pleasant that they could sit upon the piazza long after supper. The days seemed longer too, and John was able to push his work with all speed. The splendid agricultural advantages of the country became more and more apparent to John the longer he studied them. He could not understand how men could have neglected the land so long.

Jack Foster's plantation was about as badly run down as any of them. Jack had but little ambition to improve his place. He had been satisfied to "make a living." After talking with John, however, he really went to work with some sort of system. He bought stock, and did his best to imitate John's methods of work.

Jack had given up all hope of speaking to Lucy again, and he hardly knew why he was anxious to improve his place. But it is certain that after every visit to John's house, and every talk with Nellie, he went back home with some new plan for work. If the rest of his neighbors had looked upon him differently, no doubt he would have joined the majority of them in saying that John's system might do for a Yankee, but that it never would work at the South. His neighbors did not trust him and he knew it. John was the first man with whom he had talked confidentially since the war. The two men were placed in such a peculiar position that they developed their friendship and grew towards each other more and more.

Whenever Nellie went to town, she did her best to

get a glimpse of Lucy. She saw her whenever they went to church, for Lucy was sure to be there. It made Nellie's heart ache to see poor Jack Foster watch Lucy as she sat in church. Lucy seemed pale and ill. There were deep lines of suffering on her face, and she had lost most of her beauty. She never looked at Jack, but sat cold and stern, except when at the last prayer she knelt with her face in her hands. Nellie learned more of her story as time went by. Her mother had died a few years after the war. She lived now with an old aunt in the house where Jack had met his doom. Jack pointed out the place to Nellie one day. He had lived so near it for years, and yet he had never dared to enter since that morning, when Lucy's scorn had driven him away. Nellie wondered what she could do to soften that proud heart. She seemed powerless. There appeared to be no tenderness in that stern face, and yet Nellie could not help feeling how *she* would have felt had she been placed in like circumstances, and been told the true story. She longed for a chance to talk to Lucy and tell her what she had told Jack.

It was a great mystery to John at first how farmers had so much time to sit about the stores in the town. He found them there on all occasions when he knew there must be work to be done at home. Seated on comfortable chairs, smoking their unfailing pipes or chewing tobacco, they all seemed to take life as a remarkably pleasant dream. He could not understand how these men ever made a living. With him a "living" had always stood as the representative of a number of hard days' work. The lazy men at home were generally paupers. Here, they seemed to be leading citizens. One of these stationary farmers said to him one day: "I reckon I kin make mo' money right yer in my chair than I kin out on ary farm in this country."

This only served to heighten John's perplexity, and he went to Colonel Fair for an explanation. Colonel Fair had a most supreme contempt for these loungers. They were a part of that class of citizens that he insisted would have to "die off" before the country could ever come to anything.

"They live on the niggers," he explained, when John came with his question. "They rent out their land to niggers, and make the poor black fellers do all the work, while *they* hold down them chairs and take the money. There's a heap of men in this country that jest cuss the nigger up hill an' down, an' yet them same men would starve to death if the nigger should go away. It's mighty easy, I reckon, to make money outer niggers if a man only has a tough conscience. I reckon a heap of the men here have got consciences like sole leather. A man with a little cash can buy half a dozen mules in the spring o' the year, an' make 'em support him.

"A nigger comes in an' wants to buy a mule. Them fellers sell him one for, say, $150. The nigger gives a lien on his crop for the money. The nigger goes out an' makes his crop. The white man sells him meat and corn enough to run him through the summer. The nigger works out in the sun, and the white man sets in the shade. When they come to settle up, the nigger is always behind. He can't never git ahead. He loses his mule, an' he loses his crop. The white man can figger, an' the nigger can't. The nigger, like enough, signs his name to whatever the white man draws up. Nine times out of ten, he can't read any way. When he comes up with his crop, he finds a statement about like this."

Colonel Fair picked up a piece of board as he spoke, and wrote with his pencil the following remarkable statement of account: —

	Nigger Dr.		
Mule and Harness	. . . .	$200	
Rations	. . . .	75	
		$275	
Interest at 2 1-2 per mo.	. . . . . .	40	
			$315
	Nigger Cr.		
By Cotton	. . . .	225	
Bal. against Nigger	. . . .	$90	

"Then the white man," continued Colonel Fair, "says, 'I'll allow you $50 for that mule and harness, an', as you've had hard luck, I'll knock off $25, so you'll only owe me $15.'

"So the nigger, after workin' hard all summer, only finds himself in debt. The white man has his mule to sell — like enough to the same nigger next year. That's the way them fellers live. I know one mule that's been sold that way six times.

"That's why I claim the nigger ain't never gonter be nothin'. He won't never git no chance. The nigger is the cleverest-hearted mortal in the world.

He'll work his hands off fer a little flattery, I reckon. These fellers down here know how to work it sharp, an' the nigger is always goin' to do the work, while the white man pulls in the money."

John kept the board, and showed it to Jack Foster a few days later.

"Is that true?" he asked.

"I reckon a heap of it is," said Jack, slowly. "It's a little exaggerated, of course, but a heap of it is true, sure enough. It's a mighty bad thing for the country that labor is so unreliable."

CHAPTER XXI.

THE NEGRO QUESTION

THE more John studied the negro question, the more difficult of solution the problem seemed. Not long after the election he listened to a discussion that did much to point out still more clearly the difference between the Northern and Southern methods of studying the question. In one of his visits to town John found a young Northern man who had come to the South for his health. This man, at John's invitation, spent a week at the plantation. He was a man of fine education, who studied with keen interest the curious problems of Southern life. He was an ardent Republican, and something of a theorist as regards the negro. He found in Jack Foster a man who would discuss the negro question without getting angry, and who could give him many new points. Jack had done considerable reading. During his lonely life he had thought a great deal and studied hard at the social problems of the day. He could not drop his old belief in the inferiority of the negro, but he could discuss the question with a much better spirit than most Southern men. His great friendship for John gave him a certain respect for a Northern opinion, though he could not be converted. John was never tired of listening to the discussion that was sure to come up whenever Jack and the young Northerner met.

"The nigger," Jack would say, in all seriousness, "is an inferior man, and never can be the equal of the white man."

"How do you know that?"

"Because in all the history of the world there never has been a black race that ever showed superior intelligence. The niggers are different from white men "— and Jack would describe the difference in finger nails, hair, and head. "The nigger was made to serve, and it is against all ideas of religion and morality for us to dream of him as an equal. The bare idea of such a thing would drive a Southern lady nearly crazy. No one can imagine what a horrible disgust the very suggestion of such a thing brings up. Petting the nigger, and making him think he is anything but a slave, only tends to spoil him forever."

"How spoil him?"

"It gives him fool-notions, and would in a short time break up all the safety of our society."

"Then you believe in keeping the negro in ignorance?"

"No, *I* do not, though I must confess that too many Southern men do. I am in favor of educating the nigger, because I know that his educational powers are limited. The nigger learns quickly, but he gets filled up in a very short time. Take a white boy and nigger boy, each, say, nine years old, give them equal advantages, and the nigger will beat the white boy all to death. When the nigger gets to be fifteen years old you can't get anything more into his head — he is filled up, while the white boy goes on gaining every week. There are some niggers who are smart and know how to learn. They are so few that they seem like any other freak of nature — simple monstrosities. I can't think of any more undesirable position than that of an educated nigger who knows what the rest of his race must be."

"Then it is not possible, in your opinion, for the negro to master enough of an education to fit him for the society of white men?"

"No, sar, it makes no difference how refined and talented a nigger might be, I never could ask him to my table and have any more respect for myself. A sensible nigger will realize his position, and never step over it. Do you mean to say that you would sit at the same table with a nigger?"

"To be sure, I would; there are plenty of negroes in the country who are superior to me in education and manhood. I should be proud to sit at table with them."

"I'm mighty sorry to hear it. If that was known here, how many people do you suppose would invite you to their houses? Do you reckon that these Republican leaders up North, who have so much to say about the nigger, would really invite a regular black nigger to their houses, and let him eat with them and sleep in their beds?"

"Certainly they would, if he was deserving of it. I know plenty of men that would do so."

Jack shook his head a little doubtingly. He could hardly bring himself to believe this. Southern men generally have little faith in the sincerity of the Republican leaders who urge the elevation of the negro. The experience that the South has had with Republicanism leads her people to think that the Republicans simply wish to use the negro as a tool, to spoil him for work, and then leave him to injure political enemies.

"But what are you going to do when the negroes all learn to read and write, and the 'freaks of nature,' as you call them, increase in number, as they are sure to do?"

"I reckon we'll have to keep them down. They don't know enough to organize, and they never will. We know that they are an inferior race, and we know from experience that we must keep them down."

"How are you going to do it?"

"We know how. It is a matter of self-preservation with us and we cannot afford to let the nigger dream of social equality. I might as well ask you how you propose to keep down the workingmen and foreigners at the North. They will multiply so in a few years that you will have work to control them. You know perhaps how the work will be done, and in the same way *we* know how we are going to keep our niggers in shape."

"But we have no thought of keeping our workingmen 'down' as you call it. We aim to educate them and bring them up to a higher plane of usefulness."

"That is well enough to talk of white men, but you can't tell *niggers* such stuff. It would spoil them in no time."

"Did it ever occur to you that the Saxons were at one time as low down as these negroes are now? History shows that the ignorant obstinate Saxons held together for centuries, kept their language and religion, and in time forced the superior Norman to the rear. Why is it not possible for American history to repeat, in part at least, this record? The negroes are not breaking up politically. They draw away from the whites and have begun already to be an exclusive race. Fifty years from now, when every negro can read and write, when the race has increased in numbers and crowded itself upon a smaller area, when it has a literature of its own and can show in black and white its *own* story of its wrongs, — what will you do then?"

"That's not a fair argument — not a fair way of talking. The Saxons were white. The nigger is black and you cannot show in all the history of the world an instance where a race of black men have ever proved themselves capable of coping with white men, or of forming a literature.

"You speak from a theorist's point of view. You don't understand the nigger, how ignorant he is, and how easy it is for us to manage him. Niggers are the cleverest people in the world, but they are good for nothing but work. Understand me, I don't want the nigger to go back to slavery, but I want him to keep in his place. What he did in the days of the 'Radical' rule shows that he is incapable of governing."

"But how can you tell by the conduct of the negro at that time, what he is capable of doing?

You remember perhaps that familiar quotation from Macaulay's Essay on Milton: — 'Till men have been some time free they know not how to use their freedom. The final and permanent fruits of liberty are wisdom, moderation, and mercy. Its immediate effects are often atrocious crimes, conflicting errors, dogmatism on points the most mysterious. It is just at this crisis that its enemies love to exhibit it . . . and ask in scorn where the promised splendor and comfort is to be found.' Now why is not this true in the case of the negro government?"

And so the two men would discuss, neither convincing the other, and each one proving his own idea to his own satisfaction.

CHAPTER XXII.

AUNT JINNY'S FAVORITE STORY

THE warm, pleasant weather continued all through November and to within two weeks of Christmas. It seemed strange enough to John and Nellie to think of eating their dinner at Thanksgiving with the doors wide open and the sun shining hotly on them. At home, Thanksgiving usually came with a white mantle of snow or a rough overcoat of frozen earth. Thanksgiving is the great day of New England country life. City people prefer Christmas, but the plain, honest folks who wrest their living from the rocky hillside farms hold to the old Puritan holiday. It is the day when great families come together, when old scenes are pictured, old stories are told, old memories are brushed to life, when the golden grains of the past are brought from beneath the dust of years. The social nature of the Thanksgiving celebration somehow appeals to the lonely country life as Christmas never can.

Thanksgiving was a very thoughtful time for John and Nellie. It was the anniversary of their marriage. All the old days were brought to their minds. They did their best to appear merry and thankful for the sake of the little girl, but it was hard work. How gladly would they have changed this great plantation and the beautiful weather for the rocky old farm at home. Go where he will, improve his circumstances as he may, the New England man can never repress the yearning for the rough old hills that seem so dull and barren to a stranger.

A short time before Christmas, a heavy rain set in that seemed, in a few hours, to double the distance between the plantation and the town. The road was changed into a mass of deep mud through which an empty wagon could hardly be pulled. The little family seemed to be shut out from the rest of the world. John was obliged to make his trips into town on horseback. He would come back completely covered with mud, longing for the frozen ground and packed snow of a New England winter.

As Christmas drew near, the negroes began to show signs of an increased jollity and merriment. Even Sol and his mother joined in the fun.

Aunt Jinny told little Nellie a series of such remarkable stories that the child came to have an entirely new idea of Christmas and Santa Claus. She had lost considerable faith in the old story the year before at home, when by an accident she discovered that Uncle Nathan had endeavored to take the place of old Saint Nick. Aunt Jinny's stories put such a new face upon the matter that the little girl resolved to give Santa Claus another fair trial. Aunt Jinny could not understand much about little Nellie's description of the reindeer and sledge that formed so important a part of the Christmas procession. Snow and ice were unknown to her. Santa Claus came through the mud on a stout mule or in a hack. The deer and the sledge were entirely out of place.

"I reckon dey's a heap ob folks, honey, dat done know nuffin' about dese tings. I reckon dem raindeer ud git stuck mighty bad in de murd. I knows a heap about Santa Claus, I does, bekase I heard all about de man what done seen him onct."

"Tell me all about it, Aunt Jinny," little Nellie would say, bringing her chair up to the side of the old slave.

"Well, honey, I reckon it ud take a heap ob time ter tell all about it. 'Pears like I'd better tell about one p'int at a time. Whar you reckon I'd better begin?"

The little girl, after much thought, would at last decide upon some "p'int."

"What do people hang up their stockin's for, Aunt Jinny?" Nellie soon came to know that this was Aunt Jinny's favorite story.

"What make dey hang up dere stockin's?"

Aunt Jinny was in her glory, surely, when this point was raised. She claimed to be one of the very few people in the world who could answer this leading question. She never would impart the coveted information except to those who she felt sure would make good use of it.

"What make dey will hang up dere stockin's? Wall, chile, dere is a mighty cur'us story about dat. Hit's de cur'uses story dey *is*, I reckon. I reckon I's hev ter tell yer, chile, bekase youse gonter 'member it, an' it look like you done git yo' idees sorter shuck up like, on dis p'int.

AUNT JINNY'S FAVORITE STORY

"Onct dey wuz a man dat lib 'way back yunder in de country. He wuz a po' man — a mons'us po' man, sho' 'nuff. An' de longer he lib de po'er he git, tell bime by he didn't hab nuffin' skersely."

"Where did he live?" the little girl would ask in breathless interest. She meant to mark the fatal spot in her little geography, so that papa never would go there.

"Whar he live at?" Aunt Jinny proposed to tell one thing at a time. "I don't reckon you'd know, honey, ef I wuz ter go an' tell you. You jes' wait tell youse go over de groun' an' den you'll know sho' 'nuff. Dis man wuz po'ful po'; corn an' meat dey wuz 'way up yunder, an' when Christmas come along, he done hab nuffin'."

"But why didn't he wait for Santa Claus, Aunt Jinny?"

"It's a-comin' ter dat p'int, honey, right away. I reckon ole Santy Claus he jes' whip his mules when he drive fru dat country. He mighty glad ter git away frum it, an' he make mighty few calls, I reckon. But the night afo' Crismus, dis po' man he go out ter git him sum light wood, an' while he wuz pickin' it up, he year somebody way off in de swamp holler. De man he ain't gut nuffin' ter do, so he sorter walks down ter de swamp fer ter see who dat is. Who you tink he fine down dere, honey?"

"It wasn't Santa Claus, was it?"

Aunt Jinny felt a little disappointed to have the point of surprise thus taken out of her story.

"I reckon it were Santy, sho' 'nuff."

"How did he know who it was, Aunt Jinny?"

"Why, chile, dey is a heap ob tings about Santy Claus dat is dif'rent frum odder people. I reckon *you'd* know him de minnit you see him, an' den agin, I reckon he tole dat po' man who he wuz. You see, honey, Santy were stuck in de murd. His hack wuz 'way up to de hubs in de road, an' one mule wuz kickin' while de odder wuz backin' up agin de hack. It were a hard place fer Santy, sho' 'nuff, fer he had a heap ob groun' to cover yit. Dat po' man he stan' by, wid his han's in his pockets, an' sorter watch der doin's. Bime by he ask Santy Claus have he gut nary a piece ob terbarker. Dat sorter interjuice 'em, like, an' Santy he up en' say dat his hack wuz full ob tricks, an' dat he'd fill up enyting dat po' man had ef he'd help him out.

"Dat po' man he look in dat hack, an' he see a heap ob tings dat he wanted. He sorter made up his mind what was what. He talk mighty brash at dem mules, but de mo' he talk de mo' dey pull back. Den he borry Santy's knife, an' cut him a big pole in de woods, an' while Santy he push agin de back ob de hack, dat po' man he jes' tan de hides on dem mules po'ful, till dey pull togedder, an' jes' yank dat hack outer de murd. You jes' orter see dem mules pull, honey."

"But wasn't it too bad that they had to whip them so?" said the dear little girl.

"No, I don't reckon it wuz. Mules is mighty ornery. I reckon dey ain't nuffin' but lickin' will do 'em eny good. Dey is a heap ob folks, honey, dat is jes' like mules about dat. Ole Santy Claus he mightily tickled about de way he git outer dat murd, an' when he come to de po' man's house, he say, 'Now you jes' bring out de biggest ting you gut, an' I'll fill it up.'

"Dat po' man he mighty sharp, I reckon. He done scratch his head, an' den he bring out a big stockin'. Ole Santy Claus he tink he git out mighty easy, but when he come with his truck, he fine dere is a mighty big hole in de heel ob dat stockin'. All de truck run fru the hole, an' take mighty nigh all dey is in de hack ter fill it up."

"That man didn't do right, did he, Aunt Jinny?"

"Wall, chile, dat's a mighty hard question, dat is. Dere's a heap ob folks dat ud 'a' done de same ting — an' mighty good folks, too, I reckon. Dat po' man he uz mighty tickled about de way he beat ole Santy Claus, an' he tole all de folk dey cud do de same ting. When Santy he come along de nex' time, he fine all de holy stockin's hung up fer 'im ter fill. Hit mighty nigh busted ole Santy ter fill 'em up. Santy he sorter figgered on de ting, an' he see dat dere weren't no money in dem holy stockin's, so he say dat he gib a prize to de one dat hung up de bes'-lookin' stockin'.

"Santy Claus he mighty sharp, I reckon. Everybody goes in fer de prize an' all de holy stockin's is sorter patched up like. So, honey, done yo' nebber hang up no holy stockin's, but jest take de bes' one yo' hab."

CHAPTER XXIII.

FADED FLOWERS OF ANDERSONVILLE

JACK FOSTER had promised to eat his Christmas dinner with John and Nellie.

The day had always been a melancholy one with him, bringing back, as it did, the memories of happier days. He hoped for a pleasant time with his new friends, but he hardly dared to hope for the great happiness that the beautiful holiday brought him. Jack had been a little ill. He caught a severe cold at the opening of the rainy season. Three days before Christmas he rode back from town through a severe rain. He stopped at the plantation, and was easily induced to stay to supper. His head ached and he grew hot and cold by turns. He was surprised to find how weak he was when he rose to go home. He almost fell as he staggered to the door. Nellie quickly saw that Jack was a sick man. She insisted upon his staying all night, and Jack, after one bewildered look at the blackness and rain, helplessly consented.

"I shall be all right in the morning, I reckon," he said, as John led him back to a seat by the fire. They all thought this, but when the morning came, Jack was unable to stand. He lay in a daze, with his eyes wide open, muttering and whispering to some imaginary person. He roused for a time and seemed to know John, but at last the look of intelligence faded out of his eyes, and he lay vacantly staring at the wall as before.

John and Nellie grew frightened as the hours went by and Jack never ceased staring and muttering. They could not understand what he said, but Nellie could imagine, for there was one name that was always pronounced more distinctly than the rest — it was Lucy. At last John sent Sol for a horse that he might ride to town after a doctor. The rain was still pouring down, and the road was a great mass of mud, but John did not think of this at all. As Sol brought the horse up to the door, an old negro woman came up from the gate. She was drenched with the rain and covered with mud, but she hobbled bravely up to the door.

"Whar's Massa Jack at?" she asked, peering dimly about her. "I's his ole mammy, I is done nuss him, an' 'pears like dey ain't nobody kin take car ob him like I kin. Whar is he at, Missy? I reckon I can't lib no longer if Massa Jack die."

Nellie brought the poor old woman in and gave her a seat by the fire. Old Mammy dried herself as hastily as possible, and then asked again to see Jack.

"I knows a heap mo' about Massa Jack dan eny one else do," she explained, and so it proved, for when Nellie led the old woman to Jack's room she was surprised to see how quickly old Mammy understood what to do.

The old slave watched her master as a dog might have done. Jack turned his vacant eyes upon her, and something like a gleam of intelligence passed over his face. Mammy sat down by the bed and placed her hand on Jack's head.

"I reckon you'd better send fo' ole Massa Lawrence," she muttered to Nellie. "'Pears like he know about Massa Jack like nobody else do."

John was just mounting his horse as Nellie came down and told him of old Mammy and her advice. Mr. Lawrence was the old gentleman that John had met at the hotel. Jack had often spoken of him as an old physician and friend of his father's. John decided to follow old Mammy's advice. He rode down to the gate and turned past Colonel Fair's place. An hour later he returned with Mr. Lawrence. The old gentleman came at once when John told his story. He had known Jack from his earliest childhood, and had treated him for many a serious illness.

The two men were covered with mud and drenched through with the rain. They dried themselves before the fire, and then the older man went above into the room where old Mammy was watching her "boy." John and Nellie waited anxiously for the report. They read it in the grave and sorrowful face that Mr. Lawrence brought back from the sick-room.

"It is a very serious case. I am afraid he will have a hard struggle for life. There has been something on his mind for years that has tortured him continually. He is thinking of it now, and unless something can be done to drive it from his mind, I do not think my medicine can ever help him. I speak plainly, for I think you know, judging from what you said to-day, what this matter is. I have known it for a long time, though I never told John Foster that it was so. *She* told me about it years ago. I feel that I am free to speak of it now, for the end that I have been fearing seems to have begun."

Nellie's eyes were filled with tears, and even John's strong hand shook as he brought a chair for the visitor. How well they understood what awful thoughts were filling the brain of the sick man. John and Nellie had but to place themselves in his position. The older man found that sweet romance of his youth forcing itself into his heart again.

Nellie quietly stole from the room at last to dry her eyes. Something seemed to draw her to the chamber, where, with dazed brain, the sick man was lying. She entered softly, and sat in one gray, shadowy corner to think. The gloom of the dismal day seemed to force itself into the silent chamber. Old Mammy sat at the head of the bed, rocking herself to and fro, and muttering some old song that had hushed the sick man years before. Jack lay in the old position, with his eyes wide open and his chin fallen. His hands worked occasionally, and once they were raised in a gesture of entreaty, but in an instant they fell feebly down. Jack's muttering was louder and more distinct than before. Nellie could easily understand him now. His words seemed to cut her very heart, and she listened with streaming eyes as she thought how this man had suffered for her.

"He'll do it, I reckon," the sick man muttered.

" That little one don't know what he's saying. Suppose Lucy's brother should ask me to do that. I reckon I'd do it — but I must shoot him."

One hand was raised slightly, and the eyes opened wider than before.

" I couldn't do it " — the voice trembled a little. " My dear little woman, I know you wouldn't have me shoot him. I'm glad you looked at me as you did."

He was silent for a time, but at last he reached out his hand, as if in the act of picking something from the bed.

" I'll take this anyhow, I reckon. Poor little chap. How much he looked like her. I'll carry this to her, I reckon. I'm glad, after all, I didn't shoot him."

His voice died away in a whisper, and he went on so low that Nellie could not hear him. At last he said, in almost a shout, " My *dear* little woman, listen to me. I *do* love you — I'll sell my soul for you. I did it because I loved you — because I loved you."

Nellie could not listen longer. She hurried away with a mighty resolution in her heart. Old Mammy followed her out.

" Yer's suffin' fer youse, I reckon, Missy. Massa Jack sorter reckoned dat it uz you's. I foun' it on de flo', near whar his coat is at."

How the old woman had read the sick man's thoughts no one can tell. Nellie opened the little package. It was an envelope filled with cotton, in which was a little bunch of dried violets. She placed the package in her pocket, and then went down to the room where John and Mr. Lawrence were sitting. The men looked at her in surprise, for her purpose was written on her face. She placed her hand on her husband's shoulder, and said, simply : —

"John, I am going to ride to town at once."

John looked at her in wonder. She had never yet made a proposition that had not been carried out, but this was so strange and unexpected. Nellie noticed John's look of wonder, and patted his cheek to reassure him.

"I mean to ride to town and see Lucy," she said, simply. "I shall never feel that I have done my duty until I try to show her how he has loved her all these years. It may do no good, but I must try. If you could only hear him talk, John," — and the brave little woman faltered as she thought how Jack had spoken.

Mr. Lawrence rose from his seat, and grasped Nellie's hand.

"God bless you, madam," he said, huskily. "You are a noble woman. Your husband has told me all the story. I hope and pray that you may succeed. She has always loved him, I know — it is her pride that holds her back. I cannot tell you what to do. You are a woman, and know far better than I how to reach a woman's heart. I know it is a matter of life or death with John Foster, and I think I know how you long to bring him happiness."

"But I must go with you," said John, sturdily.

"No, John," said Nellie, gently. "You cannot

help me in this — stay here and wait for me. I shall take Sol, and there will be no danger at all."

She made her preparations as quickly as possible. Sol brought the horses to the door. The rain glistened on the negro's heavy face as he glanced down the road.

"Don't you let nothin' touch her, Sol," said John, as he went out to inspect the horses.

"I reckon I'd die fust, boss," said the negro. He opened his coat, and showed the bright handle of a revolver.

"Please let me go with you, Nellie!" pleaded John, as his wife came to the door all ready for the ride.

"No, John," she answered, gently. "I must do this alone — this is nothing to what you did for me once" — and she smiled up at him to try and hide the tears that *would* force themselves into her eyes. She kissed little Nellie, and shook hands with Mr. Lawrence. When she came to John he gathered her up in his arms and kissed her again and again, and carried her to the horse. With one last word of caution to Sol, John reluctantly withdrew his hand from the bridle of his wife's horse, and then, into the early twilight that came creeping darkly upon them, they rode away upon their errand of love. John and Mr. Lawrence waited at the gate — heedless of the rain and storm — till the slow toiling horses passed out of sight behind the trees. Then they went sadly back to the house.

"Your wife is an angel — God bless her," said the older man, with a strange tremor in his voice, as he shook John's hand. "She is strangely like one I knew years ago, in New England. Is she like her mother?"

"Very much," answered John. "The same hair and eyes, and the same face."

The old gentleman smiled sadly as he listened. He said no more, but his head fell on his breast as he sat watching the fire. At last, he rose to go to the sick man's room.

"I have to thank your wife and yourself," he said, with old-fashioned courtesy, as he shook John's hand again, "for a great happiness that you cannot understand. There are many things in our lives that we cannot always explain or understand, yet I think we are able to see at last, that under every fancied wrong there lies a blessing that must gain in strength as the years go by."

He bowed gravely, and passed out at the door and went to the sick-room, where Jack lay, with vacant eyes, still muttering the old story.

The gloom came settling down over the house. It crept in at the windows and gathered about the sick-bed. The savage fire on the hearth snapped bravely at the intruder, and sent its sparks out to man the outworks. Still the gloom deepened, and still the old gentleman sat with bowed head, thinking of Nellie's mother. In the other room, with little Nellie on his knee, John sat praying for his wife's safe return. No wonder that the little girl, when she said her prayers that night, added: "God bess my mamma, an' *please* let her come home all safe."

The anxious watcher waited far into the night.

The fire snapped and snarled at the darkness, the old slave still crooned by the bed, and the sick man still talked vacantly on. At last, John caught the gleam of a lantern far down the dark road. It turned in at the gate. A splashing in the mud and water followed, and John rushed out into the storm, hardly daring to speak for fear lest Nellie had failed.

Covered with mud, his black face shining in the light, Sol stood holding two horses. The tired beasts hung their heads wearily.

John's heart gave a great throb of joy, as he saw two faces in the dim light. Nellie smiled at him with the face of an angel. The other face was white and still — ghastly in the light. John silently lifted the women from the horses. He carried Nellie, and half led, half carried Lucy to the hall. There Nellie's courage gave way. She laid her head on John's breast and sobbed like a little child. Her brave task was ended, she was only a woman now.

Lucy steadied herself against the door. Her face was pale as death. Her black hair, wet with the rain, fell about her shoulders. Her eyes were filled with a strange light as she looked at John inquiringly. He understood her, and pointed silently to the room where Jack was lying. She walked with a firm step to the door and noiselessly opened it. Gently she crossed the floor and knelt at the side of the bed where old Mammy was sitting.

"Dear Jack," she whispered, "I *do* love you, and I have come to ask you to forgive me. You are nobler and truer than I knew."

The vacant face slowly turned to her. She bent forward and kissed him. A flash of intelligence gleamed in the staring eyes, and he said, in a clear tone, as his feeble arm passed about her neck : " My dear little girl, I did it because I loved you."

There is little more that we can say. We cannot tell how Lucy's proud heart melted when the little Northern woman knelt before her, and told the story of the Andersonville Violets. The curl, the letter, and the faded flowers touched her, and the love that she had fought down for years mastered her at last. Back through the wild night they came. Back through the gloom and darkness to save a life. For Jack did not die. How could he die when the gates of an earthly paradise swung open that he might better fit himself for that higher one?

The four people whose lives have been thus strangely brought together live on through many years of happiness. Jack and Lucy grow closer and closer together as the years trail past them.

John and Nellie live the same self-sacrificing lives. They live for little Nellie. The years bring them prosperity, but they are glad only that they can do more for their little one. The old longing for home never dies out. They can never forget that they are "strangers in a strange land." That mighty gulf that opens between the two sections can never be bridged in their lifetime. Even their little girl must be sent away to be educated. But patiently and trustingly they work on, thanking God that they are permitted to develop so grandly the beautiful little life he has given them, and treasured above all else, binding their hearts closer together, filling their lives with the sweet perfume of romance, Nellie still keeps the little bunch of faded flowers that have brought so much misery and yet so much happiness — the *Andersonville Violets.*

DAVID RACHELS AND DAVID MADDEN, *Series Editors*

The Battle-Ground by Ellen Glasgow
Introduction by Susan Goodman

Manassas: A Novel of the War by Upton Sinclair
Introduction by Kent Gramm

Andersonville Violets: A Story of Northern and Southern Life by Herbert W. Collingwood
Introduction by David Rachels and Robert Baird

Cudjo's Cave by J. T. Trowbridge
Introduction by Dean Rehberger